P9-CBJ-802

The Night Before Christmas

Joyce Sullivan

Harlequin Books

TORONTO • NEW YORK • LONDON
AMSTERDAM • PARIS • SYDNEY • HAMBURG
STOCKHOLM • ATHENS • TOKYO • MILAN
MADRID • WARSAW • BUDAPEST • AUCKLAND

To Alain, my own hero, husband and friend

I would like to thank Paul V. Polishuk, M.D.;
Lynn Peterson, Archaeologist; Lorraine Vassalo,
Criminologist; Constable Joe Fitzpatrick, North Vancouver
Detachment of the RCMP; and Jean Tremblay, Chemist, for
sharing their knowledge and expertise.

ISBN 0-373-22352-8

THE NIGHT BEFORE CHRISTMAS

Copyright © 1995 by Joyce David

She was beautiful...and scared.

Laurel made a lonely figure, watching over her little girl in the semidarkened room. Her back was to him and her tawny hair gathered in mussed honey-tinged clouds just below her shoulder blades. Her shoulders were quivering beneath the red robe. There was a naked vulnerability in the scene that made his throat ache. Whatever he thought of Ms. Laurel Bishop, she'd loved his aunt. That much was plain.

Quietly, he backed into the sitting area and called her name. She came around the partition, wiping her cheeks with her slender hands. He was careful to keep his expression neutral. "The police are here."

The wariness instantly returned to her eyes—wariness tinged with fear. Ian felt an instant knee-jerk reaction of suspicion solidify in his gut. *Why was she so afraid of talking to the police?*

Dear Reader,

Be prepared to meet a "Woman of Mystery"!

This month we're proud to bring you another story in our ongoing WOMAN OF MYSTERY program, designed to bring you the debut books of writers new to Harlequin Intrigue.

Meet Joyce Sullivan, author of *The Night Before Christmas*.

Joyce credits her lawyer mother with instilling in her a love of reading and writing—and a fascination for solving mysteries. She has a bachelor's degree in Criminal Justice and worked several years as a private investigator before turning her hand to writing romantic suspense. A transplanted American, Joyce makes her home in Aylmer, Quebec, with her handsome, French-Canadian husband and two casebook-toting kid detectives.

We're dedicated to bringing you the best new authors, the freshest new voices. Be on the lookout for more "women of mystery"!

Sincerely,

Debra Matteucci
Senior Editor & Editorial Coodinator
Harlequin Books
300 East 42nd Street
New York, NY 10017

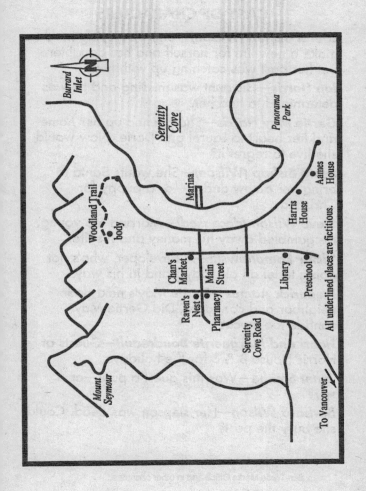

Burrard Inlet

N

Serenity Cove

Panorama Park

Marina

Mount Seymour

Woodland Trail

• body

Chan's Market •

Main Street

Raven's Nest •

Pharmacy •

Serenity Cove Road

Library •

Preschool •

Harris House •

Aames House •

All underlined places are fictitious.

To Vancouver

CAST OF CHARACTERS

Laurel Bishop (Wilson)—She was trying hard to make a new life for herself and her daughter, but her past was catching up with her.

Ian Harris—His aunt was missing and he was determined to find her.

Gertie May Harris—She opened up her home and her heart to Laurel and Dorie. Now would she live to regret it?

Dorie Bishop (Wilson)—She wants Santa to bring her a new daddy—or a puppy for Christmas.

Steve Wilson (deceased)—Married too young. He gambled away his money and his life.

Victor Romanowski—A developer, who's not going to let an old lady stand in his way.

Frederick Aames—Gertie May's next-door neighbor and confidant. Did Gertie May confide too much?

Henri and Marguerite Boudreault—Guests at Harris House B & B for the holidays.

Janet Smithe—Was this guest a poet—or a spy?

Barbara Wilson—Her stepson was dead. Could she bury the past?

Prologue

Nelson, British Columbia

"Come to Nana, Dorie. Your mom will be home soon—I hope." Barbara Wilson couldn't keep her disquietude from choking her voice as she hoisted her granddaughter onto her hip and glanced at the kitchen clock.

What was keeping her daughter-in-law? Laurel had been at the police station for three hours. What was happening? Had she been arrested for murder? Or would the results of this second polygraph test confirm that Laurel was telling the truth? That she wasn't responsible for Steve's death.

Barb paced the galley-style kitchen and crooned a sing-song of soothing words that took the fearful chill out of the deathly still house as she watched the carport for Laurel's red Tercel. There was a better view of the quiet street from the living room window, but the thought of entering the room where her stepson had died so violently on Christmas Eve was beyond her capabilities.... The pain was still too fresh. Too raw.

Dorie grew limp as a rag doll in her arms. Ah, asleep at last. They could both use a little peace. Barbara kissed Dorie's sticky brow, and laid the toddler in her crib, tucking her special bunny blanket around her tiny body to ward off the dampness of the March rain. Dorie caught colds so easily....

Barbara hovered over the crib rail. "I may have lost Steve, but I still have you, child," she whispered softly, her voice catching. Of course, she wasn't Dorie's nana by true blood relation. Steve's mother had died when he was ten. But still, she deserved the title....

She'd been a good stepmother. None better! She'd been there when Steve needed a hug or a word of encouragement. She'd stood by him during the turbulent years of his adolescence and into adulthood, always smoothing things over when he had blowups with his dad. She'd slipped him money when he needed it. They'd both grieved when Steve lost his dad.... Barbara squeezed her eyes tight; her cheeks ached from the struggle of holding back her emotions. Thank God, Charlie never knew about the gambling, but what did it matter now, anyway? Steve was dead, too. And the innocent were taking the brunt of the blame.

Barbara's hands fluttered onto her chest, trying to rub away the deep spasm of pain in her heart. Oh, the things people were saying in town about Laurel. Unfounded lies.... It was so unfair. Not that newspaper reports were any more accurate. It was none of their business anyway.

Her glasses misted over and Barbara removed them, dabbing at the thick lenses with the hem of her sweater. There was too much humidity in these old houses. In the distance she could hear the splashing of tires navigating the puddle on the driveway. Then an engine cutting out. *Laurel's home.*

Barbara threaded her way through the house, avoiding Dorie's push toys. She arrived in the kitchen just as Laurel entered by the back door. One look at Laurel told the tale: her brown eyes shone with a luster that had been missing for the past three months. A smile trembled on her lips.

"I'm free, Barb. The police believe I didn't do it." Her words carried the joyful ring of the vindicated.

Barb hugged her tightly. "I'm so glad. So very glad." Laurel felt so thin and fragile beneath the thick folds of her coat. They clung to each other, shedding tears of sorrow and utter relief, until Barbara remembered that tearful displays of affection were not in her nature. She wiped her glasses again and put the teakettle on to boil. "Now, what do you say we put this behind us? I think you and Dorie could use a change of scenery. I have a friend in North Vancouver...."

Chapter One

Brazil, South America

Mission accomplished. Ian Harris deposited the priest's white collar in the overflowing garbage can of the men's washroom in the São Paulo International Airport. The subterfuge was over, monies and gems safely exchanged. He had to make one more business stop in Los Angeles, then he was going home for Christmas. *Home.*

Ian shook his head with a wry smile. For a man who'd lived his life traveling the globe without ever laying claim of ownership to a single piece of property, he still clung tenaciously to the boyhood memories of the holidays spent within the loving walls of his elderly aunt's ramshackle house. It hadn't exactly been his *home,* he'd had parents, but the feeling he'd had there—the normalcy of having a room that was especially his and not some sterile hotel room or sparsely furnished rental home—had always stayed with him. Sometimes, particularly at Christmas, he needed to see Gertie May.

Ian dug into his toiletry kit for a razor and shaving cream, ready to begin another transformation. The sandy beard that had hugged his square jaw for the past six months came off easily. He wouldn't miss it. A couple days in the sun would take care of the paler skin underneath. Next he put on a pair of eyeglasses with round, brown-and-amber-toned frames. He looked different already. The expensive, trendy frames focused attention on his eyes. Made them look more brown than gray.

But his hair still didn't look right. It was too ragged. Too long. Maybe something upscale, *GQ*-ish, like the young studs in the nightclubs in Rome. A little long on top, enough to fall onto his forehead, and clipped short on the sides. And he'd need some new clothes. Black just wasn't his color; he felt downright sacrilegious. A cigar-colored suit, with a green paisley tie. That should do it. He was thinking of making one of the most important and difficult decisions of his life, and he wanted to look the part when he discussed it with his clients.

With a sense of purpose, Ian gathered up his belongings and emerged from the men's room. Only the faint, nagging twinge from a recent wound in his left leg—a nasty souvenir from a *bandito* on a lonely stretch of road in Colombia—slowed his progress as he went in search of a barber.

North Vancouver, British Columbia

TWILIGHT SPREAD a darkening hand across the still, lavender waters of Serenity Cove and crept slowly toward the snow-encrusted shore where it leapt up to clasp the drooping arms of evergreens mantled with pristine snow.

From her icy perch atop the antiquated porch railing of Harris House Bed and Breakfast, Laurel Bishop paused in the midst of replacing a burned-out Christmas bulb to appreciate the tranquillity of her view.

With Christmas two days away, lights of every color glowed from the masts of sailboats moored in the cove. They also bordered windows, doorways and rooflines of the cottages huddled side by side along the shoreline of the Burrard Inlet. The scene was Christmas-card perfect and Laurel's heart filled with hope.

Surely here, in Serenity Cove, in this quiet North Vancouver village, she and Dorie were safe from the ghost of Christmas past.

"Rudolph the Red-Nosed Reindeer..." she sang cheerfully as a red bulb illuminated in her gloved fingers.

"No, Mommy. Stop that singing. That's my song," Dorie protested, her pink-mittened hand held up in the sudden outrage of a three-year-old.

"Okay." Smiling, Laurel tried another version. "Dorie, the red-nosed lit-tle girl, had a—"

"Mom-my. I don't like that."

The sound of the front door opening saved Laurel from explaining that people over the age of three were allowed to sing, too.

"Hello, Gertie May," Laurel said as her friend/landlady/employer appeared on the veranda. The elderly woman was bundled from head to ankle in an outrageous orange wool coat and slacks. Orange leather gloves protected her hands from the $-4°C$ weather and an orange beret was balanced on her iron gray hair, which she wore in a smooth bob. Since orange winter boots were hard to come by, Gertie May Harris had settled for a rugged pair in black leather.

Laurel carefully lowered herself down from the railing.

"Oh, it looks so bea-u-ti-ful." Gertie May covered her rouged cheeks with her hands. "Dorie, I see you made sure your mum didn't miss any lights. Good girl. Heavens, Laurel, I don't know what I'd do without you. You and Dorie have brought such joy to my life. You've been a godsend."

Sudden tears of gratitude stung Laurel's eyes. She could easily say the same thing of Gertie May! For the past twenty-one months Gertie May had provided them with a safe harbor far from the nightmarish Christmas Eve when she'd found Steve murdered.

"What a per-fect Christmas this will be. Now, if only Ian would come...."

For a moment the brilliant light of Gertie May's blue eyes faded. "No package has arrived," Laurel reminded her optimistically. Ian Harris, Gertie May's nephew and sole living relative, only visited his aunt at Christmas and always without notice. Whenever he failed to show, a package would arrive in the mail—a doll from one of the countries where his work as an international gem dealer took him. Last year Gertie May received a set of Guatemalan worry dolls to add to her collection.

"That's true."

"And don't forget Barbara will be here after Christmas, as soon as she's done with those tests the doctor ordered."

Gertie May smiled. "Thank you, dear. I'm off to the drugstore to photocopy the petitions for the Serenity Cove Heritage Society. And I have to buy a lottery ticket at Chan's Market before five. You know the machine closes then." Gertie May's dedication to the Lotto 6/49 equaled that of a soap opera fan. She couldn't miss one.

"Remember the Boudreaults, the couple from Quebec who were here last year?" Gertie May continued. "They're coming to visit their grandchildren for the holidays. I expect them at any time. Put them in the lilac bedroom. Miss Smithe, that poet lady, is still in her room."

"I'll just finish clearing the sidewalk and the drive, then I'll put some apple cider on the stove for the Boudreaults." Laurel picked up a snow shovel and handed a smaller plastic model to her daughter.

"I won't be long. I know you have to work tonight."

"Thanks, Gertie May."

While Dorie industriously cleared a snowdrift from the front steps, Laurel tackled the walkway. She loved being outdoors in the snow. Everything looked pristine and pure. All the faults of everyday life were covered up.

But Laurel's next-door neighbor, Frederick Aames, a spry septuagenarian, apparently didn't share her thoughts. He hailed her from his yard and grumbled, "I'm getting too old for this kind of weather." He gave the foliage of his beloved viburnums a vigorous shake to remove the weight of the day's snowfall.

Laurel leaned on her snow shovel and suppressed a laugh. "Oh, Frederick, you don't mean that. You've got the most beautiful winter garden in town and you know it."

"Bah! The eyes of youth. In a few years, when you hit thirty, we'll discuss it. So, what did you think of Monday's district council meeting?'' he added gruffly, moving on to his prize rhododendrons that were the size of haystacks. ''The town won't be the same if we lose the park.''

Frederick's home bordered the gentle slopes of Panorama Park, which, to the dismay of the citizenry of Serenity Cove, had apparently never been officially designated parkland. Now a developer wanted to purchase the land and rezone the site for a condo development. The influence of the Hong Kong market had tripled property values in the region over the last five years and the district council was looking to ease its dwindling coffers with new tax revenues. Gertie May and Laurel were spearheading the committee to prevent the overdevelopment of Serenity Cove's waterfront to maintain the town's quaint character.

For Laurel it was a pleasant way to stay active in community affairs even though she'd been forced to abandon her dreams of running for office. ''The issue's been deferred until the council meeting after the holidays. Gertie May's sure we'll have everything worked out by then. I know Romanowski's hoping no one will bother.''

''Maybe we shouldn't. These developers always get what they want anyway. Money talks.''

''Not always. It's our community. We can, and should, have a say in it.'' Laurel refused to be put off by Frederick's dour tones. Frown lines framed his thin mouth like parentheses, giving him a sour expression. She knew his negativity came from the burden of caring for his wife, Anna, who had Alzheimer's.

Frederick shrugged his narrow shoulders. ''I'll believe that when the Realtors stop phoning to ask if I'd be interested in selling this place. I got an offer yesterday for five hundred thousand dollars. As if I'd ever sell! My father built this house. It's the only place Anna finds familiar.''

''How is Anna today?''

''So-so. She has a cold. Keeps asking why her mama doesn't come to tuck her in. She thinks I'm her papa.'' Frederick shook his head.

Laurel smiled sympathetically. "How 'bout if we come over for a Christmas Eve tea party tomorrow? Dorie's made something special for Anna for Christmas, haven't you, love?"

"Shh, Mommy. It's a surprise."

Frederick stooped over the snow-flanked cedar hedge, his mouth easing into a rare smile beneath the brim of his stern, gray felt hat. "Don't worry, Little Miss. Your secret is safe with me. I won't breathe a word to Anna, but I shall look forward to our tea. We have a gift for you, too." He tipped his hat. "I should go in now. I don't like leaving Anna alone. Sometimes she slips out the back and I have trouble finding her."

Laurel finished shoveling the driveway, then stripped holly leaves off a twig to serve as arms for the snowman Dorie was making. "Know what, Mommy?"

"What, lovey?"

"Gertie May says after this nighttime we have to leave Santa some cookies by the chimmy—and carrots for Rudolph."

Laurel laughed as a warm, motherly glow spread through her. This was what Christmas was all about: playing in the snow with her daughter, baking cookies, and making surprises for the special people in their lives. Steve's murder was safely in the past.

"We won't forget the cookies or the carrots. Now come inside, I need a helper with the apple cider."

By the time Gertie May returned, the Boudreaults had checked in and Laurel had changed into her waitressing outfit: a short, black leather skirt, black stockings and a feminine, white organza blouse. Her crystal earrings bobbed in a sparkling cascade from her earlobes as she filled plates for supper. If she had a good night of tips serving drinks at the Crow's Nest, she'd have enough money to finish paying off Steve's car loan. That was her Christmas present to herself. Of course, there were still the credit cards and the other debts Steve had accumulated, but at least she was making progress. In two years she'd be debt free. And once she finished her business courses, she could provide Dorie with a future.

"Mommy, I don't want chicken," Dorie announced, eyeing her supper with distaste.

Laurel sighed, taking a seat next to her. It would be her last opportunity to sit down tonight. "Good, because we're having pork chops."

Gertie May tapped Dorie's plate. "You might want to eat a bite or two, Dorie-girl. Santa makes it his business this time of year to see which boys and girls are keeping their rooms tidy and emptying their plates. Hey, what was that blur of red at the window? Say, you don't suppose that was Santa...?"

Brown eyes wide as acorns, Dorie popped a piece of pork into her mouth.

Gertie May beamed, her china blue eyes forming upside-down crescent moons. "By the way, Laurel, I found this card addressed to you at the door when I came in. Maybe you'd like to open it for your mum, Dorie."

"That's odd—I wonder who it's from. We were here. I guess whoever dropped it off didn't have time to ring the bell."

Dorie eagerly tore at the stiff, buff-colored envelope. "Look, Mommy, an angel."

"Oh, pretty. Let's see what it says." Smiling, Laurel reached for the ornate card imprinted with a Renaissance angel. "'Seasons Greetings,'" she read the gold-embossed type out loud. Then her smile dimmed as she felt the blood drain from her face. Below the salutation someone had scrawled *I know about your past—murderess* in black felt lettering.

Laurel dropped the card on the scarred pine table as a cold, terrible fear crept like a ghostly finger over her spine. Oh, God. What did this mean? No one but Gertie May knew about Steve's death.... She'd been so careful. A wave of panic mounted in her breast and she pressed her hand to her heart in a feeble attempt to calm herself.

"Laurel, what is it? A card from a secret admirer?"

Perspiration beaded on her forehead as she struggled to squeeze words past the paralyzing tightness in her throat. "N-not exactly an admirer." Laurel cast a meaningful glance in Dorie's direction, worried that her small daughter might pick up on the fear that had taken hold of her heart. "Tell me what you think, Gertie May."

"Where's the secret mirror?" Dorie demanded as the elderly woman retrieved the card.

Gertie May's pale, freckled fingers trembled. "Oh, dear."

"I want to see the secret mirror in the angel, Gertie May."

"Not now, Dorie-girl. Eat your dinner."

Laurel watched as Gertie May promptly crumpled up the offending card and marched it over to the trash container under the sink. The cabinet door rattled alarmingly against the childproof latch when she slammed it closed.

"Nonsense. The foolishness of some people," Gertie May muttered, returning to the table. "Don't give it another thought, Laurel."

Laurel felt coils of tension tighten in her shoulders. Not think about it? Someone knew her secret. Laurel pushed her plate away. She was suddenly in no mood to eat.

The card's threatening message preyed on her mind as she kissed Dorie good-night, slipped on her coat and walked the three blocks to the Crow's Nest. The card had been hand-delivered to her door. Someone in Serenity Cove knew about Steve's murder...knew that she had been accused of the crime.

Laurel felt a hot flush of shame, followed by a surge of anger. She glanced back uneasily over her shoulder. Was someone watching her now? What could they possibly hope to gain by tormenting her like this?

Snow crunched beneath her boots as she moved closer to the curb, grateful for the Christmas lights that illuminated the darkened shop doorways with fairy rings. Safe. But for how long?

THE CROW'S NEST was unusually empty for a Saturday night. The regulars were snug at home drinking eggnog, wrapping presents and planning last-minute shopping strategy. Home, where she should be, making sure Dorie was safe in bed.

Laurel anxiously scanned the patrons; there were only two unfamiliar faces in the smoky bar. And she was sure she'd never seen either of them in her hometown of Nelson. Finally, she allowed herself to relax.

As she approached the bar around ten, Laurel came face-to-face with Victor Romanowski's dark, flat features. Victor reminded her of a bulldog; he was all chest and stubby legs. She gave him a polite smile and stepped past him. He smelled of musk and new leather. "A Rusty Nail and a Zombie, please, Simon."

Laurel felt a heavy hand settle on the small of her back. Great. Just what she needed. With a faint shake of her head, she expertly moved out of the developer's range.

Undeterred, Victor gave her a broad-lipped smile and patted a vacant bar stool. Even his fingers were short and stubby. "Take a load off, Ms. Bishop. Maybe it's about time we got personally acquainted—aired our differences. Who knows, maybe we can reach some sort of mutual understanding?"

The double meaning in his tone grated on her nerves, and Laurel didn't like the way his eyelids lowered to shade his black eyes as they conducted a lecherous perusal of her body. She slowly counted to five under her breath and added more cocktail napkins to her tray. She hated having to be friendly to jerks like this. "Sorry, Mr. Romanowski. I'm working now and I've already taken my break. There's a time for work..." She paused for effect, smiling ever so sweetly. "And a time for civic pursuits. Right now, my time is money."

"Is that so?" Victor removed his wallet from his back pocket and opened it to her view, obviously of the opinion that she would be impressed by the thick layers of green, red and brown bills. "Well, I got all the money a pretty thing like you could want." He extracted a crisp one-hundred-dollar bill. "Would this cover five minutes' worth of conversation?"

Laurel flicked her eyes over him, unable to conceal her contempt. Did he really think he could buy her off? "It wouldn't cover five-tenths of a second."

"Well, then, I guess I'll have to order something. How about Sex-on-the-Beach?"

She'd rather put ice in his pants—the arrogant pig. She gave him a smile chilly enough to freeze South Africa. "Simon will be happy to take your drink order."

The ice cubes tinkled against the glasses in a chorus of merry laughter as she headed back to her tables. What rotten luck. The last two hours would feel like an eternity if she had to ignore Victor every time she placed an order.

Fortunately, within a few minutes, Victor was joined by a pink-faced man wearing a heavy jean jacket. Laurel thought she recognized him from the last council meeting as being one of Victor's general contractors. From the way their heads were bent together in deep conversation, she imagined they were planning their strategy for the January council meeting. Laurel grinned. She and Gertie May were going to stop them in their tractor tracks.

The Crow's Nest closed at midnight and Simon saw Laurel home. Simon had six grown daughters and he didn't like the idea of his waitresses walking home alone at night—even if Serenity Cove was a safe place to live.

As Laurel stepped onto the veranda at Harris House, her warm breath misted in the cold, sharp air and her heart stilled. *Oh, God, not again.* Fear settled like a heavy stone in her stomach. Tucked inside the doorframe was another buff-colored envelope with her name clearly visible in thick, black letters.

Laurel squeezed the envelope between her mittened fingers like it was a poisonous snake. After fumbling with the house keys, she finally got the front door open. Once inside, she slid the dead bolt into place and stood for a moment peering through the diamond-shaped sidelight. Her heartbeat echoed in her ears. Was someone out there watching her? But her own frightened image was all she could see reflected in the window glass.

Dorie.

Laurel kicked off her boots, tossed her mittens onto a table beside a pair of pruners and hurried down the basement stairs to the suite she shared with her daughter.

Gertie May saved the second-floor bedrooms with views overlooking the cove for guests, but Laurel much preferred the cozy quarters of the B and B's basement over the spacious turn-of-the-century home she'd shared with Steve. She'd never imagined she could be this happy again. A hydrangea-flowered partition separated one end of the suite into two semiprivate sleeping cubicles. There was also a tiny bath squeezed next to the laundry room. The other half of the basement was used as storage.

Laurel rounded the partition. A halo of light from Dorie's night-light illuminated the bed, chasing her darkest fears away. Dorie was sound asleep in bed, surrounded by an army of stuffed playmates. Thank God! Laurel adjusted a straying blanket, then quietly moved to her own cubicle.

Shrugging out of her coat, she sank onto the bed, the buff-colored envelope carefully balanced in the trembling palms of her hands. Should she open it? Maybe she should just throw it away. It couldn't harm her—or Dorie—if she didn't look at it.

But that would be like running away. And she was tired of running. Laurel opened the envelope.

Inside she found another Renaissance angel on the card's front, though in a different pose. Was there supposed to be some metaphoric meaning in that? The gold-embossed letters on the inside of the card bore the generic message "Happy Holidays And Best Wishes For The Coming New Year." To which the same dark, malevolent pen had added, *History Can Repeat Itself.*

Laurel bit down so hard on her lower lip she tasted blood. What was that supposed to mean?

Nothing, she finally decided. Someone was obviously trying to frighten her—and doing a very good job of it—but she'd be damned if she'd give someone that power over her. She refused to be sucked into a life governed by fear again.

Strengthened by her decision, Laurel returned to the main floor and hung her coat in the front hall closet. Then she went upstairs to ensure that a light had been left burning in the hallway for the guests.

A strip of light was visible beneath Gertie May's door. She paused in the hallway, uncertain. It wasn't like Gertie May to fall asleep with her bedside light on. Was she feeling ill? Laurel tapped softly on the door. "Gertie May?" she whispered.

There was no answer. Laurel eased the door open and looked into the room. The bed was neatly made. Laurel felt a ripple of apprehension. The clock on the bedside table read 1:15 a.m. Where was Gertie May? A light was on in the adjoining en suite and she crossed the room in quick steps, worried that her friend had slipped in the bathtub or on the tile floor.

The bathroom was empty, but Laurel noticed signs of use. The clothes Gertie May had worn earlier lay draped across the storage cupboard under the window. Her flannel men's pajamas and chenille robe were missing from the hook on the bathroom door.

Gertie May was dressed for bed. She had to be somewhere in the house. Maybe chatting with one of the guests? Quietly, Laurel returned to the hallway and listened for sounds of conversation coming from one of the two occupied guest bedrooms. But all she could hear were the normal sounds of sleep and the rustle of bed coverings. The unreserved guest bedroom at the front was still empty.

Laurel returned to the main floor, racking her brain for logical explanations. Had she somehow missed Gertie May? She remembered that a light had been left on in the living room, but she decided to try the dining room first, noting that the place settings for breakfast had already been laid on the mahogany table.

"Gertie May?" Laurel called softly as she entered the kitchen again. The sound of her hopeful voice echoed in the room. No one answered.

Goose bumps rose along her arms and stole over her shoulder blades as Laurel experienced a disturbing sensation of déjà vu. Terror cut through her heart like a sharp knife. She didn't want to go to the living room. That's where she'd found Steve that horrible morning....

Rubbing her arms to combat the goose bumps, Laurel began a methodical check of the remainder of the rooms on the main floor: the alcove Gertie May used for an office; the front hall closet; a guest bath; and, finally, the living room.

Laurel took a deep, steadying breath before she went in. The Christmas tree lights were off, giving the tree an eerie cast—a look of falseness much like viewing the layers of makeup on a theatrical performer's face in daylight. Her gaze rested on the painted face of the porcelain angel that was slightly askew on her treetop perch. The cupid's-bow lips no longer seemed to sing for joy, but to smirk with the knowledge of a secret.

A cold, deadly secret.

"Please, God, don't let me find her body...." she whispered hoarsely, forcing her gaze downward to the floor. She saw nothing but the red-and-black arabesque patterns repeated in the Persian carpet. Then her eyes locked on the concealing bulk of the divan. This couldn't be happening—again.

She skittered across the room, her body quivering with near hysteria. "Calm down, Laurel. Gertie May's okay."

So why was she looking behind the sofa? And why was she talking to herself? Laurel braced her hands on the sofa back, steeling herself for the worst as she looked down at a gray...furry dust ball.

"Oh, God!" Laurel collapsed onto the sofa and massaged her temples with trembling fingers.

Gertie May wouldn't leave Dorie alone. It wasn't like her, especially with strangers in the house. But even if Gertie

May had gone out, where would she go dressed in pajamas and robe, in the middle of winter?

Laurel returned to the front hall closet and grew more perplexed. Gertie May's winter boots and beret were in the back of the closet, but Gertie May's coat and Laurel's rain boots were missing. She couldn't have gone far. Had there been an emergency? Maybe Frederick had had a problem with Anna, but Laurel couldn't find an explanatory note anywhere.

Laurel struggled into her coat and boots and grabbed her mittens. The pruners caught her eye and she placed them up high out of Dorie's reach. Then she took a heavy-duty flashlight from the closet. She'd have a look around the outside of the house first, then see if there were any lights on at the Aameses'.

The cold air stung her cheeks and seeped into her lungs as she made a slow tour of the front and back yards. Shining the light into the shadows of the snow-shrouded shrubbery skirting the house's stone foundation, she saw nothing out of the ordinary. No fresh tracks in the snow. Gertie May hadn't slipped on a patch of ice while taking out the garbage. The wooden cage that kept raccoons and coyotes from scavenging the garbage cans was undisturbed.

An icy blast of wind coming in from the water swirled under her coat, numbing her thighs. Laurel shivered and kept moving, making a diagonal set of tracks across the front lawn. As she rounded the end of Frederick's laurel hedge, the sight of the Aameses' darkened house brought her to a halt. Could she be mistaken? Laurel experienced a tremor of misgiving that she immediately tried to counteract with a dose of common sense. Frederick and Gertie May were probably having a cup of tea in the kitchen. She followed Frederick's immaculately swept brick walk to the back of the craftsman-style home. But the rear facade was also dark, the windowpanes gleaming like mirrors in the moonlight.

Suddenly, Laurel felt very much alone and very much afraid. What was she supposed to do now? And where was Gertie May?

IAN HAD NEVER thought of himself as a sentimental man, but when the cab approached the bend in the road, he felt spurred into spontaneity. He tapped the cabbie on the shoulder. "Pull over here. I'll walk the rest of the way."

"Are you certain, sir?" The cabbie's tone carried an edge of wariness. Tall evergreens bordering both sides of the road turned the bend into a tunnel of darkness. A good spot for an ambush at two o'clock in the morning.

Ian sensed the man's uneasiness, and relented. "The town begins just 'round the bend. You can let me off there. Careful, it's a blind curve. It might be icy." The headlights of the cab swerved sharply to the right and Ian leaned forward in anticipation. He'd always fancied the way the angle of this particular bend situated at the north end of town made Serenity Cove suddenly appear as if out of nowhere—as though you were encountering something unexpected and special. Serendipitous.

And there it was, quaint as ever in its Christmas finery of jeweled lights and snow-dusted rooftops with the light standards wrapped like candy canes. *It still looks the same,* he thought at first glance, oddly pleased.

The cab pulled over in front of Jorgen's Pharmacy. Ian paid his fare and climbed onto the wooden sidewalk, slinging his bulky duffel bag over his shoulder. The frigid air was refreshing, but hard on someone who had no hat or gloves. Aunt Gem's was only two blocks away. He'd be okay.

He walked with long, quick strides, marveling at how little Serenity Cove had changed in the four years since his last visit. Indeed, since his childhood. The two-block village constructed in a mix of architectural styles supplied the basics of civilized life: a market, a take-out pizza joint, a pub, a bakery/café, a coin-operated laundry, a pharmacy, a post office and a hardware store.

At the end of the street he paused to fill his soul with the silvery dance of the moonlight on the waters of the Burrard Inlet against a shadowy backdrop of mountains on the opposite shore. But it was too cold to linger; Ian turned down his aunt's front walk.

The house hadn't changed, either. The same parchment shingles, creamy white trim and perky orange door. As always, the long railings of the front steps seemed like white, soft arms flung wide in an eternal gesture of welcome. Looking up, his eyes followed the vertical lines of the house to the dormer window nestled under the gabled roof. The room where he always stayed. The window was dark, but pools of light glowed from the downstairs windows. It was almost as though "Aunt Gem" had known his flight out of the concrete jungle of Los Angeles would be delayed.

Ian smiled, enjoying a rare moment of complete happiness. He could almost smell his aunt's apple cider simmering on the stove. And just thinking about her chocolate fudge made his mouth water.

Then Ian's thoughts were lost to him completely as something landed with great force on the right side of his skull.

Chapter Two

"Oh, my God," Laurel whispered in dismay, shining her flashlight over the prostrate form of the man lying in the snow at her feet. "What have I done?" What she had thought was Gertie May's body thrown over the man's shoulder was, in fact, a large, overstuffed duffel bag!

She shone the light in the man's suntanned face. She didn't recognize him. His features were lax. He was out completely. But for how long?

Laurel had only a few seconds to recover from the shock of committing the first violent act in her life. It was too much of a coincidence that a stranger would be lurking around the outside of Harris House on the same night Gertie May had disappeared. She pulled off her mittens with her teeth, her heart galloping at a frenzied pace, as she knelt down and felt the man's pockets with shaking, tentative fingers. Where was his wallet? What if he came to before she could get his ID and phone the police?

He'd fallen on his left side. No wallet shape jutted out from his jean-clad buttocks. She unzipped his brown leather jacket and slipped her hand into the cozy haven of warmth against his chest. The leather had a fine, crackled patina like the glaze on old china. As her fingers skimmed over the lining of the jacket, searching for a breast pocket, she noticed he wore a lightweight denim shirt. He must be freezing. *There!* She felt something . . . the corner of his wallet.

Laurel pulled, hearing the wrench of fabric as the pocket tore. A second later the man moved in a sudden twisting motion. The next thing she knew, he had flipped her onto her back and was sitting astride her, pinning her arms above her head in a viselike grip with one hand, while his other hand smothered her screams.

IAN KNEW IMMEDIATELY by the suppleness of the body beneath him that his assailant was a woman. He stared at her in amazement, vaguely aware of the sharp pulse of pain above his right ear. The hood of the woman's duffel coat had fallen back in the struggle and her long, pale hair radiated in a scallop shape over her upraised arms and onto the blanket of snow beneath them. Ian felt a tight curl of disgust in his gut at having to manhandle a woman in this way. Her mouth felt soft beneath the unrelenting strength of his hand and he saw quite clearly in the moonlight the details of her beautiful face—thin, arched brows, wide, frightened eyes, and a slender nose with nostrils flared. What the devil was going on?

He cast a wary, practiced eye around the yard to ensure that another assailant wasn't lurking in the shrubbery waiting for a chance to put a matching dent in his skull. What had the woman hit him with, anyway? He saw the flashlight and winced, grateful that her aim wasn't precise.

Satisfied the woman had acted on her own, he loosened his grip on her mouth. "I won't hurt you," he said calmly, trying to gauge her reaction to his words from her gemlike eyes. Twin spears of moonlight reflected in them like a cat's-eye. But he couldn't quite tell what color they were. A deeply ingrained sense of self-preservation warned him not to trust her.

His instinct proved dead-on, for in the next instant she snapped at his palm with her teeth and tried to buck him off her. "Ouch! I can see you don't play fair."

She was strong despite the slender width of her torso, twisting and turning between his thighs like a fish trying to escape from a net. Her wrists were thin and delicately boned. He applied pressure, knowing he could snap them with one squeeze.

She kicked him soundly in the back with the heel of her boot.

Ian chuckled, settling a larger portion of his 185 pounds on her pelvis. If it weren't so bloody cold, he might enjoy this. Something about this spirited she-devil got his blood pounding. "I'm probably an idiot for doing this, but I'm going to take my hand off your mouth and ask you a few questions. If I like your answers, I'll let you go. Seeing as it's Christmas, I might not even file assault charges." The woman made a small sound against his palm. Of agreement? Or protest? "Do you understand?"

She nodded and Ian removed his hand, letting it hover inches from her mouth in case she started to scream. Her breath came in shallow, misty puffs fanning his face, and he was very much aware of the intense cold seeping into his kneecaps and the cushioned warmth of her body between his thighs. Anger glittered in her eyes like sparks from a fire.

"What do you want from me?" she demanded, as though she was in the position of power. He could feel the tension coiling in her body. He braced himself for another attack, admiring her courage. She should be scared as hell, but she wasn't showing it.

"Hey, I'm asking the questions. Why'd you try to put a crater in my head?"

She gave him a doleful look. "You wouldn't believe me if I told you."

"Try me."

"I thought you had my landlady slung over your back—my mistake. It was your duffel bag."

"What? You think the hole you put in my head made me senseless? You just tried to mug me, lady. I caught you red-handed, fingering my wallet."

A dark flush spread over her face. "I can explain that—"

"I can hardly wait. An' make it quick—I'm cold, and frostbite makes me cranky."

"I wasn't trying to take your wallet. Just your ID."

"Right. And maybe a few credit cards. Hey, you didn't escape from a mental hospital or anything?"

She glared at him. "No! Now get the hell off me. You're wasting time."

"What's your rush?"

She exhaled a long breath, her eyes hard with determination. "I told you already. My landlady is missing and I'm trying to find her."

Perhaps it was her forcefulness that finally convinced him he wasn't being ambushed for his money. Ian felt an odd premonitory prickle at the back of his neck. "Yeah, so who's your landlady?"

"Gertie May Harris. Have you seen her? I'm so worried—"

"Aunt Gem!"

Ian jumped up somewhat awkwardly and helped her to her feet, uttering an apology and trying to dust the snow from her coat with frozen fingers. "My aunt is missing? I'll help you find her." The wound in his left leg was numb as he bent to retrieve her mittens, handing them to her.

The woman's face registered surprise, her small mouth forming a dark *O*. "You're Ian?" She clasped the mittens to her breast. "Of course you are...who else could you be?" She laughed with relief and a deep shudder passed through her slender body. She looked white as a ghost in her dark coat.

Ian slung his duffel bag over his shoulder, walking stiffly. "Let's go inside where it's warm and you can tell me what's happened."

They hurried into the house, shedding coats and boots in the front hall. Ian sucked in his breath when he saw the short, black leather skirt and filmy blouse the woman wore beneath the plain duffel coat. Aunt Gem's boarder was a real looker.

"My name's Laurel Bishop," she said through chattering teeth. "I just came home from work and noticed Gertie May's absence. I don't know where she could be...." Her voice faltered. "Gertie May wouldn't leave Dorie alone. N-never."

"Dorie?"

"My daughter. She lives with me downstairs."

Laurel lifted her gaze to meet Ian's. She'd been hoping to meet Gertie May's nephew, but not like this. The way he'd handled her in the yard had scared the daylights out of her. For a terrifying minute she'd thought she'd come face-to-face with Steve's murderer. She'd never been at the mercy of a man's strength before, and after this experience, she hoped to never be again.

He'd taken off his glasses when they'd stepped inside. His eyes were not like Gertie May's cheerful blue, but rather a cool, flint gray—as emotionless as a rock—beneath thick slashes of gold-tipped eyebrows. He was handsome in an ordinary way. She studied his features warily, noting that his nose wasn't quite straight and his mouth had a hard, studious set to it. Only the oblong shape of his face reminded her of his aunt—and that vague resemblance didn't suggest he also shared Gertie May's friendly disposition.

"You're shivering," he said brusquely. "Let's change into warmer clothes. Then we can search the house again from top to bottom. Okay if I change in the bathroom?"

Laurel nodded, rubbing her hands over the thin sleeves of her organza blouse to warm her goose-pimpled flesh. Then she hurried downstairs.

"That settles it," Ian said almost an hour later, curling his square-tipped fingers around a steaming mug of black coffee. "We've searched the yard and the house, with the exception of the guest rooms, and there's no sign of Aunt Gem. I say we wake the guests and phone that neighbor you mentioned. If they don't know where Aunt Gem is…we call the police."

We? Laurel stifled a tremor of alarm as she set her empty mug on the blue-tiled kitchen counter. He was assuming an awful lot for someone who'd shown up barely an hour ago. She wasn't about to give him complete control. He didn't know all the facts. And the last thing she wanted to do was tell this tough, unapproachable man about the Christmas cards she'd received. She rubbed her forehead, feeling as though Ian were steadily backing her into a corner. "I should be the one to wake the guests," she said finally, with more firmness than she felt. "They might be alarmed to see a strange man in the hallway. Especially at this time of night."

"Point taken. I leave it to your discretion, Mrs. Bishop. I'll wait here."

Laurel wrapped her red, terry robe, which she'd put on over black leggings and an oversize red sweater, more tightly around her waist as she headed for the stairs. She couldn't seem to get warm enough. Her heart had been seized by a tight fist of fear. What if no one knew where Gertie May had gone? What then?

She chose the Boudreault room first, because the couple were repeat customers. She rapped softly on the door, calling out in French, *"Monsieur Boudreault? Madame? Excusez-moi..."*

Henri Boudreault opened the door, dressed in yellow flannel pajamas. *"Oui...*what is it?" he asked sleepily, squinting against the brightness of the hallway light.

"I'm sorry, *monsieur*...but Miss Harris is missing. I wondered if something had happened while I was away this evening?"

Henri shook his balding head and rubbed his hand over the black stubble on his jaw. "I'm sorry, *madame.* We came back from my son's house early, by nine o'clock. Midnight for us, because of the time difference. Mademoiselle Harris was here—all smiling. She took our order for breakfast, then we said *bonne nuit.*"

"Do you remember what she was wearing?"

He frowned, thinking for a moment. "Yes, a sweater with a pumpkin pie on it. I hope Mademoiselle Harris is all right. I tell our friends in Quebec about her hospitality."

Laurel smiled faintly. "Thank you. I'll ask Miss Smithe. Perhaps she'll know something...."

"I come with you. This is a grave situation." His round, dark eyes were sympathetic as he stepped barefoot into the hallway, quietly closing the door behind him so they wouldn't disturb his slumbering wife.

It took several rounds of knocking to rouse Miss Smithe. Laurel was on the verge of opening the door herself when it was yanked open and Janet Smithe emerged headfirst, her spiky, henna-tinted hair giving her the appearance of a porcupine on the offensive. "This better be good...." She yawned noisily into her hand. "Or I'm deducting money from my bill."

Laurel stifled her anger. Janet was one of those people who delighted in being difficult. "I apologize for waking you, Miss Smithe, but I'm very worried about Miss Harris. She seems to have disappeared from the house, I thought you might know where she is."

Miss Smithe's narrow, pointed face twisted into a scowl. "Why would you think that?"

"What I mean is, perhaps Gertie May was taken ill and a friend drove her to the hospital?"

Janet Smithe's expression softened and her tone lost its edge of irritability. "I'm sorry, I can't help you. Miss Harris seemed perfectly fine when I came home this evening. Too fine, if anything. She really goes overboard on Christmas—"

"What time was that?"

"Just after ten o'clock, I suppose. She was in the living room, watching the news in her bathrobe and rearranging the ornaments on the tree. She looked like one of those people you see on TV commercials who look so happy they can't possibly be real. I told her I'd be sleeping in tomorrow, and not to disturb me."

Henri brushed Laurel's elbow politely. "My wife and I were asleep the moment our heads touched the pillows. But perhaps the *mademoiselle* heard something before she fell asleep—the phone ring?"

"Come to think of it, I did hear the doorbell."

The doorbell? There, a simple explanation: someone had come to the door in need of help and Gertie May had responded instantly—only pausing long enough to grab her coat and boots.

The consistent, muffled creak of footsteps sounded on the stairs and Laurel whirled around, hoping Gertie May had suddenly materialized, full of apologetic smiles and dramatic explanations. But her high hopes sank into a deep valley of disappointment when Ian came into view instead. She'd almost forgotten about him.

But Ian, apparently, was not a man who wished to be forgotten, especially where his aunt was concerned. At the sight of the stranger, Henri stepped protectively in front of Laurel and Janet.

Ian came forward, his hand outstretched and his tone carrying just the right note of friendliness to put Henri's wariness instantly to rest. "Obviously Mrs. Bishop hasn't had an opportunity to tell you about me. I'm Ian Harris. Miss Harris's nephew. My flight into Vancouver was delayed several hours—that's why I've arrived so late. Everyone wants to be home for Christmas, you know. I couldn't wait any longer downstairs not knowing..." His last words hung uncomfortably in the crowded, overly lit hallway. His eyes met hers, questioning.

Laurel's stomach churned, her cheeks flushing with guilt. Did he hold her responsible for his aunt's disappearance? She made herself return his gaze with a calmness she didn't feel, annoyed that he hadn't remained downstairs as he'd promised. "Janet was just saying she heard the doorbell as she was drifting off to sleep."

"What time would that have been?" Ian shifted his frank, assessing gaze to Janet, who blinked repeatedly under his fixed granite expression, her pale blue eyes taking on a foggy, unfocused appearance.

"Between ten-thirty and eleven." She rubbed her chin with her fingers, causing the acne-dotted skin to redden. "I didn't look at my watch and there's no clock in my room."

"Did you hear anything else?" Laurel asked. "The door slam? A car start up?"

Janet shook her head. "Sorry."

Laurel sighed. "You've been a big help, actually. I'm sure this will turn out all right. Go back to bed, now. I insist." She held up her hands when Henri Boudreault protested. "There's nothing more you can do. Mr. Harris and I will handle it from here." Had she really said that?

Laurel dialed Frederick's number on the kitchen phone, the knuckles of her fingers white from the strength of her grip on the receiver. Ian hovered by the kitchen counter, near enough to listen to her side of the conversation. Laurel turned her back to him on the pretext of peering between the panels of the café curtains toward Frederick's house to see if a light now pierced the darkness of his windows. Ian's hovering made her even more nervous. The phone rang four times before Frederick responded with a grunt of a hello.

"Frederick?"

"Laurel, is that you? What time is it? Is everything all right?"

Laurel made a soothing noise, then, speaking slowly, explained the reason for her call. "I was hoping Gertie May was over at your house giving you a hand with Anna."

"Gertie May here with Anna? No. Anna's sleeping." Frederick sounded disoriented and Laurel could hear noises that suggested he was sitting upright in bed and turning on the bedside lamp. Sure enough, a faint arc of light filtered through the drawn drapes in the room Laurel knew to be his bedroom. "You say Gertie May can't be found? You did right to phone me. I'll be over as soon as I've dressed."

"No, Frederick, that won't be necessary." Laurel heard her voice crack with the agonizing despair of a last hope exhausted. She struggled to regain her composure. "I—I've had some help searching the house and the yard. Besides, what if Anna wakes up while you're gone? I'm going to phone the police. I don't know what else to do."

Oh, Gertie May, where are you? she thought wildly. She turned to face Ian, the receiver still clenched in her hand. His expression was grave and a raw ache settled in her chest, compressing her lungs to the point that it hurt to draw breath. A string of terrible possibilities paraded through her mind. What if Gertie May had gone for a walk and got lost in the woods? What if she'd gone to help someone and an accident had befallen her? What if, God forbid, some crazed envelope-bearing hoodlum had abducted Gertie May with some heinous intent? What if...

Ian pried the receiver from her fingers and dialed 911. Laurel watched, appalled. Would she ever see her beloved friend again?

SHOULD SHE TELL the police about the Christmas cards? Laurel asked herself for the hundredth time as she sat at the foot of Dorie's bed, watching her daughter sleep. She looked so peaceful with a pink, stuffed bunny nestled under her chin. As soon as Ian had finished his call, Laurel had retreated to her suite, presumably to check on Dorie, but in truth she'd come because of the envelope.

At first she'd been afraid to touch the expensively grained envelope again. Afraid that touching it would make the threat it contained a reality. But now it lay on the floor at her feet like junk mail, having slipped through her fingers as she considered her options.

Her indecisiveness was worsened by fatigue and anxiety. She'd been up twenty-one hours straight. How was she supposed to make a snap decision like this? If she showed the police the malice-laden words written on the Christmas cards, Steve's murder would come out. It might even end up in the papers. Everyone would know she'd been suspected of the crime. That the murder had never been solved....

Laurel buried her face in her hands.

She couldn't deal with the public humiliation again. The taunts. The innuendos. Steve's murder had cast shame onto her parents' sterling memory and onto Steve's stepmother. Steve's gambling had become the topic of table conversation in every home in Nelson. Her parents, Penelope and Hubert Lang, had been well-respected leaders in the small, history-proud town located in the interior of the province. Your past stayed with you in a town like Nelson, where people were known for their links with the iron and silver mining of days long ago, the logging and sawmills, or their ingenuity in creating prosperous local businesses. Colorful stories became part of the fabric of the town. Permanently.

And Dorie was older now. Not an infant any longer. She'd be affected, too. The kids in her preschool might say hurtful things.... They'd have to leave Serenity Cove and find a new place to live. Start over again.

A new name. A new place. Bishop was her middle name. Her married name had been Wilson, but of course, it would have been asking for trouble to have used it when she'd relocated to Serenity Cove.

But what if there was a perfectly logical explanation for Gertie May's disappearance—an explanation that had nothing to do with these cards or her past? Then she'd have left Dorie and herself open to gossip and scandal again. The injustice of the situation riled her. She hadn't killed her husband. It wasn't fair that she should be victimized and have her reputation ripped to shreds in the press. She was innocent!

And the last thing she wanted was to be the subject of a police investigation. Again.

The knots in Laurel's stomach tightened and her slender frame trembled violently. Her fingernails dug into her cheekbones as she struggled for control over her body and her thoughts.

On the other hand, her reputation was a small price to pay for Gertie May's safe return. If the Christmas cards were linked to Gertie May's disappearance, then she owed it to her friend to show them to the police. When Ian wasn't looking, she'd retrieve that first card from the kitchen garbage. Then she'd decide when to show both cards to the police.

Lifting her head from her hands, Laurel felt a deep sigh escape her as she gazed at the lacy pattern Jack Frost had left on her window. It was Christmas and she should be thinking about peace, joy and love. Instead she was dealing with murder, threats and possible abduction.

THE ANTIQUE grandfather clock in Aunt Gem's living room chimed five melancholy notes as a police cruiser pulled up into the driveway, its red-and-blue flashing lights sending a swirling glow across the snowy lawn and the bare branches of the broadleaf maple. Ian had never felt so helpless. By his calculations Aunt Gem had been missing for six hours, and so far, he couldn't do a damn thing to help her.

A cold rage gripped his gut and refused to be dislodged as he considered the possible ramifications of a six-hour disappearance in the middle of the night. He couldn't imagine his aunt leaving a small child unattended, emergency or no. Something had happened. Every instinct he'd honed as a gem dealer—and he'd been in more than a few precarious situations—told him so.

Ian turned away from the window and silently descended the basement steps to find Laurel. He didn't know what to make of Aunt Gem's partner. His head still smarted from the blow she'd given him with the flashlight. She was gutsy. And scared.

He'd noticed the chalky pallor of her face earlier when he'd asked what her last name was in response to a question posed over the phone by the RCMP's complaint taker. There was a certain wariness in her eyes when she'd spelled out B-i-s-h-o-p that made him curious. Or was it just her eyes that made him wary?

In the front hall he'd stared deeply into her eyes as, indeed, they'd both sized each other up under the pool of light cast from the crystal chandelier. Her eyes were translucent cabochons of honey brown and possessed a true cat's-eye phenomenon of appearing as though they were lighted from within. Yes, intriguing eyes. Treacherous to dream of such eyes—or so the legends said. People had once used cat's-eyes for charms to guard against evil spirits.

Was Laurel Aunt Gem's charm?

Ian shook his head. His mind was working overtime. Still, he couldn't dismiss the way Laurel had peered over his shoulder, scrutinizing the notes he made on a pad of paper: the file number and the name of the officer assigned to the case.

The basement had been transformed from the dingy rec room with orange-plaid furniture that he remembered to a comfortable suite with a homey feel to it, courtesy of an emerald carpet, fresh white walls and lavender moldings. There was a small seating area. Ian recognized the shapes of the couches under the new purple-print slipcovers. Aunt Gem had always been thrifty. There was also a wall unit with a built-in desk, and a play area decorated with artwork and crayoned drawings. At the end of the room was a wallpapered partition, behind which he found Laurel in the second sleeping cubicle.

She made a lonely figure, watching over her little girl in the semidarkened room. Her back was to him and her tawny hair gathered in mussed honey-tinged clouds just below her shoulder blades. Her shoulders were quivering beneath the red robe. There was a naked vulnerability in the scene that made his throat ache.

Whatever he'd thought of Mrs. Laurel Bishop, flashlight wielder, she loved his aunt. That much was plain.

Quietly he backed into the sitting area and called her name. She came around the partition, wiping her cheeks with her slender hands. He was careful to keep his expression neutral, not wanting her to guess that he'd been spying on her in a private moment. "The police are here."

The wariness instantly returned to her eyes—wariness tinged with fear. Ian felt an instant knee-jerk reaction of suspicion solidify in his gut. *Why was she so afraid of talking to the police?*

Chapter Three

Laurel shivered as much from fatigue as from anxiety when RCMP Constable Sean Rafferty entered the living room. He was a tall man with a long face made distinguished beneath the authoritative brim of his forage cap. A black, bushy mustache threaded with gray shrouded his lip. Her stomach lurched as he withdrew a small black notebook from the inside breast pocket of his patrol jacket.

"Could you tell me what happened, ma'am?" he asked somberly.

Laurel looked away from him toward the Christmas tree. A Douglas fir this year, heavily laden with one-of-a-kind baubles that Gertie May picked up at craft fairs. Gertie May apparently hadn't finished her redecorating as a crocheted Santa, a pasta angel and a miniature rag doll were poised on the arm of a nearby wing chair, waiting to be rehung. On the coffee table, shriveled holly that Gertie May had removed from a centerpiece overflowed from a paper bag. Laurel felt a hot lump swell in her throat and the burning of tears in her eyes. Surely this couldn't be happening. *Gertie May was her best friend.*

"Ma'am?"

The smell of fresh cedar greens from the exuberant display on the mantel invaded her nostrils, making her gag as she stumbled over the words, trying to give details in proper time sequence. She'd learned the hard way that the question of time was very important in police work. When she came to the part about Ian's arrival, the constable interrupted her and asked Ian for some identification.

Laurel inhaled sharply, twisting her fingers in her lap. She should have thought of that. Ian had arrived in the dead of night and she'd taken his identity for granted. She was considerably more cautious with the B and B guests.

"What's your line of work?" Constable Rafferty asked Ian, thumbing through the pages of his passport. "You're quite the traveler."

"I'm a free-lancer," Ian explained, tucking his hands into the back pockets of his jeans. "I specialize in geology and mineralogy. I'm an expert on beryl, corundum, spinel . . . they're minerals, you know. I collect samples and sell them to wholesalers."

Rafferty nodded vaguely.

"I'm sure there are a few photographs of me in my aunt's albums that could clear up any doubts as to my identity."

His answer threw Laurel even more off-balance emotionally. What a gross misrepresentation of the truth. Gertie May had told her Ian was an international gem dealer. He transported tens of thousands of dollars' worth of gems at a time. Mostly colored stones. He bought the gems from mines all over the world and sold them to wholesalers. It was very dangerous and the stakes were high. She saw no reason why he should withhold the true nature of his occupation from the police. Unless he had something to hide? She gave him a speculative glance. Why, indeed?

"Was the front door locked when you returned from work, Mrs. Bishop?"

"Wh-what? Oh, yes." The door. She'd had trouble opening it because she was so scared. Her voice trembled with the memory of fear. "I distinctly remember hearing the lock click as I turned the key. I believe Gertie May has her coat and my rain boots on over her pajamas and robe. I don't understand why she'd take my black rain boots—she's never done that before. But maybe her winter boots were wet . . . and she wasn't planning to go far. She's not wearing a hat, either."

"What about her purse?"

"She doesn't have one. Just an apricot leather wallet that she carries in her coat pocket."

"I see. What about her car?"

"She doesn't use it much. It's the red beater in the driveway."

"Have you contacted Miss Harris's relatives?"

"I'm her only living relative," Ian put in.

"What about friends?"

Laurel shook her head. Should she have? "I phoned one neighbor. I thought Gertie May would only leave Dorie to give him a hand with his wife. Mrs. Aames has Alzheimer's disease...."

"How long has it been since you last saw your aunt, Mr. Harris?"

"Four years."

"Did you keep in touch with her through letters or phone calls?"

Ian ran his hand through his hair. "No. With the nature of my work, it's difficult to have a fixed address. We have this ongoing understanding that I'll come for Christmas— if I'm able."

Rafferty looked up from his notebook. "You didn't phone her to tell her you were coming?"

"No, I've always just shown up on her doorstep. It's more dramatic. My aunt loves dramatics."

"I believe he's telling you the truth, Constable," Laurel said hesitantly. "Gertie May's told me any number of times that she loves the way Ian just shows up for Christmas."

"Is your aunt a wealthy woman?"

"I've no idea. She's comfortable, I suppose. The subject of finances has never come up between us. Do you think my aunt could have been kidnapped?" Ian experienced a dawning horror at the prospect of his aunt being held for ransom.

"We're not ruling anything out at the moment. How about enemies?"

Enemies? Aunt Gem? He wasn't sure. But he certainly had a few enemies. The meetings with his L.A.-based clients had ruffled a few feathers. But enough to do this? "I don't know," he replied after a pause. "Aunt Gem's a mover and a shaker. Laurel would be able to answer that better than I."

Rafferty looked at Laurel expectantly.

Ian wondered if it was his imagination, but Laurel seemed even more pale. "No, no enemies," she said, choking on the words.

"Have you noticed anything unusual in the house?" Rafferty continued. "Things out of place? Missing items?"

Laurel shook her head.

Constable Rafferty snapped his notebook shut. "Well, ma'am, we have at least a dozen missing-persons reports a day. But a responsible adult doesn't leave a preschooler alone in the house, and the fact that Miss Harris is elderly is cause for concern. I'm going to ask you and Mr. Harris to assist me with some of the groundwork by contacting Miss Harris's friends. In the meantime, I'm going to have a look around and call in some support units."

FROM THE SOUND of Laurel's phone calls, Aunt Gem had not gone off to help a friend, Ian thought morosely as he sipped a cup of strong, black coffee. Laurel's voice grew hoarse as she flipped through Aunt Gem's address book, making call after call. He tried to keep her well supplied with tea. But watching the helplessness grow in her eyes as she explained Aunt Gem's disappearance over and over again, and hearing the frustration in her voice when she was forced to leave a message on an answering machine, was almost more than he could bear.

Ian clenched the pen in his fingers and kept an equally tight grip on his emotions as he made notations on the running list of names they were compiling for the police. But there was nothing he could do to diminish the stab of guilt-riddled pain he experienced each time Laurel's voice swelled with gratitude when she was momentarily buoyed by someone's offer of assistance. It was no surprise to him that Aunt Gem was well-thought-of in the community.

There was a lot to love about Aunt Gem. He'd loved her, more than his own parents. She had a gift for making people feel welcome. Wanted. Loved. He could kick himself for having stayed away so long. For trying to prove to himself that work was more important than family. But wasn't that what his parents had taught him?

Constable Rafferty entered the kitchen to advise them that the support units had arrived. By "support units," Constable Rafferty was referring to the German Shepherd dog squad. "The cold, moist climate is good for holding human scent," he explained to them quietly when Laurel had finished her calls. "The lawn looks a bit like Swiss cheese with footprints everywhere. But there may be some tracks on the ground and the dog is checking to see if there's a body stashed close by."

Laurel shuddered and clamped her hands over her mouth.

Despite his suspicions, Ian slipped his arms around her. "Hey, don't imagine the worst," he murmured as Rafferty left the kitchen. She curled into him, resting her hot forehead against his chest. Her back was taut with tension and her shoulders heaved as she wept. He rubbed the knotted muscles in her back, not minding that her tears were dampening his shirt. He was so close to the edge with worry about Aunt Gem that he derived some comfort from the contact.

After a while, she lifted her head and started to pull away, but he gently contained her with reassuring words. He was determined to do—or say—whatever he had to, to gain the trust of the woman who shared his aunt's home. Aunt Gem's life could depend on it.

Constable Rafferty returned a short time later to inform them that the perimeter search had come up negative. The dog was now on a leash conducting a radii search, working in a circular pattern in an effort to detect any signs of human effluent: sweat, blood or vomit. The officer's dark, guarded gaze seemed to take note of the fact that Laurel still remained in the shelter of Ian's arms. Ian felt a twinge of uneasiness at the base of his spine. Exactly what was going on in Rafferty's mind?

"There is an area of some concern just to the right of the front path," Rafferty said carefully. "The snow is flattened as though a struggle may have taken place."

"Ah, that I can explain," Ian replied with more bluster than he felt. "You see, Mrs. Bishop was searching the yard for my aunt at the time of my arrival and mistook me for an intruder. We had a scuffle until introductions were properly made."

"Actually, I tried to knock him out," Laurel said flatly. Ian gave her a bolstering squeeze. "With my flashlight."

"I see," Rafferty responded in a tone that implied the contrary. "Would you care to lay assault charges against Mrs. Bishop?"

Ian felt Laurel stiffen in his arms. He chose his reply to put her at ease. "No. Given the circumstances, I believe it was perfectly understandable. I have a small bump on my head. It's nothing serious."

"You won't mind if I have a look at this bump, then?"

"Of course not." Laurel discreetly moved aside, leaving the sweet-scented warmth of her body imprinted on him. Ian lowered his head for Rafferty's doubting fingers, feeling suddenly irate. "Ow, there. That's it." He scowled. "I understand you have to ask us all these questions, Constable, but may I ask what you're doing to find my aunt?"

"I've spoken to my supervisor and requested assistance from the General Investigations section and the Identification section. They should be here shortly. You'll have to wake your daughter, now, ma'am. It's possible she may know something that could help us. In any case, the Ident officer will want to go over her room. It's customary procedure."

While Laurel led Constable Rafferty downstairs, Ian tidied the kitchen for lack of anything better to do. Rafferty's questions had rattled him. What if one of his clients had stooped to abducting Aunt Gem to ensure his continued services?

A baker's cap of used coffee grounds and soggy tea bags was cluttering up the sink. Ian tried to open the trash cupboard, but a plastic latch held the door closed. It took some fiddling before he mastered the knack of opening it. The trash container was full and he pulled it out of the cupboard to compact it with his foot.

On the very top were pork bones and a fancy gold Christmas card that had been savagely mangled—not surprising, considering there was a kid in the house. Ian was about to tamp down on it when he noticed the dark, handwritten wording on the card that spelled—*murder?* He eyed the grease-stained angel as he smoothed out the card. He must be nuts, but his aunt's unexplained disappearance and Laurel's wary expression had primed the pump of his intuition. He flipped the card open anyway.

The salutation made his blood run cold. *I know about your past—murderess.*

"Would you mind, Constable, if I went in first to wake my daughter?" Laurel asked weakly, hoping he would misconstrue her nervousness and knocking knees for motherly concern. "She's only three and a half. I don't want to frighten her any more than necessary. Perhaps I could bring her into the sitting area so you could examine her room?"

He nodded. "Nothing seems to be disturbed here. Try not to touch anything in your daughter's room."

"I understand." Laurel slipped around the partition, her legs trembling as she retrieved the card and envelope that she'd slid underneath Dorie's mattress for safekeeping. What should she do with it now? She looked around the room in desperation for a hiding place. She didn't have any pockets in her leggings and her robe pockets were too obvious.

Dorie's pink, fabric Gloworm doll peeped out at her from a mound of animals. The plastic battery case concealed inside the doll's soft, padded, elongated body was empty. She'd been conveniently forgetting to buy batteries for ages. They were too expensive.

Laurel quietly unzipped the doll's back, rolled the Christmas card and the envelope into a tube, and slid them inside the battery case. Then she zipped up the doll and tucked it into the zoo of other animals, firmly squashing any feelings of guilt at her actions.

"Dorie. Dorie, honey. It's Mommy." Laurel gently stroked her daughter's warm, silken cheek. Dorie awakened with a smile and instantly raised her arms for a good-morning hug. Laurel snuggled her close, breathing in her little-girl scent of baby shampoo and strawberry bubble bath. Her heart constricted in a painful knot. Dorie was the most precious thing in her life. She'd do anything to protect her. "Did you have a good sleep?"

"Mmm-hmm."

"Good. Dorie, Mommy's very worried about Gertie May. She's lost and I can't find her. She wasn't here when I came home from work last night." Laurel tried to keep the fear from tainting her voice. "Do you remember when the policeman came to visit your preschool? He told you the police are your friends, and they help you when you have a problem?"

Dorie nodded and recited, "You always ask a policeman for help when you're lost."

"Right. Well, there's a policeman here who's going to help me find Gertie May. Can you answer his questions for Mommy?"

"Yes."

"Good girl." Laurel scooped her out of the warm nest of blankets and carried her into the sitting room where Constable Rafferty was sitting on the smaller of the two couches. He'd removed his hat, Laurel noticed, and looked less frightening. His eyes had a friendly twinkle. He waited until Laurel had sat down, with Dorie nestled next to her, before he held out his hand to the preschooler.

"Hi, my name's Sean. What's your name?"

"Dorie."

"How old are you, Dorie?"

Dorie held up four fingers, then changed her mind and pushed one down. "Three."

Constable Rafferty smiled encouragingly. "That's great. I was three once, too. It was a long time ago, but I still remember what it was like. Do you remember what you did yesterday morning?"

Gradually, Constable Rafferty worked through Dorie's detailed descriptions of her meals and her playtime in the snow. Laurel admired his patience. "After your mom went to work, what did you do?"

"I dried the forks and spoons and put them in the drawer. Gertie May lets me stand on chairs. But Mommy doesn't. I'm a good helper. Then I had a bath with bubbles and put on my jammies all by myself. Gertie May said if I brush my teeth well I can have two stories."

"Did you have your stories next?"

Dorie shook her head. "No. I watched TV with Gertie May for the numbers."

Constable Rafferty looked puzzled.

"For the Saturday night Lotto 6/49 draw," Laurel explained. "The numbers are drawn on BCTV at 7:00 p.m. Dorie's bedtime is at 7:30 p.m."

"After the numbers, we played ring-around-the-rosy fast, fast, fast. Then Gertie May read me three stories. She was very happy 'cause Santa's coming, so she said I could have an extra story. I love Gertie May this much—" Dorie spread her arms wide, then flopped against Laurel's side.

"You're lucky to have such a good friend," Constable Rafferty said. "What did you do after the stories?"

"Go to sleep."

"Gertie May stays down here and reads until Dorie's asleep."

"Were you tired? Did you go to sleep right away?"

Dorie hunched her small shoulders forward and tucked her hands between her knees. Her dark brown eyes shone impishly as she looked up, then down, and away from her inquisitors. Laurel touched her shoulder. "It's okay if you didn't.... What did you do?"

"I played a trick on Gertie May. I pretended to be asleep."
She giggled. "An' Gertie May went upstairs. Then I played
tea party with my baby and my bunny. And you know what,
Mommy?"

"What, sweetie?"

"I saw him."

Him. Laurel felt a clammy chill of apprehension slide over
her like a damp sheet. She caught Rafferty's eye, and with
a faint movement of his hand he encouraged her to continue asking the questions. "Saw who, sweetie?"

"Santa. He looked in the window just like Gertie May
said."

"Are you sure it was Santa?"

Dorie's giggles evaporated and her arms folded across her
chest as thunderclouds formed on her rounded brow. "Yes.
He looked two times, Mommy, 'cause he knows when
you're sleeping and I wasn't really sleeping. No kids can fool
Santa. I wanted Santa to bring me presents so I closed my
eyes and went to sleep." Dorie clapped her hands. "I know,
Mommy, maybe Gertie May went with Santa to visit the
North Pole. Can you phone Santa and ask?"

"I'll do that first thing," Constable Rafferty promised,
rising to his feet.

Laurel smoothed her daughter's fine, honey gold hair,
half listening to Dorie's chatter about reindeer and elves and
the sound of Rafferty's boots thundering up the stairs. What
was it Dorie had said? "No kids can fool Santa." But can
Santa fool kids?

WITH THE CHILD'S awakening, the day had begun. Ian noticed a subtle change in Laurel from the moment she reen-
tered the kitchen wearing her daughter like a comfortable,
pink, fuzzy sweater. Gone were the sharp edges to her manner; she seemed all soft words and curves as she unhooked
Dorie's arms from around her neck and settled her in a
chair. Her hands lingered on Dorie's shoulders in a gesture
of protective reassurance as she made introductions.

Ian didn't quite know what to think of this sprite of a girl with her big brown eyes and pearly skin, a miniature version of her mother—or what to say to her. He knew zilch about kids. Where was her father? Laurel wasn't wearing a wedding ring....

But Ian quickly realized that making conversation with Dorie wouldn't be a problem. Dorie made plenty. He did his best to follow along with the flow while Laurel prepared toast and cereal.

"You're Gertie May's Ian?" Dorie asked with great awe and respect worthy of Mickey Mouse.

"Yes." He suddenly felt bigger in his boots.

"Goody! Gertie May knew you were coming this year. She bought you a present, but I can't tell you what it is. It's a secret. But you know what?"

"What?"

"I helped Gertie May find a hiding place. Did Mommy tell you Gertie May is lost? But don't worry, the nice policeman will find her, okay?"

"Okay." Ian patted her head awkwardly. "Thanks, kiddo."

Dorie hoisted a spoonful of Cheerios to her mouth and Ian took advantage of the opportunity to have a private word with Laurel at the counter. "The police are interviewing the guests upstairs. We're to stay in the kitchen for now, but Rafferty said Dorie could go to a sitter—only we should go out the back door."

Laurel nodded, buttering a slice of toast with short, nervous strokes until it crumbled in her hand.

"Let me do that," he said, taking it from her trembling fingers. "Phone the sitter. You're exhausted, and we could have a long day ahead of us." She would definitely have a long night answering his questions once the police had departed. And his interrogation methods would be far less civil.

After Dorie was safely dispatched, bundled up as though for a trip to the Arctic, the guests filed into the kitchen, their faces grave.

Laurel jumped up from the table, offering apologies and breakfast. Ian was relieved they had the good sense to refuse her offer, even the waspish redhead. Laurel reassured them that they could have their rooms over the holiday as agreed. Then the conversation was broken up by the appearance of an Identification officer requesting to take their fingerprints.

"Why are you taking our fingerprints?" Laurel asked, wiping her hands nervously on a kitchen towel. Ian smothered his angry fascination with her actions. What murderess wouldn't be worried about having her fingerprints taken?

"Your fingerprints will be used to eliminate those found on the scene to point to an intruder's fingerprints," the officer explained.

It was a disquieting ceremony. Ian volunteered to go first, then maneuvered himself near the back door where he could observe the guests. Henri Boudreault went next, his features drawn into a sorrowful expression, followed by his wife, Marguerite. She was a petite brunette, neat in appearance, with watchful eyes the color of dark chocolate. A big voice in a little package, Ian thought as she expressed her shock and outrage at Gertie May's unexplained disappearance to the officer until her husband finally succeeded in shushing her. "I will say a prayer for your aunt at midnight mass *ce soir,*" she murmured to Ian, taking her husband's arm for assistance down the icy back steps.

Miss Smithe seemed impatient for the procedure to be finished with as quickly as possible. She scrubbed at her fingers with an alcohol-soaked wipe, then slipped her arms into a drab olive coat and scurried out the back door. Ian noticed Laurel's hands shook as she held them out to the officer, her face a stiff, white mask.

She was hiding something . . . he knew it. But if he turned her over to the police right now, he'd never find out what happened to his aunt. She'd be too inaccessible locked away in a jail cell.

He moved up behind her. She was lost in thought, dabbing at the ink stains on her fingers with a wipe. She jumped, startled, when he touched her arm, and dropped the wipe, bending over quickly to retrieve it. Her face was suffused with color when she straightened.

From guilt, or exertion? He wanted to shake her by the shoulders until the answers he needed came rolling out of her mouth. Was she a murderess, as the card suggested? Her name had been on the envelope.

He bit back his questions and pulled a chair out for her, dragging it ruthlessly across the wood floor. It was an effort to keep his voice calm. "Let's sit down, reserve our strength. We don't know what could lie ahead."

She nodded wordlessly and sat down.

Periodically, Ian looked down the hallway to check the progress of the forensics experts in white coveralls, who were combing the house. They didn't have long to wait.

Forty minutes later Constable Rafferty loomed in the doorway like a dark-winged angel of death. Two senior officers were behind him. "I'm very sorry to tell you, folks, but we've found a smear of blood on the side of a table in the hall...."

"Bloo-ood." Laurel moaned the word, a hoarse cry of pain. She'd half risen from her straight-backed chair when she'd seen Rafferty, but now she sank back down. Disbelief whitewashed her face as her fingers pressed over her lips.

"Are you suggesting my aunt may have been murdered?" Ian fought to gain control over the blinding rage that was ripping him apart. Christ, this couldn't be happening! He cursed the plane for being late and cursed the woman seated within arm's length of him. If only he'd gotten here sooner...

"I can't say anything more at this point. Only that blood has been found and we're investigating all possibilities and ruling out nothing."

Investigating all possibilities... Ian's jaw hardened and it was all he could do to prevent himself from pointing an accusatory finger at Laurel as Rafferty droned on. "There have been no reports of injured persons matching your aunt's description admitted into the hospital, or unidentified bodies found. Mr. Harris, I'd like a private word with you."

Ian nodded. He noticed one of the other officers stayed behind with Laurel in the kitchen. Did the police know something about Laurel that he didn't? Rage bore down on his chest until he thought he was ready to snap under its unrelenting weight. All he could think about was confronting her when they were finally alone. Then he'd ask her about the Christmas card.

"Wouldn't I be of more use if you'd let me search the waterfront and neighboring yards?" Ian said testily, limping as he paced the alcove's narrow width. It was exactly five strides. "You already know my aunt was missing before I got here."

"Yes, we've confirmed the arrival time of your flight. We were more concerned with how well you know Mrs. Bishop."

Ian froze. Caution masked his expression. "I just met her. But I gather she's worked for my aunt about two years. Why?"

Rafferty skirted the question. "Do you know where she's from?"

"No." But he was determined to find out.

"Has your aunt ever mentioned her?"

"No. If you'll recall, I haven't spoken to my aunt in years."

On the way back to the kitchen, Ian wondered what the hell kind of flimsy answers Laurel was giving to the other police officer.

He wasn't the least bit fooled by Laurel's sudden interest in cleaning as soon as the officers returned to their work. He was bitterly amused by the haste with which she dragged a broom around the immaculate floor and the uncommon length of time it took her to empty the dustpan into the trash container. He knew exactly what she was looking for—the Christmas card. He figured she had to be plenty worried to risk removing the card from the garbage right under his nose.

She pulled open a drawer and began rummaging through its contents. He took a deep breath and willed himself to say calmly, "What are you doing?"

She looked up, startled, her beautiful face pale. Lines of tension tightened along her brow and created indentations in her cheeks.

"I can't find the Christmas tea towel that hangs on the oven door. I want everything to be nice for Gertie May when she comes home...." Her words trailed off, punctuating her uncertainty.

Not that he believed her for a second. Her feeble explanation was just another nail in her coffin as far as he was concerned. Ian rubbed the stubble sprouting on his jaw, feeling the beginnings of a headache pound at his temples. Why shouldn't he have a headache? She'd whacked him pretty dang well.

The source of his headache ran a dishrag over the countertops and he studied her covertly, finding her slender frame and pear-size breasts very much to his liking. Frowning, he sat up taller in his chair, trying to distance his mind from his body's physical reaction to her figure. *Damn,* he thought with a sudden awareness that chilled his soul. *This woman is trouble.*

Ian hadn't prayed since he was fourteen. Then he'd asked God to forgive him for not being sorry his parents were dead. Now he prayed that Aunt Gem was still alive, and that the police would soon leave. He wasn't sure how much longer he could remain in the same room with Laurel without confronting her.

Darkness came. The police cars and vans disappeared into the night, one by one. It was Christmas Eve. The house grew eerily silent as Ian tracked Laurel's desperate flight down the hallway from the front door to the kitchen, straight to the cupboard under the sink.

Ian slipped the Christmas card out of his back pocket. When he was directly behind her, he gripped her arm and whirled her around to face him, plastering the Christmas card to her chest. "I believe this is what you're looking for," he said in a deadly tone.

Her shriek of dismay was not the least bit gratifying.

Chapter Four

Ian felt the rage that had been building in his chest burst in an overwhelming wave of heat as Laurel's fingers closed around the card. "You shouldn't leave incriminating evidence like this lying around during a police search." He slid his hand up to grasp her neck, pressing her back against the counter. "What'd you do to my aunt?"

Laurel's eyes widened with fear. "N-nothing. I love Gertie May. She's the best friend I've ever had. I'd never hurt her—I swear!"

Ian applied persuasive pressure to her throat, feeling her pulse throb against his thumb. It seemed to mingle with his own ragged pulse. "This card suggests otherwise. If you're so innocent, why didn't you show it to the police?"

He felt her sag against the counter and he was unprepared for the wave of misery that welled in her eyes. Tears dribbled down her cheeks. "Oh, Ian, you don't understand—"

Her chin was trembling and Ian found himself loosening his grip ever so slightly. Something about the darkness of his hand against her lily-white skin sickened him. She had the strangest effect on him. "I'm listening."

Laurel was oblivious to the tears that dampened her cheeks. Ian's expression was cast in unrelenting granite. His hard, abrasiveness terrified her. Somehow she had to make him understand... Convince him not to go to the police with the Christmas cards. At least, not yet.

She drew a deep breath and let it out slowly, grateful that he'd let go of the death grip on her neck. "Two years ago, on the morning of Christmas Eve—the same as today—I found my husband in our living room. He was d-dead... murdered by a blow to the head. The police said he'd been killed the night before—"

"Who killed him?"

"I—I don't know. The police never solved the crime."

"Whoever sent this card seems to think you did it."

"They're wrong!"

"Where were you when this happened?"

The bluntness of his questions rattled her. She felt so very cold. The card seemed to be sucking all the warmth from her fingers. She knew if she told Ian the absolute truth, he'd drag her through the streets of North Vancouver to the police station. "Dorie and I were spending the night at my mother-in-law's for Christmas. Steve was going to drop by our house after work that night—he often worked late as a car salesman—to pick up a Christmas gift I'd forgotten. He n-never arrived at Barb's. I phoned the house the next morning, thinking he'd been too tired to drive after work. There was no answer, so I went over and that's when I found him." Laurel swallowed hard. As long as she lived, she'd never forget the horror of finding Steve's body.

"If you loved your husband so much, why aren't you wearing his ring?"

"I sold it to pay for his funeral," she said, surprised by the bitterness in her voice. Why would she want to keep it anyway? Their whole marriage had been based on lies.

Ian remained silent, judging her, she knew. She hoped Gertie May would forgive the white lie she'd just told.

After a pause she said quietly, "I didn't kill my husband. The police investigated me quite thoroughly. I even took a polygraph test twice to prove my innocence."

Ian let go of her and his fist hit the countertop. Laurel jumped. "Look, lady," he said in a clipped tone. "My aunt is missing—coincidentally, two years to the day from when your husband was killed—by some unknown assailant.

There's blood on the hall table and a nasty note here that makes you look damned guilty. You may not want to show this to the police, but I certainly do." He moved toward the phone.

Terror sliced through Laurel's heart. She leapt in front of him, restraining him physically with her palms pressing firmly against his chest. His fingers tightened around her wrists like handcuffs.

"No, please! You can't do that. They'll take Dorie away from me. I *won't* let you do that to her." She searched her mind, desperate for something factual to add to her argument. "B-besides, I have an alibi. I was working, remember? The bartender walked me home. He can verify what time we arrived...I'll give you his phone number...I didn't have the opportunity to do anything, much less hide a body." She paused for a moment. He was listening to her, perhaps believing her—those cold eyes seemed to be calculating everything she said.

Her forearms were beginning to ache from the force she was exerting against him. "Besides, we don't even know for certain what's happened to Gertie May," she continued. "Maybe it's all some crazy misunderstanding. The front door was locked when I came home. Gertie May had to have locked it before she left. Maybe the blood that the police found belonged to someone else—like the person who came to the door. It's quite possible that Gertie May took this person to their home or to the hospital and hasn't had a chance to phone me yet. Isn't it?"

"In nineteen hours? I doubt it," he said harshly.

Laurel winced.

"How do you know that this note isn't a prelude to extortion, or part of a kidnapping plot? Or, for that matter, some emotionally unstable person's idea of a good time? Did it ever occur to you that some lunatic is hell-bent on harming the people closest to you?"

A lunatic? After her and Dorie? Laurel suddenly felt faint and she swayed against him, her fingers twisting in his tan chambray shirt. "No, I d-don't know."

"All the more reason to show it to the police."

Laurel closed her eyes and licked her lips, fear spiraling through her. Beneath the soft fabric of his shirt she could feel the implacable wall of his chest and the steady, determined rhythm of his heartbeat underneath. He was going to show the cards to the police—and she couldn't stop him.

"Have you ever been the subject of a police investigation, Ian?" she whispered, laying bare the deepest humiliation of her soul. "They peer into every corner of your life, even corners that you didn't know existed. Steve was heavily into gambling. We were on the verge of losing our home and I had absolutely no idea. I was so involved with Dorie at the time...she was just a baby. Of course, the police didn't believe me. In their eyes, they'd found my motive."

She drew a ragged breath. "They even spoke to my neighbors and friends, who were all quite eager to share the details of our private conversations, because it was their civic duty to assist the police in building a case against me.

"Did I mention the newspapers? It was the big Christmas tragedy story. Widow Suspected of Murder, the headlines read. It's rather interesting to see the whole of your life set out in tidy rows of print. Of course, when I was cleared of all charges, just a tiny blurb appeared. No big headlines. No apologies for turning my life inside out."

The warmth of Ian's strong hands encompassed her own, and Laurel felt a stirring of hope. If she had someone like Ian on her side, someone strong and tough and incapable of being intimidated, she might stand a better chance of finding out what happened to Gertie May, and who was hounding her with the Christmas cards.

"Don't you see, Ian, with *my history,* it will start all over again. If I'm arrested and taken in for questioning, they'll take Dorie from me and put her in a foster home with strangers."

"Don't you have a relative who could look after her if that happened?"

His question struck her full force in the heart. She wrenched her hands free from his. How could he think a mother was replaceable by a relative? "We're talking about a child here, not an object that can be moved around from place to place with no ill effects. There's no one I can leave her with. The only family I have left is Steve's mother, and she's ill."

Laurel raised her eyes to meet his cold, steady gaze. "If you turn me over to the police, Ian, the investigation will come to a grinding halt and you'll never discover what happened to Gertie May. If her disappearance has something to do with the Christmas cards, you'll need my assistance. Couldn't we please wait a day or two and see what happens?" His silence tore mercilessly at her soul.

She tried one last-ditch argument. "Besides, you weren't honest with the police, either. That free-lancing business was a stretch of the truth. I'm rather curious why you wouldn't want the police to know you're in the gem trade. How do I know you didn't arrive earlier and harm Gertie May?"

Ian spread his arms wide, anger infusing his tone. "Wait a minute. Did you just say Christmas cards, as in plural? You mean, there's more?"

"Yes—"

He swore and pushed his glasses up to the bridge of his nose. "How many more?"

Laurel remained silent, weighing the risks of telling him the truth. "It would be rather stupid of me to tell you that before we've struck a deal, wouldn't it?"

He took a menacing step toward her.

Laurel's knees trembled.

"Here's the deal," he said sharply, "I'm willing to wait forty-eight hours, and there's a condition."

"What?"

"That you entrust me with the other cards you've received. I'll hang on to them until it's time to turn them over to the police. Deal?"

Laurel had no choice. She had to trust him for Dorie's sake. "It's a deal." She gave him an impulsive hug, then stepped back quickly, embarrassed by his stiff reaction. "There's only one other card. It's downstairs."

"I'll come with you. But first, I'll need some plastic bags."

Laurel found the bags and watched as Ian dropped the card and the envelope into separate bags and sealed the tops to protect them from gathering any more fingerprints. Then they went downstairs to Dorie's room. To Laurel's relief, the second card was still hidden inside the Gloworm doll.

"Not a bad hiding spot," Ian commented with a wry smile as he eased the card out of the battery case with a facial tissue. "I'll have to remember it. A handful of gems could be concealed in there quite easily." He arranged the card in the plastic bag so the message was visible. "'History Can Repeat Itself.' It sounds like a threat."

Laurel grew uneasy again. "That's why I think the cards may have something to do with Gertie May's disappearance." She laid her hand on his arm. "You're not going to back out on our deal, are you?" A sudden nervous awareness coursed through her as she felt the tension stiffening in the muscles of his forearm. Blushing, she eased her hand away. He was obviously a man who needed his own space and wasn't comfortable with casual physical contact.

"No. I'm not backing out on our deal."

"Good. That was the second card. They both came yesterday. One in the late afternoon. The other was on the door when I came home from work."

"Hmm. It's obvious someone in Serenity Cove has a grudge against you."

"But that's the strange part. I'm originally from Nelson. Dorie and I moved here *after* my husband's death. No one but Gertie May knows about my past, or even where I'm from. I've been very careful to put that part of my life behind me."

Ian looked at the objects in his hands and grim lines formed at the corners of his mouth. "Evidently, you weren't careful enough."

THE NIGHT was cold and crisp, the stars twinkling at their brightest so that Santa would have no trouble navigating his sleigh. Ian felt angry to the core as he limped along the icy sidewalk next to Laurel. Aunt Gem was missing and the rest of the world was celebrating Christmas Eve. He cursed his bum leg under his breath, the stab of pain he experienced with each step was nothing compared to the deep ache in his heart.

He glanced at Laurel, who was peering into each snow-draped yard they passed for some sign of Gertie May. "Caroline Nicholls lives five houses down," she explained as they turned onto a narrow lane crowded with parked cars. "She goes to preschool with Dorie." Ian kept his eyes averted from the windows of the homes. He was in no mood to see the families inside enjoying the festivities of this holiday.

Laurel obviously had similar thoughts. She was about to knock on the door of a white stucco cottage when her hand fell to her side and she turned to him, her eyes huge and dark in her pale face. Music and laughter seeped through the thickness of the door. "I—I don't know if I can go through with celebrating Christmas tomorrow...."

"We won't, then," he replied tersely. "We'll just post-pone it until Gertie May comes back. That is, if you think your little girl won't be too disappointed."

"No, not if we handle it just right. I'll figure out some-thing to tell her." She touched his arm with a mittened hand, the fourth time she'd touched him since they'd met, and he felt as though she'd touched his heart. "Thanks, I thought you'd understand."

He nodded, unable to break her gaze, wondering how she could have such an intimate effect on him—despite the enormous distrust he felt for her—and how she could so easily break through the reserve that normally held others at bay.

It was Laurel who pulled her eyes away first, squaring her shoulders and knocking briskly on the door. Dorie hurtled into the foyer as soon as she heard her mother talking with Mrs. Nicholls.

"Mommy!"

Laurel scooped her up and hugged her hard.

"Oh, I missed you! Give Mommy a kiss."

Ian felt a lump form in his throat at the sight of them clinging together. Laurel's back was to him, but the way her hand lovingly stroked Dorie's head was a deeply telling gesture. Had his own mother ever loved him that much? He couldn't remember an instance in his childhood when his mother had fought valiantly to keep him at her side. Or had even given him an extra hug at a parting to show her affection.

On the contrary, his parents had been academic in their care for him, sending him to boarding school for discipline and stability, which they couldn't provide from an archaeological site on the Seward Peninsula. He'd spend a few weeks with his parents in the summer, wherever they happened to be working, then he'd be off to camp. Christmas was the only time his parents left their work behind to celebrate the holidays at Aunt Gem's.

With deft fingers, Laurel laced, zipped and fastened Dorie into her winter gear. Then they retraced their steps home, three lone figures in the night. Ian remained silent, observing them with sidelong glances and half listening to their conversation, though his ears pricked up when Laurel brought up the delicate subject of Christmas Eve.

"Mommy's going to leave a note for Santa tonight and ask him to please wait to bring the presents until after Gertie May is home. Okay?"

Dorie was silent for a moment. "Are you sure Santa takes notes?"

"Of course. He answered your letter, didn't he? A note is a short letter. Besides, if I know Santa, I'll betcha when he reads the note he'll decide to leave you something special to play with until Gertie May comes home."

"Okay, Mommy. Let's wait for Gertie May. And I'll save my presents for you, too."

Ian felt his facial muscles relax into a bemused smile. He was beginning to like this kid.

His thoughts were interrupted by a sharp, painful nudge in his ribs courtesy of Laurel's elbow.

"Look. Is it my imagination or is there someone on the veranda peering through the windows?" she murmured in his ear, pointing at Harris House.

Ian scanned the veranda and quickly spotted the dark shape silhouetted in the glow of the porch light.

"Maybe it's Gertie May," Laurel whispered excitedly.

"Or maybe someone's delivering another card. I'll see who it is. Stay behind me," Ian ordered in a quiet tone as he moved cautiously up the front walk. He got within tackling range of the person, then spoke out in a loud voice. "Can I help you?"

The figure whirled around awkwardly, as though unsteady on his feet. "What? Who's there?"

"Frederick? Oh, Ian, it's Frederick, our next-door neighbor." Laurel rushed up the walk and made introductions.

Frederick shook Ian's hand. "We've met a few times, I believe. Your aunt has told me a lot about you. Actually, your aunt is the reason I dropped by. I noticed the police were here earlier and I was getting worried. Is there any news?"

Laurel cleared her throat and made a signal with her eyebrows. "Uh, maybe I'll take Dorie inside and get dinner started, so you two can speak privately."

"Sure. I can take a hint." Ian unlocked the door and held it open for them to pass, then turned to Frederick. The old man appeared genuinely upset. "I'm sorry, there's nothing."

"I can't believe such a thing could happen in Serenity Cove...."

"That's just it. We don't know what's happened yet. The police will keep us posted. I don't suppose you noticed anything unusual last night around ten-ish?"

"Me? No, I'm usually in bed at that hour. My wife is an early riser. I said as much to the officer who came by this afternoon. I did see a fella, though, just before supper. He went up to the front steps and left real quicklike. I thought he might be delivering handbills, but he didn't come to my house. He just took off on foot across the park."

Ian's pulse quickened. "Do you remember anything more about him? What he was wearing?"

"Sorry. Come to think of it, it could have been a teenager or a small man. I was taking vegetable peelings out to the compost bin and it was dark. It's a shame your holiday has taken such an unexpected turn." Frederick turned to go. "Let me know if there is anything I can do to help. I'll say a prayer for Gertie May's safe return."

DINNER WAS a somber affair around the kitchen table. Laurel was too sick with worry over Gertie May and too tired to do more than nibble on a cracker and sip a few spoonfuls of soup. Eating just wasn't worth the effort. Yet somehow she had to summon enough energy to do the supper dishes, get Dorie to bed, and plan tomorrow's breakfast for the guests.

Ian, too, seemed to have pushed himself beyond his limits. She'd noticed his limp on the walk to the Nichollses'. His expression as he ate his meal was drawn and tight. Was he in pain?

"Why don't you go to bed early?" she suggested, meeting his gaze after she got Dorie busy drawing a picture for Santa's note in Gertie May's office. "The guests probably won't be back until after nine. You can have the bathroom to yourself. I'll get you some fresh towels. I don't suppose I have to show you to your room—Gertie May kept it vacant for you."

"Forget about the towels. I can get them myself," he said, scowling. "I think you should ask the guests to go. It's too much for you—having to deal with the guests and Dorie, and Aunt Gem's disappearance."

Laurel lifted her chin. "Gertie May will be found soon— I'm sure of it. She wouldn't want me to turn guests out. It's Christmas. Where else would they go?"

"And what sort of atmosphere is this for them to stay in?" he countered. "If it's a question of money—"

"I can handle the finances, thank you very much."

His short guffaw infuriated her. "You're so translucent—like brittle needles of crystal. I only wanted to help out until Aunt Gem's found. You can consider me a paying guest, if you like."

Laurel snorted. "And what would Gertie May say about that? You can just keep your money, Ian Harris."

"Well, then, let me help. What does it take to run this place?"

"Oh, laundry, cleaning, dishwashing, breakfast, handling reservations, yard work, bookkeeping." She ticked them off on her fingers, her skepticism showing. She didn't know what to think of his offer. "I'm sure you're very proficient in all of those areas."

Ian pushed himself away from the table and she pretended not to see him wince as he tested his weight on his left leg and kneaded his thigh. "I guess I'll just have to prove to you how proficient this jack-of-all-trades can be. I'll start by giving you a hand with the dishes."

"But you don't have to—your leg is obviously bothering you."

He started stacking plates, ignoring her.

Laurel blinked and rubbed her eyes, admitting to herself that she was not up to dealing with him. Gertie May had never mentioned how stubborn her nephew could be. One thing about being a loner, Ian was probably used to always getting his own way. "In that case, you do the dishes and I'll make the cranberry waffle batter for tomorrow. Once I get Dorie tucked in, we can go to bed...." Her voice trailed off. Ian was looking at her, his eyebrows drawn up in a questioning manner and his gray eyes infused with a sudden warmth. Had she said something?

"What's the matter? Why are you looking at me like that?" she said irritably, feeling a flush of heat invade her cheeks.

"Nothing's the matter. You mentioned going to bed. The idea sounds so appealing."

Laurel had heard more come-ons at the Crow's Nest than she could count, but there was something about the way Ian drawled out those innocent-sounding words that knocked her off-balance.

She stared at him as he rolled up his sleeves, dismayed to find herself responding to his broad shoulders and lean waist in a womanly, insides-melting way. His forearms were as tanned as his face and liberally sprinkled with fine, sandy hairs. Limp and all, he commandeered the kitchen with his masculine, take-charge attitude in much the same way he'd commandeered the secrets of her life. Or most of her secrets, anyway.

Laurel pulled a cookbook from the shelf, feeling her irritability grow. She didn't care if he was attracted to her. Ian Harris was the last kind of man she'd fall into bed with.

The phone rang as she was placing the batter in the refrigerator. Laurel froze, her eyes meeting Ian's. The question of Gertie May's safety hovered unspoken in the room. "Do you suppose that's the police?"

"There's only one way to find out." Ian picked up the phone. "Yes, Constable. Sure, I understand." His eyes continued to hold her gaze as he spoke into the receiver. "That's certainly an option. When would you like to do it? The morning will be fine. I'll inform Mrs. Bishop. We'll be ready."

"We'll be ready for what?" Laurel asked when he'd hung up. She grasped the refrigerator door handle for support, trying not to give in to the fear that held her heart hostage.

"Constable Rafferty said they've decided to conduct a grid search of the park tomorrow morning."

"A grid search. Why?"

Ian's voice lowered, each word forming painfully on his lips. "He said that in his experience a big park like that with easy access by car is the most logical place to stash a body."

"Oh, my God!"

"There's more.

"Rafferty would like to call in the media. Have some TV cameras brought in here and broadcast Aunt Gem's picture on the news. To see if anyone's seen or heard anything. It might provide the police with some viable leads."

The media. Laurel's stomach tightened reflexively. "Oh, Ian, I can't."

The anger crept back into his voice. "I thought you said my aunt was your best friend?"

She felt as though the police and Ian had slipped a noose around her neck and were drawing the rope tighter. "She is! But what if they show me on the news? Someone could see it in Nelson, and then my past will all come out. There'll be no stopping it. We'll lose our chance to find out what's really happened to Gertie May."

"I hadn't thought about it that way." He put his hands on her shoulders. The warm, even pressure of his touch steadied her, pulling her back from the fringes of panic. His irises, she noticed, licking her dry lips, were like a fine gray tweed blended with flecks of gold and green. Why had she only thought him ordinary? He had good bone structure.

With trembling fingers, she touched his cheek. "Could you do the interview?" His skin was warm against the icy coolness of her fingers. His gold-flecked eyebrows rose in surprise as an undercurrent of heat flickered in his eyes, igniting an answering flame in her belly. Then his eyes cooled again to the fine tweed. Noncommittal, again. Yes, she thought now, there was a quiet handsomeness about him. Ian Harris didn't make waves, he moved with the undercurrents.

He was a secretive man with a secret life. Maybe he had his own reasons for not wanting to appear on television.

"Of course," he said after a long moment had passed. "But maybe it's time you faced up to the fact that sooner or later your past will come out. And it may not be up to you to decide when."

His comment sounded like a warning.

IAN AWOKE from a deep sleep, his heart thudding at an accelerated pace. Where was he? Moonlight spilled through the window, making a parallelogram of ghostly white on the familiar patchwork coverlet. Then he remembered. Aunt Gem. Laurel. He remembered Laurel coming up to say good-night, her damp hair curling on the shoulders of her red robe and smelling fragrant as sweet peas. He still didn't trust her, but every second he spent with her seemed to pull him deeper into the web of her troubles.

Cold air whispered around his bare chest as he sat up in bed, listening. Something must have awoken him. A noise? He strained his ears. Beyond the rhythmic ticking of the travel clock on his bedside table, and the odd creak of the house settling, he heard a faint scraping sound. Then silence.

Ian checked the time: 3:00 a.m. He'd been asleep for almost six hours. Why was someone roaming around the house at this hour?

He reached for his clothes and dressed quickly in the dark, then eased his door open, squinting against the glare of the hall light. The other doors in the hallway were closed. Barefoot, Ian quietly moved to the stairs and descended slowly, keeping close to the wall. The downstairs hall light was off and he stepped into a pocket of shadows. From somewhere in the back of the house he heard a small noise. Was someone fixing a late-night snack? He peered into the living room and dining room, but the rooms were soaked with darkness. The kitchen, too, was still and dark, a yawning blackness at the far end of the hall.

He inched down the hallway until the scrape of a drawer opening made him pause in midstep. The sound came from the alcove, just ahead of him, to the left. He waited for a moment, listening to the movements of paper being shuffled. Aunt Gem used the alcove as an office. Was Laurel doing paperwork this late? Or hiding paperwork? Another faint creak echoed down the hallway... a drawer was being closed.

Ian cautiously approached the arched opening. A faint pool of light, probably from the desk lamp, lapped the darkness of the hallway. The lamp suddenly switched off. Ian molded himself against the wall and froze. His ears strained to hear the faintest sound as he waited to pounce on whoever was rummaging through his aunt's desk.

He didn't have to wait long. A few seconds later he heard the rustle of clothing rubbing together. He could sense another person in the hallway, coming closer. Closer...

Ian reached out, entrapping his unsuspecting target's neck in a viselike grip that had no mercy for screams. The person struggled against him as Ian dragged his quarry back inside the alcove and hit the light switch.

"Miss Smithe. I was expecting Santa," he said in a deadly tone, without the slightest trace of amusement. Reluctantly he let her go. She slumped against the wall, her hands tentatively exploring her throat for bruises. She was dressed in a long, purplish nightgown. "Would you mind telling me what the hell you're doing wandering around here in the dark?"

"You know, you're an awfully big boy to believe in Santa Claus," she whispered faintly. Her eyes traveled suggestively from his face to the waistband of his jeans. He hadn't bothered to button his shirt.

Ian took a threatening step toward her. "Answer the question."

Janet pursed her lips and ran her fingers in a sensuous trail from the base of her throat through the valley of her tiny breasts, and on down to the curve of her hip. "I couldn't sleep. I remembered there were some books on the shelves in here, so I thought I'd borrow one." She glanced toward the desk. "I was going to leave Mrs. Bishop a note. I was looking for some notepaper in the drawer—I didn't think she'd mind."

Ian followed her gaze to the rows of bookshelves suspended above the desk, not quite believing her. "Where's your book?"

She sashayed into the hall where she retrieved a paperback from the floor. "I must have dropped it when you attacked me. That wasn't terribly hospitable of you, but it was wildly exciting foreplay."

Ian met her statement with stony silence. He found her and her cloying cheap perfume repulsive. Why did Aunt Gem let these weirdos into her home?

Janet shrugged her shoulders. "I picked out one of those glitzy novels filled with sex and lies. It's the next best thing to the real thing. Merry Christmas, Mr. Harris." With a throaty laugh, she disappeared into the darkness at the end of the hall.

Shaking his head, Ian examined the desk and checked inside the drawers. There was nothing he could see that would capture Miss Smithe's interest. No money or bankbooks. Just the guest registry, a few files with bills tucked neatly inside, some tourist brochures and maps, a pile of photocopies secured with a rubber band, and postage stamps. Nothing too interesting or worth harming an affable elderly lady over. So why, then, did the lingering scent of Janet Smithe's cheap perfume still disturb him?

Ian sighed and headed for the basement. Since he was up, he planned to do some middle-of-the-night investigating of his own.

Chapter Five

When Ian peered into her sleeping cubicle, Laurel was all
curled up in that feminine way women have of sleeping. He
checked on Dorie, too. The stuffed playmate she had
clasped against her chest brought a smile to his lips. Pink
bunnies were definitely not allowed at the boarding school
he'd attended.

Moving silently, Ian turned on a table lamp in the sitting
area and began a tour of the room, looking for clues to
Laurel's past. There was a cluster of photographs on the
wall he hadn't noticed before. One of a middle-aged couple, with matching stern expressions. Her parents, probably. A baby picture of Dorie. And a wedding photo of
Laurel and Steve. He removed the photo from the wall and
carried it closer to the light to examine Laurel's radiant
smile, the baby's breath tucked in her hair, and the virginal
white gown. She looked young. Eighteen. Nineteen, maybe.
Her groom not much older, wearing a navy suit. Steve had
the build of a high school athlete and what Ian called "persuasive good looks"—dark hair, clear blue eyes and a dim-
ple in his chin. The kind of guy you couldn't say no to. A
born salesman.

Ian put the photo back. There was a shelving unit with a
desk area piled with business course books. He opened a
filing cabinet drawer. It didn't take him long to find the
ledger and Laurel's bank records. He sat down at the desk
and started to read.

By the time he'd scanned the last page in the ledger, he was ready to throttle Steve. What kind of husband and father left his wife and daughter thirty-five thousand dollars in debt? Here was Laurel diligently cleaning up her husband's mess, steadily paying off the accumulation of bills. And doing a fine job of it, too. The tiny balance in both her checking and savings accounts was a testament to her thrifty management. Of course, it helped that Aunt Gem wasn't charging her rent.

Ian made a list of the creditors and tucked it into his back pocket. He'd hire a private investigator to check them out. Make sure they were legitimate businesses. If Laurel paid them off with checks it could explain how this anonymous card sender had located her. Ian carefully put everything away. Then he went to check that Laurel was still asleep.

LAUREL LAY still in her bed with her eyes closed. Her heart thundered so loudly in her chest that she felt sure Ian could hear it from where he stood near the foot of her bed. She thanked God Ian hadn't caught her peering around the partition at him. What was he doing searching through her belongings? The fact that he obviously didn't trust her worried her. What would he do when he found out she hadn't told him the whole truth?

Laurel didn't relax until she heard the familiar sound of wood squeaking as Ian tread on the third step from the bottom of the basement stairs. He'd obviously finished for the night.

"STOP FUSSING and have some breakfast," Ian grumbled at Laurel from the kitchen table the next morning. "The Boudreaults have gone out and Miss Smithe will probably sleep till noon, so you might as well sit down and join us."

"I'm not hungry," Laurel said sharply as she put the mixing bowl to soak in the sink. Anxiety frayed her nerves. How could she eat? It was Christmas Day and Gertie May wasn't here to feast on her famous waffles. *Please be okay, Gertie May,* she prayed silently, looking through the window at the chilly winterscape. *Wherever you are, whatever's happened. Please, come back to us.*

Ian came up behind her, and Laurel started. "Nervous about the media interview?" he asked, refilling his coffee cup.

She didn't like the hint of censure in his tone. She flicked her eyes over him. He'd pulled on the same jeans from yesterday and a gray sweatshirt that made his eyes appear a darker gray, or was it worry about his aunt that darkened his eyes so? Laurel sighed. She couldn't blame him for his suspicions.

"Don't worry. I'll handle the interview. You just stay out of sight downstairs with Dorie. I'll say you're too upset to go on camera if the reporter asks about you. Whatever you do, don't come out until I tell you the coast is clear. You never know what these media types will do to get a story. Rafferty said four stations would show up."

She turned to face him, sensing an introspective wariness stealing over him. The upcoming ordeal with the TV cameras didn't seem like such a threat with Ian in charge. "Thanks, Ian. I'm glad you're here."

Deep down, she knew he could help her. He was the kind of man you could rely on in an emergency. If only she could get him to hold off going to the police for a few more days. Gertie May was sure to turn up. . . .

"Mommy, is Gertie May coming home today?" Dorie asked, cuddling the doll Santa had left for her under the Christmas tree. Santa had responded to her note just as Laurel had promised.

"I hope so, sweetie," Laurel said quietly. "We'll just have to wait and see."

"I miss Gertie May, Mommy." Dorie's eyes glistened with tears.

Laurel went to give her a hug, trying not to cry herself. "Me, too, sweetie. Me, too."

Ian cleared his throat. "Me, three. But it seems to me there's too much talking going on here and not enough eating." He pointed at Laurel's vacant chair. "Sit, lady. Eat."

"Yes, sir." Laurel sat down promptly as ordered.

Dorie giggled and hopped out of her chair. "My turn, my turn," she chanted. "Do it to me, Ian."

Laurel suppressed a smile as Ian made a great show out of ordering Dorie to eat, his expression parentally stern. *If only Gertie May were here to see this* . . . Laurel thought sadly. How many times had Gertie May lamented that her nephew would never settle down and give her a great-niece or great-nephew to spoil? Good gracious, she'd even have welcomed an illegitimate great-child.

Laurel choked down three bites of waffle, then pushed her plate away and muttered an excuse about cleaning the kitchen before the reporters arrived. "What sort of advertisement for Harris House would that be?" she demanded when Ian raised his eyebrows at her questioningly.

Advertisement, indeed. Laurel scrubbed hard at the countertop, wishing she could cleanse the pain from her heart just as easily. When an elderly woman inexplicably went missing, nobody cared about the state of her kitchen. The sound of the doorbell jarred her from her thoughts, causing her to drop the dishrag on the floor. Cursing softly, she bent to retrieve it, hating her nervous clumsiness. The reporters were here. What if they already knew about her past?

Ian took the dishrag from her and tossed it into the sink, his lips pressed into a tight line. The doorbell pealed again, but he seemed in no hurry to answer it. Instead he lifted her chin a fraction of an inch with his forefinger, his eyes lingering on her mouth and chin. Laurel could feel the emotional struggle going on beneath his still features. A tiny shudder passed through her. She had no idea what he was thinking.

"That's better. That's the lady who clobbered me the other night," he said brusquely. Then, to her astonishment, he dropped a surprisingly gentle kiss on her forehead.

Laurel shook her head, overwhelmed by the unexpectedness of that kiss and the doubts that crowded her mind. Had the search he'd conducted of her belongings last night convinced him she was telling the truth? Oh, God, she needed him to believe in her innocence! "This feels like running away again, Ian, like I'm caught in a loop I can't get out of...."

The doorbell rang a third time, an insistent knock accompanying it.

"You're not running away this time ... we're waiting another twenty-four hours to see if another card shows up with a ransom demand. Then we'll tell the police everything."

So, he was going to hold her to her promise! Twenty-four hours was all she had left before her life fell apart completely. Did he think that little kiss would sway her toward his way of thinking?

She backed away from him, not trusting herself to speak, and lifted Dorie from the kitchen chair. Her heart wrenched as Dorie's legs curled around her waist. *She's still a baby*.

The basement felt as gloomy as the leaden gray clouds Laurel saw clinging to the mountains across the cove when she closed the miniblinds. The only bright spot in the darkened room was Dorie's laughter at Cookie Monster devouring a dump truck on "Sesame Street." No wonder Cookie Monster doesn't have any teeth, Laurel thought, rolling her eyes. What was going on upstairs? The interviews should be done by now. Two hours of her precious last twenty-four had passed....

How long was Ian going to make her wait? She could be out scouring the neighborhood for clues the police might have missed. And what about the grid search the police were conducting in Panorama Park? Had they found anything? She could imagine the dogs and police officers poking through snow-encrusted layers of decaying maple leaves and brown, withered salmonberry thickets for Gertie May's body. If Steve's murder wasn't still haunting her, she could be searching the park for Gertie May herself.

God, her stomach felt like cement was hardening it by degrees. Laurel prowled restlessly around the room, plucking real and imaginary cracker crumbs from the carpet.

When she couldn't stand waiting any longer, she parted the miniblinds a crack, but the sight of a TV news van in the driveway made her jump back from the window. This was making her crazy. She'd be climbing the walls soon.

The ceiling suddenly rumbled overhead with the steady tread of footsteps and Laurel gazed at it expectantly. Was the last news crew leaving? Her fingers balled into fists and she prayed that the publicity would help solve the mystery of Gertie May's disappearance. At least, thanks to Ian, she had been spared the possibility of being recognized through the media.

Ian. That kiss.

Would he really force her to go to the police?

Laurel looked at Dorie, her eyes stinging with tears that she was too stubborn to acknowledge. They'd never spent more than a day apart since her birth.... But Laurel knew she'd do whatever she had to for Gertie May's sake. Even if it meant going to the police and ending up in jail.

Laurel pushed her dark thoughts of grueling police interrogations aside and concentrated instead on the image of Ian's face. She was going to think positive thoughts. She and Dorie would be just fine. Gertie May and Ian were going to have a wonderful Christmas reunion.

Perhaps because she had been thinking of Ian, he suddenly appeared in front of her. She hadn't heard him enter. Although the room was shadowed, she knew it was him—blending what she could actually see with the reality in her mind.

"It went okay. It'll be on the news, 'round the clock. Maybe we'll hear something..." His broad shoulders seemed to have lost their confident thrust, as though in the darkness he felt it safe to let down his guard. Laurel felt something releasing inside her, slipping away, and she reached out her arms to him.... Now was her turn to offer comfort.

Ian came, a harsh groan escaping from deep in his chest as he buried his face in her hair.

"Oh, Ian..." Laurel welcomed the tense hardness of his body into the soft curves of her own, admitting to herself that she was attracted to him. Dorie was too intent on Oscar the Grouch's antics to notice that Ian had come in. Her back was to them. Laurel closed her eyes and held on tight, reacquainting herself with the stirring of sensations that holding a man could evoke. There had been no one special in her life since Steve.

Her hand slid up his back, gently soothing, gently stroking, gently exploring the ridges of muscle and bone in an effort to comfort this man on whom she was beginning to rely far too much. What kind of lover would he be if she allowed herself to be carried away? Passionate? Playful? Unhurried, she was sure. And dangerously exciting.

She could feel that in the current of awareness that passed between their bodies. Being with Ian would take her to sensual heights she'd never known, but what would be the point?

She'd only end up alone. Dorie needed a father, and Ian with his world-traveler life-style was an unlikely prospect. Laurel didn't believe in wasting time with brief flings.

The phone rang and Laurel extricated herself from the warm bond of their bodies, feeling a blush come to her cheeks at Ian's obvious reluctance to let her go. "I'll get that." Dorie turned her head briefly at the sound of the first ring, then went back to her program.

Laurel hurried to answer it before the caller hung up. "Hello?"

The voice of her mother-in-law crackled thinly over the wire. "Laurel? I just saw a newsbreak. What's this about Gertie May having disappeared? I can't believe it."

"Unfortunately, it's true, Barb—"

"Why didn't you phone me? The news reporter said she's been missing for more than thirty-six hours. At least Ian is there. It was such a shock to see him. I haven't seen him since he was a boy."

Laurel swallowed back her tears. Barbara and Gertie May had been close friends for almost forty years. "I didn't want to worry you—what with your tests and all. I—I was hoping Gertie May would turn up safe and sound. I still am.''

Barb was silent for a moment, her voice sounding even weaker when she spoke again. "Thank you for trying to spare me, dear. But I want you to promise to keep me informed.''

Informed? Laurel glanced quickly at Ian, who was opening the miniblinds, spilling pale gray light into the room. "I will, Barb. I'm going to have to tell the police about Steve...what happened—''

"What? Laurel, listen to me, don't do such a foolish thing—'' Barb stopped suddenly, gasping for breath.

"Barb? Are you all right?''

"Y-yes. Give...me a minute. Whe-he. Whe-he.'' Barb's breathing sounded so painful as she tried to slow it down with steady indrawn breaths. Laurel clung to the receiver, wishing she could transport herself to Barb's aid.

"Listen, then, don't talk. It's too much of a coincidence.... If the police find out, it could look very bad for me. You know how they think. Don't worry, okay? Everything's under control.'' Laurel spoke for a few minutes longer, editing her words in case Dorie was listening. When she hung up, she felt even more troubled. Just how ill was Barb?

"Who was that?'' Ian asked. His face looked carefully composed, his gaze unreadable. Was this the same man she'd held so intimately a few minutes ago?

"My mother-in-law. She saw you on the news. You gave her a shock.''

Ian nodded grimly. "I thought I'd walk over to the park and check on how the grid search is progressing. Want to come?''

Laurel shook her head and said quietly, "I don't think it's any place for Dorie. Especially if...it's being covered by the TV news cameras.'' That wasn't precisely what she'd intended to say, but it was a suitable substitute. "We'll be okay here. We have a delivery to make next door at Frederick's. That should keep Dorie occupied for a while.''

"And her mom, too." Ian's fingers brushed the hair off her shoulder and Laurel felt a tingling sensation radiate down her shoulder to her arm. "Just don't jump up and offer to wash the dishes—you don't want to insult the old guy."

Laurel frowned. "Hey, I don't—you're not insinuating something with that remark, are you?"

Ian laughed dryly, then his eyes grew serious again. "No, just sometimes when your heart's breaking you've got to laugh at something to ease the pain. At least, that's my way. You clean. I laugh."

Laurel folded her arms across her chest to keep from touching him again. Why did she feel so drawn to him? He didn't trust her farther than he could throw her, and yet there was something tangible between them. Was it because her heart was breaking, too? She wet her lips, saying the first thing that came to mind. "I'm sure Dorie would be happy to lend you a Sesame Street bandage to mend your broken heart. If you think it would help..."

"What good's a bandage without a kiss?"

His question was so provocative. Her gaze flew reflexively to his mouth, which seemed just a few scant inches from her own. Was he thinking of kissing her? Her face grew hot with embarrassment—and shame. *No, he couldn't! She couldn't—not under these circumstances.*

To Laurel's intense relief, Dorie chose that moment to interrupt them. She looked down to see Dorie tugging on Ian's arm.

"You have to come in the bathroom if you need a bandage. I'm too little to reach. Which do you like, Big Bird or Cookie Monster?"

Ian chuckled. "You choose for me, sprite. You're the doctor."

After Ian had gone with Big Bird stuck to his shirt, Laurel reminded Dorie that they had a tea party and a present awaiting them at the Aameses'. "Why don't you get the presents you made for Frederick and Anna?"

"Okay, but don't look, Mommy." Dorie sped across the room into a little nook beneath the basement stairs that was just big enough for a child's play kitchen and a miniature chair. Dorie called it her "mouse hole." Dorie tugged the kitchen out of the hole and opened a small access door to a storage area underneath the lower portion of the stairs. "I've got the presents, Mommy."

"Let's go, then."

Five minutes later they were ringing Frederick's doorbell.

"Who's this? One of Santa's elves, I'm sure," Frederick exclaimed, opening the door. His face looked grave as his eyes met Laurel's, but he kept his voice cheery for Dorie's sake.

Dorie giggled. "Merry Christmas! I brought presents."

"My goodness! I was just about to make some tea. Are you in the mood for a tea party?"

"Yes!" Dorie exclaimed.

"Laurel?"

Laurel blessed him for his tact, her jaw tightening as she struggled to keep her emotions in check. "That would be fine, but we won't stay long."

"I understand. Come in. Let me help you with your coats. Leave your boots by the door. That's nice. Dorie, Anna's in the living room by the Christmas tree. Why don't you go in and say hello?"

Laurel bent down to pick up Dorie's tuque, which had been abandoned on the floor. She could hear Dorie singing to Anna in the other room.

"I saw the noon news. I suppose there's no word yet on Gertie May?" Frederick inquired hopefully, slipping his wiry arm around Laurel.

"No."

"Do the police have any leads?"

"None that they're sharing."

"Well, Gertie May's a strong woman. I'm sure she'll be back with us soon."

"I hope so."

Frederick gave Laurel a supportive hug. "The water's probably whistling in the kettle. I'll go check. Sit down and make yourself comfortable."

"Did you like my new ring-around-the-rosy song, Anna?" Dorie asked, twirling around. "Gertie May taught it to me."

Laurel chose a lumpy wing chair by Frederick's cheerful fire, discovering as she adjusted a cushion to ease the lumpiness that one of the lumps was a stack of bills secured in an elastic band. She quickly shoved the stack further into the crack behind the cushion. She didn't want Frederick to think she was prying into his personal affairs.

Anna was apparently more interested in the animal figures on the bright wrapping paper than in Dorie's song. She bent her dark gray head over Dorie's honey-colored one. "Look, my little sister has given me a lovely Christmas present. I don't know where my other presents are, especially the doll Papa gave me."

"I'm sure it'll turn up," Laurel replied, forcing a smile. Anna's green eyes were dull and doubtful as she pulled a tissue from a box on the coffee table and blew her nose. "Papa says I have a cold."

"You do look ill. Did you have a nice sleep last night? That's the best thing when you're sick. Soon you'll be up and around and playing with your doll again."

"What doll?" Anna frowned.

From experience, Laurel knew better than to pursue the subject of the doll. "Here's Frederick with the tea tray. Now that we're all here, Anna, perhaps you'd like to open your present?"

Laurel didn't know how Frederick could live with this day in, day out. Though she knew sometimes he and Anna had quite lucid conversations about the past. The fact that he cared for his wife so dutifully spoke highly of his love for her. It was the kind of love Laurel wanted in her own life. Everlasting. For better or worse. In sickness and in health. A shared life, without secrets. Certainly not what she'd had with Steve. Frederick handed her a steaming cup of herb tea.

Anna tore open her package with a hoarse cry of pleasure. "Oh, pretty soaps. Thank you!"

"Smell them." Dorie held one to Anna's nose. "It smells like flowers."

"I love flowers. Papa grows the most beautiful flowers in the garden. Don't you, Papa?"

"Yes, Anna. I grow them just for you. Sweet peas and roses and English daisies. Here's your tea, now." Frederick placed a dainty china cup and saucer on the coffee table.

"Now, Frederick's turn," Dorie announced, enjoying her role as gift giver. Frederick sat down on the sofa and undid Dorie's lovingly wrapped package with shaking hands.

"What a fine bird feeder." He extracted the lid of an egg carton smeared with peanut butter and birdseed from a plastic bag covered with Christmas wrap. "Did you make this, Dorie?"

"Uh-huh. Gertie May told me how." The corners of Dorie's mouth turned downward.

Laurel swallowed hard, watching them.

"You did a good job. Thank you very much." Frederick kissed Dorie, and Laurel thought she saw a bit of extra moisture in the elderly man's eyes. "I'll find a nice safe place to hang it so our feathered friends can have a birdseed snack without worrying about the Thompsons' cat. Here's our gift to you."

Dorie brightened immediately and wasted no time in opening her present—a storybook on gardening. Although Laurel knew Frederick was probably thinking about Gertie May, too, the tea party proceeded on an almost merry note until Anna dipped one of her fancy soaps in her tea and bit into it, thinking it was a cookie. With a quiet grumble, Frederick went into the kitchen and came back with another teacup and a damp washcloth to remove the taste of soap from his wife's mouth. Neither helped, and Anna made such a fuss that she was soon coughing uncontrollably.

Laurel touched Frederick's shoulder. "I'll take Dorie home now, so you can get Anna settled."

"Yes, that would probably be best." Frederick sighed. "I'm sorry this happened."

"There's no need to be. We had a lovely time. At least it's distracted Dorie from what's happening around her. I'll let you know if there's any news about Gertie May."

Laurel hurried Dorie along. As they stepped outside the warmth and commotion of the Aameses' house, the coldness of reality seeped into her bones. It was still Christmas Day. Gertie May was still missing.

Laurel glanced anxiously at the sky where the faint yellow tinge of the sun was nearly obscured by a rumpled blanket of gray clouds that promised another dump of snow soon. Would Gertie May be found by then?

Maybe she'd just put Dorie in the sled and do a tour around the neighborhood.

IAN SURVEYED the desolate solemnity of Panorama Park from the front seat of a police car. The parking lot was jammed with police and volunteer vehicles, and news vans. The sweeping expanses of the picnic area had been churned into a brown, crusty mess by the diligent searchers. Only the branches of the towering evergreens curving downward in frosty arcs remained unsoiled. Would this be Aunt Gem's final resting place?

Why was it taking so long?

A crowd of people had gathered around a fire someone had lit in a garbage can, waiting for news of the search. Ian recognized a few of his aunt's friends. It was nice of them to show up—especially on Christmas Day. Among them was a woman wearing a drab olive coat and purple felt hat; she resembled Janet Smithe. But the distance was too far to be absolutely certain. Perhaps the wasp was losing some of her sting.

Ian turned his head at a tap on the window. Constable Rafferty opened the driver's-side door and slid inside. His face was reddened from the cold around the big, gray-streaked mustache.

Ian's stomach froze into a slab of stone. *"Well?"*

"The search was negative, Mr. Harris." Rafferty flexed his gloved fingers on the steering wheel.

Thank God. Ian closed his eyes for an instant, letting it all sink in, allowing hope to flourish anew in his chest. In this instance, no news was good news. But the constable's cautious demeanor told him it still looked bad. "What next?" he asked after a pause, keeping his tone equally cautious.

"The investigation is ongoing. We'll spread the search out over the surrounding terrain tomorrow, and the next day, if necessary. We should also be hearing back from the forensics lab soon. Go home. Get some rest. We'll be in touch."

Home. Ian was acutely aware of the fact that he didn't have a home. Especially with Aunt Gem missing. That he might never have a home. Why did it suddenly seem so important?

Snowflakes began to sift down from the sky, melting into the silvery waters of the cove as he walked back to his aunt's house. The tuque and gloves he'd pulled from a box in Aunt Gem's basement allowed him to take his time, to plan a strategy for dealing with the police—and Laurel. The imprint of her sweetly feminine body pressed against his was indelible in his memory, disturbing him even now.

Logic told him she had to be involved in Aunt Gem's disappearance. There were too many coincidences. But yet there was a part of him that wanted to believe her. That part had to do with Dorie. Laurel was a good mother to her daughter—warm, loving, fiercely protective—and on that basis alone, Ian wanted to believe her. He wanted to believe in someone who could give her child such selfless, unconditional love. It also occurred to him that just such a mother would kill to protect her daughter.

If only he could shake the feeling that Laurel was still hiding something from him.

Ian exhaled a deep, frustrated breath that misted his glasses as he limped down Aunt Gem's salt-sprinkled front walk. To make matters worse, he couldn't deny that he was attracted to Laurel; and the way she'd held him this morning suggested she was attracted to him, too. Ian pulled up short on the veranda. Maybe the means of getting the truth out of Laurel was staring him right in the face—he'd seduce it out of her.

Chapter Six

"Would you like a glass of wine?" Ian asked Laurel when she emerged into the kitchen from the basement stairs, looking tired and flustered. "There's red or white in the fridge." He suddenly felt guilty for planning to seduce her. Wisps of hair escaped the confines of her ponytail and framed her pale, oval face. She'd hardly touched her dinner.

"White, please."

He poured her a glass and she took a sip. "Ah, just what I needed to take the edge off." She gave him a sidelong glance and looked away quickly, saying with a deep sigh, "Dorie was hard to settle. Gertie May's absence is sinking in." She took another drink, nearly draining her glass.

Ian clasped the wine bottle and an empty glass in one hand and picked up a plate of cheese and crackers in the other. "Let's go sit in the living room. We need to talk."

"No." Laurel cleared her throat nervously. "I mean, I'd rather not. How about my sitting room? The guests have their own keys. We'll know when they come in."

"Fine." He looked at her closely. What was she so nervous about? Talking to him? Or being alone with him? He followed her downstairs, silently appreciating the fact that she looked great in jeans. Nicely rounded hips, slender legs. He remembered all too vividly those legs in the sexy, black stockings she'd worn beneath the black leather skirt the other night. He wanted to pull the pink elastic band that

natched her sweater out of her hair and see it fall softly
around her shoulders. Why did women grow their hair long
and then put it in ponytails so you couldn't see it—or touch
it?

Laurel flipped the switch for the overhead fixture, flood-
ing the area with light. "How's this?" She stepped hesitantly toward the seating area, choosing to sit on the larger
couch.

"Great, if you like inquisitions." He had something more
subtle in mind. Ian set the food and the wine on the wicker
coffee table, then leaned past her to turn on the table lamp
before retracing his steps to the wall switch. She watched
him warily over the rim of her wineglass as he turned off the
overhead light. The large room suddenly grew more intimate.

Ian suddenly felt uncharacteristically uneasy.

"Oh." She shifted on the couch, moving away from him
as he sat down beside her.

But he was still close enough to remain vitally aware of
her sweet-scented warmth and the change in the rise and fall
of her breasts as her breathing rate increased. He realized
with a jolt that seducing her would require very little acting
on his part.

Ian poured himself some wine and refilled her glass. Her
hand trembled on the stem of the inexpensive crystal.
"What did you want to talk about, Ian?" Her voice was
distinctly steadier than her hand.

He leaned back against the comfortable cushions, hoping she'd do the same. "Frederick told me he saw a short
male on the front porch the day Aunt Gem disappeared, but
he couldn't give me much of a description."

"Do you think this person could have kidnapped Gertie
May?" Laurel asked incredulously.

"It's possible. My gut feeling is, if we're dealing with a
kidnapping, then a ransom note will be delivered shortly in
the form of one of those Christmas cards. In which
case—" He broke off abruptly, searching her face.

"Don't worry. I'm going to hold up my end of the bargain." Her hand came to rest lightly on his left thigh for a moment, the warmth of her fingers penetrating through the thickness of denim and sending the blood pulsing through his lower extremities. Ian stilled, forgetting for a moment that this was exactly what he hoped would happen—the two of them growing closer, sharing confidences. "If Gertie May doesn't turn up by tomorrow afternoon, I'm going to talk to the police. I—I'd do anything to help her."

"I knew you would." He reached out, intertwining his fingers with hers, and carried her hand back into his lap. More exquisite torture having her slender, white fingers so close to his... He drew a shaky breath. His lungs didn't seem to be working properly for some reason. Just who was seducing whom? "Uh, I hate to bring this up again, but I don't suppose you kept any clippings of the newspaper accounts you mentioned?" Her fingers grew frigid within his grasp. "It might help to read through them. Maybe give us a lead on the anonymous sender of the Christmas cards."

Laurel sat up stiffly and tugged her fingers free, ostensibly to splash more wine into her glass. "Of course, I kept a file. I thought Dorie might want to see it someday. That she had a right to... But it's not here." She didn't look at him, just took another swallow of wine. "I—I put it in a safety-deposit box at the bank. It wasn't the sort of thing I wanted lying around, especially with so many strangers coming through the house. Tomorrow's Boxing Day—the bank won't be open until the day after."

He cursed. Her excuse sounded far too convenient to his liking. She seemed almost relieved the bank was closed tomorrow. He wondered if whatever she was still hiding from him was in the clippings.

"I'm sorry."

Her quietly spoken words hit him someplace just below the ribs. He looked at her rigid spine, her head bent down as though in silent prayer, her lips pressed together in firm determination. She was trying so hard to hold herself together. Not to cry.

He removed the wineglass from her hands. With a firm but gentle hold, he seized her upper arms and pulled her snugly against his side, draping one arm securely around her narrow shoulders. He could feel the strength of her body test the weight of his arm, then release. "It's not your fault. And I didn't mean to imply that it was," he lied. But deep down, he wished his aunt had never laid eyes on Laurel. He caressed her shoulder. "Just tell me what happened again. Everything you can think of."

"It was an ordinary Christmas..." Laurel began.

Ian listened intently, trying not to become too distracted by the sensations her body created as it gradually relaxed against his: the softness of her breast molding to his ribs; the length of her feminine thigh bordering his male one; her ponytail feathering his arm every time she turned her head.

"So, about all I know from the police is that Steve went home that night...and an intruder hit him over the head with something. One of Steve's tennis trophies was missing from the living room. The police thought it could be the murder weapon." Laurel paused, fixing him with one of her translucent gazes that reminded him of honey swirling in dark tea. "There were all those other debts. I've often wondered if Steve was killed because he'd borrowed some money from a loan shark and couldn't pay it back. Do you think it's possible the loan shark has decided killing Steve wasn't enough? That maybe he wants to be paid—and the best way to ensure he'd get paid was by kidnapping Gertie May?"

Ian thought about the debts he'd seen in the ledger last night. Laurel's theory seemed to fit with the facts.

"It's possible—especially if it was a large sum of money. From what you've told me, you've done an admirable job of disappearing. It may have taken this person two years to find you so he could collect. He may be sending you the threatening cards to intimidate you. It's not a loan shark's usual MO—they're usually more direct. Pay up or else."

"So I've endangered Gertie May by coming here...." Her voice cracked and Ian saw the gleam of tears that she'd been struggling to hold back rim in her eyes.

He turned toward her, cupping her face in his hands, his eyes narrowing on the trembling movement of her lips. "No, that's not true."

He told himself that, timing-wise, he'd never get a better opportunity to kiss her. But the truth was, he couldn't wait any longer.

He had to know what it felt like to taste her lips. He dipped his head, his lips meeting the soft, yielding warmth of hers. The shock of that first tentative touch revved his heartbeat into overdrive. Ian swallowed hard and lifted his head back slightly to stare deep into her widened eyes. Did she feel it, too?

His thoughts swirled in confusion as he reminded himself this wasn't real.

Slowly he kissed her again, her mouth opening beneath his and granting him access to the moist touch of her tongue. She tasted of wine and warmth and fantasy. Ian felt an explosion of pure pleasure deep inside him.

With a low groan he pulled the elastic from her blasted ponytail and threaded his fingers in her hair. Her hands roughly caressed his shoulders, sliding up behind his neck, inviting him closer. He shuddered, trying to control the ache of desire that was spilling through his veins. His hands trembled as they slid up under her soft wool sweater and a lacy camisole to claim her breasts. Laurel sank back onto the sofa, moaning low in her throat. Ian could feel her warm, ultrasoft flesh swell against the callused skin of his palms.

Suddenly she gripped his arms and gasped, "Oh, Ian, I c-can't. Not under these circumstances."

Slowly the meaning of her words penetrated the blood pounding in his ears. With great effort he tugged her sweater down and stood. His chest was heaving like an adolescent's. He couldn't remember ever getting so carried away.

Laurel was looking up at him through dark and wild eyes. "I'm sorry for... leading you on like that," she sputtered as a dark shade of crimson infused her cheeks. "I—I think I had too much to drink. I'm not . . . I mean, I don't usually . . ."

Of course she didn't. Ian could see it now. She was the true-blue type who'd remain loyal to a dead husband—even sell her wedding rings to pay for his funeral. She wouldn't jump into a relationship with just anyone who came along. Especially someone like him.

Scowling, he turned away from her to collect the empty dishes and the wine bottle. Anything to keep from looking at her and remembering the heavenly taste and feel of her. It had never occurred to him that a woman who could lie to the police might possess some lofty, old-fashioned morals.

The only reason she'd sleep with him is if her feelings were real. Ian swallowed hard, remembering the unfamiliar emotions that had been surging through him just seconds ago. God help him, it just might come down to that.

LAUREL AWOKE to a ringing in her ears. She slowly opened her eyes, trying to orient herself. It was pitch-black, but the persistent peal of the telephone called out to her. Her heart started to pound as she leapt out of bed and raced into her sitting room, knocking her elbow painfully against the wall in an effort to grasp the phone. "Gertie May? Is that you?" she said breathlessly into the receiver. Who else would be calling at this hour?

Silence greeted her ears. Laurel's stomach churned. *"Who is this? Answer me, please."*

Oh, God. What if Gertie May was trying to call, reaching out for help, and she couldn't speak?

Finally, Laurel heard a quick indrawn breath followed by a hissing screech. "Murderess." Then the line went dead.

Laurel recoiled from the phone in horror.

Ian.

She had to tell Ian. She moved through the house with ease in the darkness, instinctively knowing the way. It seemed like only seconds had passed before she was opening the door to his room and following the moonlit path to his bed. He was asleep on his back, one arm bent across his face, his legs sprawled wide in the large bed. She shook his bare, sleep-warmed shoulders. "Ian, wake up."

His eyes fluttered open. "Laurel?" he whispered, sounding dazed and groggy. He pushed himself upright, the blankets bunching at his waist, and reached out for her, running his hands down her flannel-clad arms. She thought she heard him mumble, "You're real. I should have known... the nightgown was all wrong..." Or something to that effect. He was still half-asleep and she didn't have time to make sense of his ramblings.

"Listen to me. I just got a crank phone call—"

"What?" Ian was instantly alert.

"The person didn't say much," Laurel babbled. "Just called me a murderess and hung up. I—I thought at first it might be Gertie May...."

"Hey, you're trembling. It's okay." His arms settled around her, anchoring her, making her feel safe and secure. Laurel was suddenly aware of the burning warmth of his skin seeping through her nightgown, of the coolness of her fingers resting on the hard, muscled ridges of his chest, of the lure of starlight and shadows and warm sheets. Of the lack of clothing covering Ian's body. "When did you say this call came through?"

Laurel gulped. "A few minutes ago."

"I didn't hear the phone."

"Gertie May doesn't have an extension up here, so as not to disturb the guests."

Ian leaned over, revealing a goodly amount of his backside in the faint silvery light as he groped for the travel clock on the table. Laurel pressed her fingers between her knees. This was crazy. Why did Ian affect her so? Because, you're under a great deal of emotional stress, she told herself.

"It's a little after 1:00 a.m.," he said briskly, turning back to her, his expression hidden by shadows. "Could you tell if the caller was male or female?"

She bit her lip, considering. "I don't know... it happened so fast."

"How about background noises? Anything unusual—a TV, computer, street noises, a dog barking?"

"Nothing. Just plain silence. Only..." She paused. "Don't you think the wording is a bit odd? 'Murderess' is not exactly a common expression. Not like 'murderer.'" She shivered.

"Here, you're cold." Ian tucked some of the blankets over her lap.

"I—I almost think the person is somewhat educated. Or has a good vocabulary anyway. Maybe a journalism background."

"Hmm, more likely a fascination with crime stories—or personal experience." Ian rubbed his jaw and Laurel could hear the faint scratch of stubble. What would it feel like against her cheek? Against her breasts? She shouldn't be here with him in the same bed. It was too dangerous... She'd never had a one-night stand in her life. Steve had been her only lover. Ian was pushing aside the covers.

"What are you doing?" she whispered, thoroughly alarmed.

"I'm getting dressed. I'm coming downstairs with you. I'll sleep on the couch so I can be near the phone if this person calls again." His voice gentled. "Are you going to watch me put my pants on, or be a lady and turn your head?"

She turned her head, but not nearly fast enough to avoid learning that he wasn't wearing a stitch of clothing. She was suddenly immensely grateful for the dimness of the room that hid the wave of heat she felt rising to her face.

"I'm decent," Ian said a few seconds later. Laurel couldn't be certain, but as she glanced his way a faint, white flash of teeth made her suspect he was grinning as he bent his head to gather the blankets from his bed. She snatched his pillow and jumped off the bed, leading the way out into the hallway. Emotional stress, that's all it was.

"Do you think we'll ever get some sleep tonight?" she grumbled over her shoulder.

"I should hope not—" a feminine voice said as a figure appeared at the top of the stairs. It was Janet Smithe, still in street clothes—apparently just coming in for the night. "Surely you two can think of something more pleasurable to do than sleep."

Laurel froze, appalled by Janet's bluntness. But since she was a paying guest for what was left of the night, Laurel decided to simply ignore her. "Good night, Miss Smithe," she said coldly. How could Janet even suggest such a thing when Ian's aunt was missing? The woman seemed purposefully antagonistic. First thing in the morning, Laurel was going to have a look at the reservation book. The sooner Janet checked out, the better.

Ian, on the other hand, couldn't resist affirming his male pride. "I assure you, Miss Smithe, that I've never suffered from a lack of imagination."

Laurel didn't doubt it. He'd probably picked up a trick or two from women all over the world. All the more reason not to get emotionally involved with him.

It wasn't until Ian started spreading his blankets on her couch that his reason for being downstairs hit home again. The phone call. Laurel felt a chill settle along her spine. Would there be others?

IAN LAY thinking in the quiet stillness of Laurel's basement suite. The couch was a foot too short for him, but he'd sacked out in worse places. He probably wouldn't sleep anyway. Not that he expected another phone call—once a night was usually enough for those creeps. But he couldn't take his mind off Laurel. He'd thought he was dreaming when he woke up and found her in his bedroom, wearing that white flannel gown primly buttoned up to her neck. The room and the hair were right, but the nightgown was all wrong. In his dream she wasn't wearing anything. And it wasn't a planned seduction. It was real.

Ian dropped to the floor and did sit-ups to work off the mad-at-the-world feeling gnawing at his gut until he felt tired enough to sleep.

The impact of something colliding with his stomach awakened him a few hours later. "Hey, kid! What are you doing?'' he growled at Dorie, who had plunked herself on his stomach and was staring down at him with pure mischief in her eyes. She giggled and bounced as though his stomach were a mattress. "I'm hungry."

"You are, huh?" He reached up and tickled her, amazed at how pleasant her laughter sounded. Her feet pummeled his chest as she twisted and squirmed, but he didn't mind. He sat up, hoisting her over his shoulder. "All right, rascal, we'll get something to eat and let your mom sleep in."

It was relatively simple to prepare a glass of apple juice and a bowl of dry cereal to keep her happy. Dorie told him exactly what to do and where everything was kept. "You want to watch cartoons?" he asked.

"I'm not 'lowed to. But Mommy lets me watch 'Sesame Street,' Barney, an' my movies."

Blessedly, "Sesame Street" was on. Ian left her alone long enough to splash warm water on his face and pull on a sweatshirt and socks. He could shave later. When he came back, Dorie was perfectly fine. He sat near her in the living room, with a cup of black coffee and the Yellow Pages to compile a list of private investigators. None of them would be open today on Boxing Day, a Canadian holiday. He'd have to wait until tomorrow to call.

Ian stirred restlessly. There had to be something more he could do. He stood quickly and went to the front door. A draft of cold air gripped him in an icy embrace as he yanked it open. Ian stared at the buff-colored envelope securely pinned to the doormat for a long, dread-filled moment. It wasn't the envelope per se that caught him off guard. He'd been expecting another one. No, what really bothered him was the paring knife. It made a nasty thumbtack.

Chapter Seven

Shh!

Ian flicked his gaze from the handwritten message on the Christmas card to the black, plastic-handled paring knife he'd sealed in a plastic bag a few minutes ago. Someone was obviously trying to make a point. Ian's interpretation: *Keep silent—or else!*

The card itself was similar to the others. The same style angel, this one blowing a trumpet. Finding out where the cards had originated from struck him as being impossible.

"Ah!" Laurel's smothered cry startled Ian from his thoughts. Her translucent eyes radiated fear as she stared at the objects he'd placed on the kitchen table. "Where's Dorie?" she demanded.

"Watching TV. I hope it's okay I brought her upstairs. I thought you could use the sleep."

"Thanks." She tied her red bathrobe more securely around her slim waist and approached the table, frowning as she read the card. "'Shh!' What's that supposed to mean?"

"That we wait *at least* another day before we talk to the police. I want to see those newspaper clippings first. They may give us a clue as to who's sending these cards. Besides, we may yet get another one."

He wondered again at the worried expression that crossed her face when he mentioned the newspaper clippings.

"You left out the knife, Ian. Where did it come from?"

"It arrived with the card as a sort of thumbtack."

Laurel paled, pressing a hand between her breasts as though to protect herself from the horrifying image his explanation evoked. "Oh, Ian, this isn't right. If someone's holding Gertie May against her will, we'll need the help of the police to get her back safely. We can't take a chance with her life."

Ian gestured toward the knife, his tone grim and intractable. "The knife seems to suggest otherwise—that Aunt Gem will be safer if we keep our mouths shut. I thought you'd be relieved to be granted this small reprieve. Don't mistake me, Laurel. She's my aunt and I'll do whatever I think necessary to keep her alive—*if* she's still alive. I've no intention of remaining passive. There are measures we can take to nail this bastard. He's after something. And sooner or later, we'll figure out what it is."

He leaned back in his chair. "By the way, what do you know about this Janet Smithe creature? Why is she staying here?"

"She's a poet, I think. She's visiting a friend for Christmas."

"Ever met her before?"

"No. Why do you ask? You're frightening me."

"Curiosity." He told her about his Christmas Eve encounter with Janet in Gertie May's office. "She came back late last night. Maybe she hand-delivered the note—"

"Maybe she made the phone call...." Laurel said excitedly. "I'll get Gertie May's registration book. It should give us her address and phone number." She left the kitchen and came back a few minutes later, thumbing through the pages of a leather-bound book. "I've got it. Janet lives in White Rock. That's one hour south, near the U.S. border. I guess her friend dropped her off or she took a bus, because she didn't bring a vehicle. Maybe she didn't feel comfortable driving in the snow. She's booked her room until January second."

Ian jotted down Janet's address and phone number. "Isn't that a rather extended stay?"

"Not for this time of year. It's considerably cheaper than a hotel."

"Still, I think it's odd she isn't staying with her friend. We should check it out. Make sure she's legit. What about the Boudreaults?"

"I hardly think that nice couple is involved in this—"

"Appearances can be deceiving." His eyes dared her to object as he took down their address. What would she think if she knew he was equally determined to check out her background?

"Just what do you mean by that?" She grabbed the pencil from his hand, anger snapping in her eyes. "I hope you're not implying that I'm deceiving you."

He straightened, schooling himself not to be affected by the indignation of her expression. "The thought has crossed my mind."

She put her hands on her hips. "Well, let me just tell you the jury's still out on *you*, Ian Harris. I'm still wondering why you lied to Constable Rafferty about your job—"

"I didn't lie. I specialize in minerals and I told Rafferty as much. The gem varieties of emerald and aquamarines come from the mineral beryl. Rubies and sapphires come from the mineral corundum. If you care to check a dictionary, you'll see that I've been completely honest and aboveboard."

"Then you won't mind if I get a dictionary."

"I'd be disappointed if you didn't." He folded his arms across his chest and followed her as she stalked into the alcove and took a dictionary from the shelf.

Her face reddened as she read the definitions. "I—I guess I owe you an apology," she said grudgingly.

He frowned, uncomfortable with the situation. It suddenly became important to him to spell things out as clearly as possible.

"You don't owe me any apologies, Mrs. Laurel Bishop, or whatever you said your real name is. I'm not the loyal Boy Scout type. Frankly, I can only be relied upon if it serves my own self-interests. I don't believe in anything permanent. My address is a post office box in Los Angeles. I deserve your distrust and I mean to keep it, so don't depend on me to do anything more than hold your hand through this madness.''

Now why had he said all that? Why did she make him feel like he had to be brutally honest with her? He wasn't completely honest with anyone. Not even Aunt Gem.

She advanced on him, jabbing her finger in his chest. "Fine. Message received loud and clear. Just remember two things, Ian. I will *not* defer to your judgment simply because you're Gertie May's nephew. I'm involved in this up to my eyebrows and I'll have an equal say in what we tell the police—and when. For now, I agree to wait a bit in the interests of Gertie May's safety. And second, let's clear up something about last night. You didn't hold my hand. You kissed me! And *you* initiated it. Yes, I kissed you back. Yes, I'll admit to feeling attracted to you, but don't delude yourself into thinking I'm going to fall head over heels in love with you. I don't think you even know the meaning of the word commitment. Now, if you'll excuse me, I have to prepare breakfast. All this shouting has probably woken up the guests.''

Oh, hell! Ian rubbed his forehead and sighed. He supposed he'd deserved that. He watched the tight sway of Laurel's shapely bottom beneath the clinging robe as she marched down the hallway. She looked incredibly sexy in red—it matched her temper. Did she say if? Maybe he'd come closer to seducing her than he'd thought.

BREAKFAST WAS STRAINED. Laurel avoided Ian as much as humanly possible, concentrating on Dorie and answering Madame Boudreault's questions on the best shopping spots for Boxing Day sales. She wanted to exchange a dress she'd given her granddaughter.

Was Christmas only yesterday? Laurel felt anything but merry. She asked Dorie to water the Christmas tree because she couldn't bear to gaze upon the holiday's most enduring symbol. Playing Christmas carols on the radio while they ate was definitely out.

Constable Rafferty phoned after breakfast with the dismal news that the blood found on the hall table matched Gertie May's blood type. He was expecting to hear some results on the fingerprints later in the afternoon. The North Shore Search and Rescue Squad was assisting the police in a foot search of the wooded, mountainous terrain to the north of Serenity Cove. Everything possible was being done.

"I hope to hell the police won't find her," Ian told Laurel when he relayed Rafferty's news. "In fact, I'm betting they won't."

Laurel tried to ignore the accusation in his eyes. She felt guilty enough for bluffing her way through their confrontation this morning. She prayed Gertie May would show up before Ian read the clippings tomorrow. Laurel wasn't sure she could get up enough nerve to tell him that she was in the house the night Steve was killed. "Do you think we'll get another note today, then?"

Ian nodded grimly.

Laurel was relieved when he went outside to clear last night's snowfall from the driveway and the sidewalks, giving her a short respite from his penetrating gazes. But it rankled to see how reluctant he was to leave her in the house alone. What did he think she'd do, hide incriminating evidence?

As soon as she had Dorie dressed, Laurel inserted a fresh tape into the answering machine in the kitchen. Now she was all set to record the anonymous caller's comments and determine the gender of the voice.

Janet appeared for breakfast at half past nine—early considering the time she'd come in last night. Laurel fixed her a pot of herbal tea and toast, and tried to engage her in conversation. "Are you enjoying your holidays with your friend?"

Janet grimaced. "The holidays aren't to be enjoyed—only endured."

"I take it your friend doesn't have children...."

"No, thank God."

Laurel didn't take her comment personally. "Well, at least you're getting your exercise. I hope your friend's place is not too far. We don't usually get this much snow."

Janet's thin lips quirked with exasperation. "Please don't take this the wrong way, but I'm having an Extra-Strength Tylenol morning. I'm not exactly in a chatty mood."

"Of course. Enjoy your breakfast. Will you be going out soon? I'd like to change your bed linens."

"Yes, but don't bother. I like them worn in."

Laurel smiled. Great. Janet was going out. She hoped Ian's leg was feeling better this morning, because she had a job for him.

"I like the way you think," Ian said with an amused grin, when she slipped outside to the driveway and explained her idea, discreetly handing him a backpack containing her camera, a notepad and pen, two muffins and Dorie's plastic thermos filled with coffee.

Laurel felt an enormous sense of relief that he was co-operating with her. Maybe he didn't distrust her as much as he claimed. "Are you dressed warmly enough? What about your leg?"

He raised his gold-tipped eyebrows. "I'll be fine, Mother."

Laurel laughed, and the strain between them created by this morning's argument faded away. At least he was being honest with her. Tonight she'd level with him. "Sorry. It's habit. You put up with my idiosyncrasies and I'll put up with yours, okay?" She squeezed his arm, warming at the answering twinkle in his eyes. "Good luck. We'll check out Janet's address when you get back."

Laurel decided to finish off the morning by searching Janet Smithe's room from floor to ceiling on the pretext of cleaning it. She gave Dorie a feather duster and a toy broom to keep her busy. Janet wasn't the tidiest of occupants. Toiletries and candy wrappers littered the dresser top. Laurel even stooped to checking the zippered compartments of Janet's soft-sided suitcase. Nothing. But the pocket of a pair of black wool pants hanging in the closet yielded something interesting—a phone number jotted down on a yellow Post-It note. The prefix was for a Vancouver business listing.

Laurel enticed Dorie down to the kitchen with the promise of a snack so she could try the number. It rang ten times before she hung up in frustration. What did she expect? It was Boxing Day. She'd try the number again after she cleaned Ian's room.

Ian's belongings were as enigmatic as his life. He possessed no less than six pairs of glasses in varying styles. He had a tin box of what looked like stage makeup, and his eclectic assortment of clothing ranged in quality from the ridiculously expensive to bargain-basement cheap. The only distinctively personal item was a can of lime shaving cream.

Laurel stared at her finds feeling vaguely disturbed. Something was missing, but she couldn't quite... Then suddenly she knew. The Christmas cards and the knife were not here. What had he done with them?

Had he lied to her and taken them to the police on his own? He'd been gone two and a half hours. Surely he should be back by now. Janet's friend lived within walking distance. As Laurel prepared lunch, she couldn't let go of the disturbing notion that Ian had double-crossed her.

Lunch came and went with no word from Ian. Several of Gertie May's friends stopped by to leave casseroles and nut bread and make hushed inquiries about what progress the police were making. Just after two, Caroline Nicholls invited Dorie over to play for a few hours. Laurel gratefully accepted. Despite everyone's kindness, Laurel felt like a spring being wound tighter and tighter. Sooner or later, the wire would snap and she'd spin out of control.

At four o'clock the phone rang and Laurel hastened to answer it, certain it had to be Ian or the crank caller. She pushed the two-way record button on the answering machine.

"Mrs. Bishop? This is Constable Rafferty—"

Laurel pressed the stop button in a rush of panic. She was recording a police officer's conversation! "Ye-es?"

"Ma'am, I'm just reviewing the fingerprint report from the forensics lab—er, an item has come to my attention concerning your fingerprints. I would like to formally request that you meet me here at the station immediately. I've already dispatched a vehicle."

Laurel gulped. *Her fingerprints?* She had no idea what Rafferty meant, but it occurred to her that the fingerprints could be a ruse Ian and Rafferty had drummed up to catch her. She should have expected Ian to set her up.... He'd been gone for six hours. He'd even told her in no uncertain terms not to trust him. Laurel wasn't taking any chances. "Of course, Constable. There was a matter I wanted to discuss with you anyway."

"I assure you, ma'am, I'd be most interested in anything you have to tell me."

Her arm shook uncontrollably as she hung up the phone. Numbly, she realized it wasn't just her arm. Her whole body was trembling.

An overwhelming sensation of déjà vu tingled along her nerves as her mind reeled back over the conversation. What was it Rafferty had said? Formal request? Yes, those same words had been used the last time and she'd gone like the dutiful citizen her parents had raised her to be, to sit at a bare table in a tiny sterile room while two police officers asked her the same questions over and over again. It was happening again...she could feel it: the police were on the way.

Laurel looked at the clock and pressed her fingers to her lips. Dorie was at a friend's house. There was no time to kiss her baby goodbye.

LAUREL JUST MIGHT be on to something, Ian thought, snapping a picture of Janet Smithe as she climbed on board the *Venture,* a forty-six-foot cabin cruiser that had chugged up to the Serenity Cove public wharf a few minutes ago. A man in black denim jeans and a floater jacket helped her aboard.

Ian took a picture of him, too, but the hood of his jacket obscured his face, making him doubt that the picture would be all that good. Laurel's 35 mm camera wasn't equipped with a zoom lens.

He had to get closer to that boat. From the sound of the engine, it wasn't stopping for long.

Ian shoved the camera and his glasses into the backpack and pulled his tuque low over his forehead. Slinging the backpack over his shoulder, he tucked his hands into the pockets of his leather jacket and sauntered down the dock.

The cabin cruiser was still there, idling alongside a sleek seventy-foot sailboat. No one was on the deck of the sailboat and, without giving it a second thought, Ian boarded it, heading for the stern. A quick glance at the cruiser told him that Janet and her friend had gone into the main salon, out of the cold. Loud music suddenly blared from the salon's interior. Someone would be coming back onto the bridge soon. It was now or never. If they were leaving, he was going with them.

Five feet of water separated the stern of the sailboat and the bow of the cruiser. Ian climbed over the guardrail and jumped, landing hard on the afterdeck of the cruiser with a hollow thud that was easily masked by the music. His injured thigh protested the force of the impact with a sharp eruption of pain. Ian winced and fell onto his backside. He saw a ladder leading up to the flying bridge and he slid toward it, dragging his sore leg and the backpack with him. The flying bridge was used to enjoy some of Vancouver's warmer weather. It would be a good place to hide. He climbed the ladder and crouched between the bolted down captain's seat and the bulkhead below the wheel, out of the worst of the wind. But it was cold!

The cruiser was heading out into the inlet, the jarring motion of the boat reverberating torturously in his thigh. He hoped it wasn't going to be a long trip.

The coffee, and thoughts of himself peeling off Laurel's prim nightgown and making love to her, kept him tolerably warm. She was getting under his skin, twisting him inside out so that he didn't know what to think anymore.

Ian kept track of the cruiser's steady course due west to the mouth of the inlet. There, he feared, they would head out to the open sea. But, thankfully, the cruiser changed course and headed south past the deserted beaches of Stanley Park, then turned east into English Bay and up into False Creek toward Granville Island—a popular public market with its colony of shops, artist studios, restaurants and theaters. He'd taken Aunt Gem there for dinner once.

The cruiser moored in the marina for the Granville Island Hotel. Ian kept himself hidden on the flying bridge as Janet jumped ashore with the lines. He heard their voices as they disembarked, and gave them time to reach the end of the dock before he trailed after them, cursing under his breath at the pain involved with each step. Damn leg! He wouldn't be surprised if he'd ripped the wound open again. The doctor in Colombia had told him it would take time to heal properly.

Janet and her friend walked with their heads bent close together in conversation. He was slightly taller than she, and stockier. They headed straight for the entrance to the hotel, which looked more like an industrial warehouse with multitudes of red girders and glass, than a luxury resort. Ian gritted his teeth and increased his pace, determined to keep them in sight. He entered the lobby just in time to catch a glimpse of Janet's distinctive coat and a brass hotel key dangling from a male hand before the elevator doors slid closed.

He'd seen enough to convince him that Janet Smithe led an interesting life. In fact, he wouldn't be surprised to learn her companion was a married man.

Ian felt a warm trickle on his left leg. Blood was seeping through his jeans. With a weary sigh, he limped back to the dock to get the *Venture*'s registration number. Then he returned to the hotel and told the doorman to call him a taxi.

By the time the doctor in the hospital emergency room had added several new stitches to his leg, and he'd popped a couple of prescription painkillers, Ian was longing for a good dinner, a warm bed and one of Laurel's soft, understanding looks. Not necessarily in that order.

What he found was an empty house and a note from Laurel that she'd been taken to the police station for questioning. Ian stared at the note as a fearful possibility leapt into his mind. Had Laurel been arrested?

Chapter Eight

One look at the RCMP interrogation room was enough to start Laurel's stomach muscles quivering nervously. She banged her knee on the metal table leg when she sat down.

A tape recorder rested on the table, a cassette spinning quietly. Constable Rafferty opened a file and pulled out a fingerprint sheet dotted with black smudges, his demeanor potently serious.

Laurel tried not to think about Dorie being told her mommy wasn't coming home because she was in jail.

"I'll get right to the point, if I may. I'm rather confused as to your identity...." Rafferty paused for an ominous half second and Laurel's heartbeat trebled. "You've identified yourself in your statement as Mrs. Laurel Bishop of Serenity Cove. However, Ottawa insists these fingerprints belong to Laurel Lang Wilson, and places you at the scene of a murder in Nelson two years ago."

Laurel swayed in her seat. It had never occurred to her that her fingerprints might be on file.

"And here's where things get interesting...." He removed a stack of papers from his file. "According to my information, your husband was murdered two years ago on December 23 from a blow to the head. I don't need to remind you that Miss Harris disappeared on the night of December 23, and that blood was found in the hallway which matched her blood type. Now, Mrs. *Wilson*— It is Mrs. Wilson, isn't it?"

Laurel nodded. *What else did Rafferty know?* She'd seen no sign of Ian anywhere. Maybe he hadn't double-crossed her. The walls of the room were shifting around her, coming closer and jerking backward in kaleidoscopic patterns. She wished she'd been able to bring in the Christmas cards and the knife with her—even the newspaper clippings—to show her intentions of cooperating fully.

"We're taking Miss Harris's disappearance very seriously, especially in light of this new information. Before we go any further in this discussion, Mrs. Wilson, it's my duty to inform you that it is a criminal offense to give false or misleading information to the police. . . ."

Laurel didn't hear any more. She fainted dead away.

IAN HAD NEVER DRIVEN so recklessly to a police station. He parked Gertie May's beater on St. Georges, near the hospital, and hobbled around the corner to 13th Street, keeping an eye out for black ice. The red lights of an ambulance parked at the curb of the RCMP detachment caught his attention.

Ian hurried toward the entrance, compelled by a strong sense of urgency.

The door opened as he approached and a stretcher was wheeled out. Ian stood to one side to let it pass, his heart stopping when he recognized the patient's pale features and honey-colored hair. The streetlamp gave her appearance a deathly glow.

"Wait! Stop! Laurel?" He stroked her cheek and her eyelids fluttered open. Her pallor and the wildness in her eyes scared the hell out of him.

"Oh, Ian, you're here," she whispered, struggling against the bindings that held her in the stretcher. He felt the wetness of her tears dampen his fingers. "They're going to arrest me. Promise me you'll take care of Dorie."

"I can't—"

"Please, Ian. I'm begging you."

He found himself responding to the desperation in her voice. "Okay, I promise." Her eyes closed. "Laurel?" Ian shook her shoulder gently. She'd slipped into unconsciousness.

"We gotta go, mister. You her husband?" one of the attendants asked him.

Ian looked at him blankly. "No."

"Then stand aside."

He watched helplessly as they loaded her into the ambulance, then he wheeled around and barged into the detachment. Rafferty was in the foyer talking with the watch commander.

"What the hell happened to her?" Ian thundered at him.

Rafferty fixed him with a warning gaze schooled to intimidate. "Mrs. Wilson fainted during the course of our conversation. I called the paramedics."

"You probably scared the daylights out of her—"

"Perhaps we should continue this conversation in private...."

"I'm going to the hospital."

"They'll keep me posted on Mrs. Wilson's condition."

"Mrs. Wilson? So you know who she is, then?" Ian said.

"Yes." Rafferty led the way to an interrogation room and closed the door behind them.

"Then I might as well show you what's been arriving at the house since the day my aunt disappeared...." Ian withdrew the plastic bags containing the Christmas cards and the knife from his coat pocket. "Did Laurel tell you about these?"

"Our conversation hadn't progressed that far. Please, sit down and enlighten me."

It seemed to Ian that it would take an eternity to explain everything to Rafferty's inquisitive satisfaction. His mind kept circling back to Laurel being raced to the hospital. Was she okay? Would she be afraid if she came to again and found herself alone in a hospital bed? Would she be worried about Dorie? Damn Rafferty and his questions.

"You should have come forward with this information sooner." Rafferty paused and stroked his mustache. "I'll have the lab check out the knife and the Christmas cards."

"What if this person calls again? Can you trace the call?"

Rafferty frowned. "Were you in the room when Mrs. Wilson received the call?"

"No."

"Did you hear the phone ring?"

"No, but—" Ian leaned forward, his impatience erupting into irritation. "What are you implying? That a call never came?"

"I'm merely pointing out that there's no evidence, other than Mrs. Wilson's word, that a call was made. You stated she couldn't tell whether the voice sounded male or female, correct?"

"I don't think she's lying. She has no reason to hurt my aunt."

"No reason that we know of—yet."

Ian shook his head, struggling to keep his tone reasonable. "I'm beginning to understand why the prospect of telling you the truth was so frightening to her."

"She has good cause to be frightened. Kidnapping and murder are indictable offences. And we can't forget that she was at home the night her husband was killed."

Ian's jaw dropped. Rafferty's statement hit him like a powerful left hook. "Laurel was home that night?"

Rafferty handed him a copy of Laurel's statement to read. "She had motive and opportunity. But the Nelson RCMP cleared her. She passed a lie detector test twice. I'd like to see those newspaper clippings as soon as possible. And I'll make the necessary arrangements to trace incoming calls to the house. If your aunt has been abducted, it could explain why we've found no trace of her. The search today was negative. Dressed as she was, it's doubtful she could have survived three nights at these temperatures unless she's found shelter. There's one remaining area we haven't covered. That will be done tomorrow."

Ian nodded grimly.

"Since you're here, you can answer another question for me. How are your personal finances?"

"I beg your pardon?"

"You deal in gems, right? It took me a while to translate that jargon you gave me. What's the state of your finances?"

"I've got about two hundred thousand dollars tucked away for a rainy day, in a bank in Los Angeles." Ian gave him the account number.

"Anyone know you got that kind of cash?"

"No. Just me, you, and the bank teller. I'm a very private man."

Rafferty smiled complacently. "I've already learned that. In my experience, private people have something to hide."

Ian rose from his chair. "Off the record, Constable, my own feeling is, why waste words talking about nothing? If you'll excuse me, there's someone I'd like to visit."

LAUREL'S FAINT SMILE touched Ian like a ray of sunshine when he entered her curtained-off berth in the emergency room, sliding the curtains closed behind him. He smiled back, feeling his stomach drop with relief at finding her conscious. There were purple smudges under her eyes and the hollows in her cheeks that were part of her delicate bone structure looked more pronounced. An IV pumped fluids into her body. How much had she eaten in the last few days? Why hadn't he paid more attention? "How are you?"

"I'm okay. The doctor says I fainted. The stress of everything." She looked past him toward the curtain, suddenly wary. "Is Rafferty coming to arrest me?"

"No. Why would you think that?"

"But I thought... Oh, Ian, I've made such a mess of everything...."

"I know." He rubbed her shoulder. "After I read your note, I went to meet you at the station. That's quite a dramatic exit you were making. Anyway, I spoke to Rafferty for a few minutes. I gave him the Christmas cards and the knife. Now they have more to work on." He cleared his throat. "Rafferty also wants to see those newspaper clippings."

He waited, feeling his body tense. He'd given her the perfect opportunity to come clean. Was she going to lie to him again?

Her hand crept out from underneath the blankets and slipped between his fingers. Fragile and cold. "There's something I have to tell you. Dorie and I were home the night Steve was killed. Dorie was sick with a virus. I went to bed early, thinking she'd be up several times as she had the three previous nights." Her voice cracked. "Dorie woke up at 5:00 a.m. and I went downstairs to get her a bottle. That's when I found him . . ." She moistened her lips. "I didn't tell you the truth because I thought you'd go to the police right away if you knew."

Ian felt an almost phenomenal sense of relief. Maybe the painkillers were making him woozy. He squeezed her fingers. "If I were in your situation, I'd have lied to me, too. Um, do you get to come home now, or what?"

"The doctor is waiting for results back from the blood tests, but he says I'm dehydrated. They'll keep me here overnight for observation. Could you phone Mrs. Nicholls and ask if Dorie can spend the night?"

"She doesn't have to keep Dorie. I'll pick her up. I promised you I'd take care of her, remember?" He smiled gently.

"I pressured you into it—"

"I occasionally keep the promises I make. I'll go call. What's the number?"

When Ian returned, Laurel looked at him anxiously. "Is Dorie all right?"

"Yep. They're making popcorn. I told Mrs. Nicholls I'd be there in an hour."

"Good. I'm glad Dorie will be sleeping in her own bed tonight." She picked at the sheet. "It's hard enough that Gertie May suddenly disappeared from her life. I'm terrified that one morning Dorie will wake up and be told by a stranger that her mommy isn't there—that she'll feel I've abandoned her. Dorie's my life. She's supposed to be able to depend on me. *Always.*"

Ian didn't know how to respond to her emotional outburst. The strength of her feelings for her daughter was so far removed from his experience with his own mother. He wondered what it would be like to be loved the way Laurel loved Dorie.

"Sorry." She smiled weakly. "Tell me what happened this afternoon when you followed Janet."

He gave her an exact account.

"How did you injure your leg in the first place?" she asked when he'd finished.

"A knife wound. I had something someone else wanted and I refused to give it up." He shrugged. "The other guy was a lot worse off. At least I walked away. It's a risk you live with in the trade."

She didn't approve of his answer, he could tell by the way she averted her eyes. He'd come as close as he could to admitting he'd killed a man in a fight for his life and sixty thousand dollars' worth of gems. It wasn't her reality. But it was his.

"What happened to your glasses? Did you break them when you jumped onto the cabin cruiser?"

The glasses. He'd forgotten about them. It wasn't like him to slip out of character like that.

"Don't worry about the glasses. They were only a prop."

She frowned. "A prop? Like an actor's prop?"

"Yes. Sometimes there's anonymity in appearances. Before this 'look,' I was a Catholic priest."

"Oh."

"Don't look so disappointed." His grin faded. Her reaction was creating a sizable rift in his male ego.

"I'm not disappointed. You're much handsomer without them. It's just ... I was wondering how you can live changing your history constantly. Doesn't lying to people bother you? I feel like the world's biggest fake telling people Steve died in a car accident."

"Why should I care what other people think? I'm good at what I do. My clients get their product delivered safely and on time. That's all that counts." His parents were never concerned by what other people thought of the way they were raising their son. Ian could see she didn't like this answer, either.

She abruptly changed the subject. "I searched Janet's room today. Don't look so surprised. There wasn't anything incriminating, just a phone number. I tried dialing it several times, but there was no answer." She reached for her purse and dug it out of the contents. "We can call the research section of the library tomorrow to see if it's listed in the backward section of the city directory...."

"Consider it done," Ian said, tucking the paper into his pocket. He'd get a private investigator working on it in the morning.

"WHERE'S MOMMY?" Dorie asked him when he came to collect her at the Nichollses'.

"Sleeping at the hospital."

"Is Mommy sick?"

"No. Just really tired. The doctor wanted her to sleep there, so I'm going to take care of you tonight. Is that okay? Come on, let's get into these snow pants. Are you old enough to zip your coat? No? I'll do it, then." He felt clumsy as he tried to get her dressed, tying her pink knitted tuque under her chin. Her bubble-gum pink boots ended up on the wrong feet, but she didn't seem to mind. He picked up Dorie's backpack. Mrs. Nicholls gave him an encouraging smile as they left. She'd already agreed to baby-sit Dorie tomorrow while he went to pick up Laurel at the hospital.

They got home at nine o'clock. Dorie had fallen asleep in the car, so Ian carried her directly to bed. She roused a bit as he pulled off her snowsuit.

"Ian, do you have a daddy?" she asked sleepily.

"Everybody has a daddy, sprite."

"I don't. It's not fair. Caroline's daddy plays monster and makes popcorn. My daddy's a picture on the wall 'cause he's in heaven. He doesn't do anything."

Ian slipped her pajama top over her head, surprised by a sudden impulse to hug her. "I know how you feel, sprite. I never got to do anything fun with my daddy, either. I used to imagine doing fun stuff with him, though. Maybe you could try that." He tweaked her nose. "And don't forget you have the absolutely best mommy in the world."

As his own words reached his ears, Ian found himself believing them. Whatever remaining doubts he had about Laurel's involvement in her husband's death disintegrated beneath the growing warmth of feeling he had for her.

"Okay," Dorie mumbled drowsily. She lifted her arms up and gave him a sweet, damp kiss on his cheek. A few seconds later she was asleep. Ian found her pink bunny and tucked it under her chin. This little sprite deserved a helluva lot more than a picture-on-the-wall daddy.

LAUREL WAS DISCHARGED from the hospital late the next morning. Ian would have carried her to the car, but a nurse insisted he use a wheelchair. She sat quietly with her hands folded in her lap as he drove home. He was going to put her to bed and threaten to stay there with her if she didn't stay put. She'd need a good lunch. He'd fix her some soup and crackers and a glass of milk. The doctor said she needed rest, plenty of fluids and three square meals a day. And if at all possible, reduce some of the stress she'd been under. He'd make sure she followed doctor's orders.

But the first thing he learned about Laurel when they arrived at Harris House was that she couldn't follow orders.

The front door was slightly ajar and Ian paused in midstep, putting a finger to his lips. "Wait here on the porch," he said quietly against her temple. "I'd better check it out. I remember locking it before I left."

"Don't be silly! One of the guests probably came back for something and didn't close it properly." She pushed past him and he grabbed her elbow, forcing her to stop.

"Humor me, please? I have a bad feeling about this."

She looked up at him with wide, frightened eyes. He realized he shouldn't have said that. God, he was a terrible nurse. What made him think he could take care of another person?

Cautiously, he nudged the door open with the toe of his boot. His instincts were dead-on. Aunt Gem's normally spotless front hall was littered with coats and umbrellas. Ian strode down the hallway, glancing from one room to another. They were in similar states of disarray. Drawers upturned. Cupboards opened. Papers and books strewn everywhere. What the hell was going on? Was someone still in the house?

"Oh, Ian, look at this mess! Have we been robbed?" Laurel's stunned expression worried him. She looked like she was going to crumple again at any moment. And he couldn't very well check out the house with her trailing behind him. Not in this state anyway.

He ushered her outside. "Come on, it's not safe for us to be here. We'll phone the police from next door. Rafferty's got his work cut out for him on this case."

Frederick was more than obliging, offering both the use of his phone and a strong cup of tea for Laurel. "Was anything taken?" he asked Laurel, joining her at the kitchen table while Ian went back to Harris House to await the police.

"I don't know. Ian wouldn't let me go inside."

Frederick shook his head in dismay. "Sometimes I think the world has gone mad. A good woman like Anna is a prisoner of her mind. Citizens have to put bars on their homes to protect their possessions. Burglaries are an everyday occurrence." He pursed his thin lips, looking dour. "Did you know that the newspaper prints a list of break and enters each week? Press clippings for the criminals. I should have gone into insurance instead of pharmaceuticals. I imagine the crime rate in Serenity Cove will skyrocket if Victor Romanowski gets his way with those luxury condos. We'll need more police. More police, more taxes. I'm already overtaxed as it is. I wonder if the district council has considered that?"

"Did you say the police were coming for a visit, Papa?" Anna croaked hoarsely from the living room.

"No, dear. Go back to your program."

"I had an uncle who was a police officer. Or was it a brother?" Anna went on, her ramblings getting drowned out by the television.

The park. Condos. Laurel sighed and stared down into her teacup. She'd forgotten all about Romanowski and the district council hearing. Where had Gertie May put the petitions to save the park? And there were notes for a speech she and Gertie May had been working on... She couldn't let Gertie May down. If there was no vocal opposition to the project, Romanowski would get the go-ahead for his development. There was too much money involved for the district to turn its back on prospective revenues.

She carried her saucer to the counter. "Thanks for the tea, Frederick. I should be going. The police may need me."

"You're right. Frankly, the last thing I need is a police officer on my doorstep. Chances are, Anna would invite him in and start reminiscing." He showed her to the door and helped her with her coat. Feeling his gaze on her as she walked down his brick walk, she turned to wave before she rounded the hedge. He looked so forlorn. A slender silhouette of a man peering through the divided lights of his front door at the world beyond.

LAUREL STOOD in the center of the kitchen and surveyed the chaos of cutlery, linens and foodstuffs at her feet. She felt angry. Violated. *First Gertie May and now this. How dare they!*

She knelt down and gathered up Dorie's artwork from the jumble of old lottery tickets and grocery coupons. Why did people keep so much junk on their refrigerators? Laurel smoothed the pictures flat and stuck them onto the refrigerator with alphabet magnets. One was torn, but not too badly.... Hot tears suddenly stung her eyes, blurring her vision. She brushed them away and picked up a fork, sniffling righteously. *Some burglar. He didn't even recognize good silver when he saw it.*

"Laurel, what are you doing?" Ian demanded, storming into the room. "One of the officers said he'd seen you come in here. We're not supposed to touch anything until they're done fingerprinting.''

"Oh." Her arms fell to her sides.

He plucked her from the floor, taking the fork from her hand and sending it clattering into the sink. "Come on, you're going to bed," he said, steering her toward the basement stairs.

"But the mess—"

"No buts. Your suite wasn't touched. Most of the mess is on the first floor and upstairs in Gertie May's bedroom and mine. The guest rooms weren't touched. Actually, I don't think much was taken. The televisions and the stereo are still here. Rafferty says it was probably someone looking for cash and jewelry." Ian propelled her all the way to her sleeping area and looked at her dresser, frowning. "Which drawer do you keep that sexy nightgown in?"

Her what? She looked at him in total confusion.

He laughed. "You know, the one that shows off every inch of your neck?"

She laughed then, a hiccuping laugh, and wiped at the tear tracks on her cheeks with the back of her hand. "I'm not going to bed, Ian. There's too much to do."

"Yes, you are. I'll undress you myself if I have to. Where's the nightgown?"

He meant it. There was a hard edge to his voice that reminded her of their first encounter when he'd pinned her to the ground. "Y-you've forgotten about Dorie. She can't stay at the Nichollses' all day."

"Yes, she can. I already spoke to Mrs. Nicholls about it. She said Dorie was fine and it would be okay if I picked her up at four. Where's the nightgown?"

"For heaven's sake, you're the most stubborn man I've ever met." She turned her back to him and jerked the nightgown out from underneath her pillow. "All right, I'll have a nap. You can pick up the whole damn house for all I care. No, don't turn down the bed. I'll do it."

"Fine. I'll be back in five minutes with your lunch. You'd better be between the sheets—or else."

"Or else what?" She swung her head around and met his narrow, uncompromising gaze, while her fingers angrily worked the buttons of her blouse. "You're going to put me there yourself? I'd like to see you try, especially with police roaming all over the house. That should be something." Her blouse fell open and she looked away from him as a bubble of hysterical laughter rose in her throat. Gertie May was missing, maybe wandering around exposed to the elements, and instead of trying to help find her, she was supposed to rest? Guilt was a lousy sedative.

What if the person who'd burgled the house had taken Gertie May? Maybe he'd left behind a clue that only she could identify.

His fingers bit into her shoulders, sinking through the thin silk of her blouse. Laurel gasped as she was spun around, her head snapping back so that she viewed his fierce expression from only inches away. What was he so angry about?

"Dammit, Laurel, I care about you," he said, grinding the words out as though he despised them.

Her eyes flew open in astonishment. Had she heard properly?

Then his mouth descended on hers, hard and unrelenting. Laurel felt herself spinning out of control. Her knees quaked as though the carpet beneath her had metamorphosed into a churning sea. She slid her arms up around his neck, holding on for dear life. The kiss lasted for a breathless, heart-pounding minute before he pulled away. Laurel gaped at him in confusion. The anger was gone now...she found only the stormy tension of desire hovering in his flint gray eyes. His mouth, too, had softened into an almost coaxing grin.

She suddenly wished those same police officers gone and wondered where this conversation would lead if they were alone and Gertie May wasn't missing.

Ian pulled the flaps of her blouse together. "*Please* lie down and rest. At least, until the police are done."

Well. When he put it in that silky, reasonable way, how could she refuse? "Promise you'll wake me as soon as the police are done?"

"Cross my heart."

Laurel sank onto the bed. The truth was, she was exhausted. She slipped under the covers, a weary smile curving her lips. Imagine, Ian cared about her.

Chapter Nine

Laurel removed the envelope containing the newspaper clippings from her safety-deposit box and handed it to Ian, letting her annoyance show.

She'd have preferred coming to the bank alone, but he'd insisted on accompanying her. Laurel wasn't fooled. What did he think she'd do, remove a clipping or two?

Probably.

Despite that kiss yesterday and the startling admission that he cared for her, he still didn't trust her. Certainly not enough to share the contents of Gertie May's will with her. They'd found it last night in Gertie May's Bible when they'd combed the house checking for items stolen in the burglary; they'd been lucky—only two hundred dollars was taken from the cash box.

But then, what did she expect from him?

He was a loner. A man without attachments, who changed his appearance as easily as other people changed clothes. His permanent address was a post office box, for heaven's sake. After her experience with Steve, she should know that men with a secretive nature were unable to share their private thoughts or their lives with anyone.

Even with their lovers.

Every day Laurel had to face the fact that she'd loved Steve for four years and had never really known him. Never known that he was capable of risking their home and savings—and his life—for the thrill of making a quick buck.

Ian was cut from the same cloth, risking his life for money and other people's jewelry. She was never going to be involved in a one-way relationship again.

They stopped at a print shop on the way to the police station to photocopy the newspaper clippings.

"I'm hungry," Dorie complained to Laurel as they waited in the car.

Laurel sighed. They'd had a particularly difficult morning. Dorie hadn't eaten breakfast and she'd refused to get dressed. Laurel had had to bribe her with lunch at McDonald's to get her moving. "I know you're hungry, sweetie. The McDonald's is near the police station—that's where we're going next. Here comes Ian."

Ian wore a composed, thoughtful expression as he climbed into the car. Laurel glanced at him anxiously. What was he thinking? He'd been in the print shop long enough to scan several articles.

Laurel felt nauseated. Was his distrust for her growing?

When they arrived at the detachment, the watch commander told them Rafferty was at the search site.

Laurel's heart filled with dread. "Does that mean they've found something?"

"Not that I know of. I'll see that Constable Rafferty gets this information immediately."

While Dorie whirled around on the McDonald's carousel, Laurel and Ian read through the newspaper articles. It wasn't pleasant reading as far as Laurel was concerned: Local Community Activist Implicated In Husband's Death. Wife Claims She Slept Through Husband's Murder. Murder Victim Mired In Debt.

The facts of the case remained the same. Steve came home that night and was in the process of straightening up the house when he'd been killed by a single blow to the head. The time of death was placed at approximately 9:45 p.m. There was no sign of forced entry. A tennis trophy was reported missing. Barb was quoted as saying, "I'm absolutely certain that my daughter-in-law had nothing to do with my stepson's death."

Good ol' Barb. If it weren't for her unwavering belief in Laurel's innocence, Laurel wasn't sure she'd have made it through those painful months of coping with Steve's death—and learning the extent of his secret life of gambling.

"There's nothing of earth-shattering significance that I can see, except that Steve was doing housework for a change," she said testily. "So, where do we go from here?"

Ian gave her a piercing look. "I'm taking you home. We'll drop off that roll of film at a one-hour developer's on the way. I'm hoping you'll be able to recognize the man on the boat. Then I have an errand—"

Laurel glowered at him. "I'm coming with you if it has something to do with Gertie May."

"The doctor said you need to rest. Besides, one of us should be home in case Aunt Gem phones, or another card is delivered, or we get another crank call."

"You're making excuses. The truth is, you don't want to tell me what you're doing. Fine. So, how's your credit?"

Ian raised an eyebrow. "I beg your pardon?"

She pointed at a newspaper headline. "Mine's shot, obviously. I think we should make a trip to an electronics store and buy some equipment. With today's technology there must be a way we can videotape the front door area at night—maybe catch the person who's leaving the Christmas cards on film."

He grinned. "How'd you do that?"

It was Laurel's turn to look confused. "What?"

"Guess the nature of my afternoon plans. I can make the purchases. I'd prefer it if you rested."

He'd stonewalled her again. But Laurel refused to play along. "All right," she agreed docilely. "You go shopping and I'll make some calls about Janet and the boat."

"Just make sure you find time for a nap," Ian said sternly.

"Okay, nurse." But she had no intention of resting.

"WE'RE SORRY, *madame,* to be checking out early, but my son insists," Henri Boudreault explained to Laurel as he settled his bill. Laurel had arrived home to find the Boudreaults packing their bags. "After we told him about the burglary, he says it's not safe for us to be here."

"I understand," Laurel assured him. "Have you found other accommodations? I'd be happy to refer you to a hotel—"

"We'll rest *avec* my son. Marguerite can get along with her daughter-in-law for two days. Can't you, *ma chère?*"

Marguerite rolled her dark eyes. "*Imagine, toi,* my grandchildren do not eat vegetables. My daughter-in-law is American. They don't eat vegetables, the Americans."

Laurel wished them luck and waved them on their way. After Janet checked out, she'd have the locks changed for her own peace of mind.

Fortunately, things were slow in the research section of the Vancouver public library and the researcher was willing to respond to more than one request when Laurel called. She verified Janet's address in the city directory; Laurel wondered if Janet found it poetically inspiring to rent a room above a Laundromat.

There was no listing in the backward section of the city directory for the phone number she'd found in Janet's pocket. And there was still no answer to the number. The company was obviously closed for the holidays.

Laurel quickly made another call to a friend she'd met through Dorie's preschool. Maybe Sheila, who owned a pleasure boat, would know how to find out who the *Venture* was registered to. Sheila was glad to help and gave Laurel the address and phone number for the area office of the Registrar of Shipping. But when Laurel phoned the registrar's office, a taped recording informed her it was already closed for the day and would be open tomorrow, Friday, until four.

As Laurel hung up the phone, Dorie skipped into the kitchen singing, "Fif' of June, eleven, two, 'tober tentynine. Ashes, ashes..."

"What's that you're singing, sweetie?"

"Mine and Gertie May's song." Dorie's face sobered. "Isn't she ever coming home, Mommy? I can't wait any longer."

Laurel dropped to her knees and enfolded her in a hug. She wasn't sure how much longer she could wait, either.

IAN LAY AWAKE on the couch in Laurel's sitting room. A table lamp isolated him in a pool of light as he stared at the two photographs he'd filched from the packet of photos that had been developed today. Laurel had left the packet upstairs on Aunt Gem's desk after she'd failed to identify the man on the boat. Ian couldn't resist helping himself to these two extra prints. How could he explain to Laurel that he wanted a picture of her and Dorie? It was a Halloween snapshot. Laurel was wearing a crazy clown wig and Dorie was dressed as a kitty. The other snapshot was of Aunt Gem blowing out the candles on her birthday cake. She'd turned sixty-six on November 2nd.

Ian held the photos next to his heart. He'd never felt so confused. Aunt Gem's disappearance had shaken him more than he was willing to admit in the light of day. And then there was Laurel. He'd slept in her bed to be near Dorie the night she'd stayed in the hospital, but the scent of her in the sheets had nearly driven him mad. She was slowly enveloping him—

A sound from the other side of the partition interrupted Ian's thoughts. He quickly slid the photos into his wallet and switched off the light.

Laurel entered the sitting room. "Ian? Are you asleep?"

He had to smile at the ghostly image of her nightgown in the dark. "No, but you should be. I'll bet you didn't take a nap this afternoon, either." Her telling silence infuriated him. "Come, sit down with me and I'll give you a massage. That should relax you. I'm told I have very good hands." He pushed the blankets aside on his makeshift bed.

"Don't expect me to ask who says so," she said darkly as she plopped down on the couch and presented her back to him.

He choked back a laugh and swept her strawberry-scented hair out of the way. Her shoulders were stiff with tension. Ian felt another brand of tension course through him as his fingers slid over her flannel-clad back to massage her neck.

"Hmm, that feels good. Do you think the minicamera you bought will catch our Christmas card bearer?"

"I hope so. The videotapes will only record for six hours on extended play." Ted, the computer-electronics whiz he'd brought home with him to set up the complicated system, had seemed confident it would serve their needs. They'd concealed the minicamera in the hall closet where it had a clear view of the front door through the diamond sidelight window. The camera was connected by cable to a VCR. Another cable ran from the VCR to a computer set up in the alcove. If they caught someone on film, they'd be able to print a picture to show Rafferty.

"Well, you're going to be the one to explain to Gertie May why you drilled holes in her house."

Ian laughed. He could feel Laurel relaxing beneath his touch. "That's a risk I'm willing to take. Besides, if anything has happened to Aunt Gem, it'll be my house. She promised it to me when I was fourteen."

She looked at him over her shoulder, her expression tender. "You're attached to the house, aren't you?"

"Yep. Why does that surprise you?"

"Ian, everything about you surprises me. It just goes to show that I don't really know you. But so far, I like what I see. And despite all your dire warnings, I trust you with my life and my daughter." She yawned sleepily and leaned into him.

His body responded instantly to her soft, pliable warmth. It was an effort to confine his hands to her back when all he wanted to do was pull her into his lap and kiss her. But he was trying to put her to sleep, not stimulate her. Or seduce her. At least not tonight.

He pulled the blankets over her as she snuggled against him. He waited until her breathing was deep and regular to whisper in her ear, "On the contrary, Laurel, I think you know me better than anyone."

HAD THE VIDEO CAMERA caught anything last night? Laurel wondered, the moment she awakened. Then she looked around, amused to find herself in her own bed. Had Ian carried her in here?

He was asleep on the couch when she tiptoed through the sitting room a few minutes later. Really, there was no reason for him to continue sleeping down here. She always hooked up the answering machine on the basement extension before she went to bed. He probably did it out of some misguided sense of male protectiveness.

Laurel hurried upstairs and cautiously opened the front door, shivering in the brisk morning air. No envelope. Only the Friday edition of the *North Shore News* rested on the doormat. The community paper came out thrice weekly: Sundays, Wednesdays and Fridays. Laurel reached for the paper, then paused in alarm.

A picture of Harris House was on the front page, with a short article detailing Wednesday's burglary. Laurel took the paper into the kitchen to read while she put on the coffee. Rafferty was quoted as saying that there was no apparent link between the burglary and Gertie May Harris's unexplained disappearance. The perpetrator entered by an open door and an undisclosed amount of cash was stolen, indicating the thief was likely someone in need of cash for a quick fix. End of story.

Laurel frowned. She still needed to get Gertie May's office reorganized. Ian had done a decent job of picking up, but she'd have to sort through the papers. Put everything back the way it had been.

The phone rang. Laurel put down her coffee cup to answer it, but Ian beat her to it on the downstairs extension. He croaked a gruff greeting and she waited to hear who was calling before she spoke. "Mr. Harris? I have that information you requested," a male voice said. "You said you wanted it A.S.A.P."

What information? Laurel put her hand over the mouthpiece as her curiosity got the better of her.

"Name a place and I'll meet you there in an hour and a half," Ian said.

"Lonsdale Quay. The Food Fair. I'll expect payment."

"Fine."

Laurel waited until after Ian had hung up the extension before she did. He walked casually into the kitchen a few minutes later, bare chested, barefoot, and the top button on his jeans unfastened. His hair was rumpled as though he'd just run his fingers through it. She suddenly felt angry that he could behave so casually when he was holding out on her again—keeping her in the dark on what he was doing. He hadn't told her he'd requested info from anyone. She poured cream into the creamer for the table. "Good morning. Who was on the phone?"

He leaned against the doorframe, hooking his thumbs on the belt loops of his jeans. "A client wanting to know if I was available to do a job."

Laurel yanked the silverware drawer open and pulled out a teaspoon for the sugar bowl. "You can lie better than that."

"I beg your pardon?"

"I listened in on your telephone conversation," she explained flatly. "So, what information was this person talking about?"

He shook his head. "Last night you said you trusted me."

"I do. I just want to know what you're doing." Anger crept into her voice. "I have a right to know, Ian. If you don't tell me, I'll follow you—Lonsdale Quay. The Food Fair."

He gave her a measuring gaze. "I hired a private investigator to conduct a background check on you and your creditors."

She wasn't surprised. Not really. It was a logical thing to do. What wasn't logical was the degree to which it hurt her feelings. She'd thought he was beginning to trust her, too.

"Oh. Well, maybe they'll turn up something that I've overlooked." She picked up the creamer and sugar bowl and carried them into the dining room. "You know, when I look back on what happened with Steve, I realize the biggest mistake I made was allowing him to have complete control over my life—not asking questions when I should have. I'll never let someone else have that control over me again." She looked back at him over her shoulder, unintimidated by the scowl lines gouging his lean cheeks. "Did you want some breakfast?"

He pushed himself away from the doorjamb. "I'll go see if any deliveries were made during the night."

"There weren't any. I've already checked. But you could check the tape to see if Janet came back alone. And by the way, *put* some clothes on for breakfast. We have a dress code around here. No shoes. No shirt. No service—" She broke off, hearing footsteps on the stairs.

Janet was up.

Laurel served her a plate of coffee cake and fresh, sliced fruit. "So, what do you have planned for today?"

"Not much. My friend is otherwise occupied for most of the day, so I thought I'd cozy myself up in the local library. I've already finished this paperback I borrowed from the office." She gestured toward a book she'd brought downstairs with her. "I was hoping to read something a little more intellectually stimulating."

"The library's next to the high school. I'm sure they have a nice poetry selection. Are you published?"

Janet's mouth tightened. "Only in a few literary magazines. The prestige goes a lot further than the money. By the way, I'd like to stay on past the second. Would that be all right?"

Laurel stared at her thoughtfully, trying not to let on that Janet's request had aroused her suspicions. "I'll check the bookings and let you know." She paused delicately. "There's also the situation with Miss Harris to consider."

Janet nodded. "I see."

"Have you got special plans with your friend for New Year's Eve? The Crow's Nest is having a big bash."

"I'm not one for crowds. I prefer more intimate surroundings."

"I take it your friend is a *he,* then? Is it serious?"

A guarded expression crept over Janet's acne-spotted face and acid dripped from her tone. "Actually, since you're so interested. My friend is a *she.* And yes, it's serious. Isn't that your little girl calling you?"

Laurel was unperturbed. Today she was bound and determined to find out what Janet Smithe had to lie about.

THE REGISTRAR OF SHIPPING office was located on West Pender Street near the waterfront. Laurel breathed deeply of the salt-tinged air as she paid the cab fare and hurried inside the government building. Ian had taken Gertie May's car to his rendezvous with the private investigator. Laurel hoped the private investigator was giving Ian an earful.

The clerk at the counter directed her toward some huge, ancient-looking indexes and helped her select the right book. Laurel flipped through the pages until she found the *Venture.*

It was registered to a Vancouver company coincidentally called V.J.R. Ventures. Maybe Janet was having an affair with the owner. Laurel wrote down the address. Then she thanked the clerk and quickly covered the two blocks to the Vancouver library.

It didn't take long to find the massive tome she needed in the research section. V.J.R. Ventures was listed in the business directory as a subsidiary of Roma Developments Ltd. Now why did that sound vaguely familiar? Laurel ran her finger down the list of officers and gasped. There had to be some mistake. No, she double-checked. There was no mistake. A prickly sensation stirred at her nape. It was no accident that Janet Smithe had chosen to spend her Christmas holidays at Harris House.

The president of Roma Developments was Victor Jacek Romanowski.

IT TOOK ANOTHER half hour of detective work in the research section and two phone calls before Laurel had enough facts to call Rafferty to tell him she was coming right over with some new information that could break the case wide open and lead them to Gertie May.

Laurel bought an apple and a muffin to eat in the cab. It was after two and she'd missed lunch. For once she ate with gusto. She was no longer a passive victim to the unfortunate set of circumstances fate had thrown her way. It felt good to fight back.

Rafferty offered her a chair when she arrived and she took a moment to catch her breath and pull her notes out of her purse. Quickly, she related the connection between Janet Smithe and Victor Romanowski, and the proposed development project for Serenity Cove.

"I think he planted Janet in the house to spy on our campaign against him. That White Rock address Janet gave us is real, but she doesn't live there. It's for an apartment above a Laundromat. The owner of the Laundromat told me he lives in the upstairs apartment and he's never heard of Janet Smithe. Her description didn't sound familiar to him, either. I also checked a phone number I found in Janet's room—the last digit is three numbers up from the office listing of Roma Developments. I'll bet it's a private extension. The question is, would Romanowski resort to kidnapping Gertie May so she couldn't block his development project?"

Rafferty looked at the notes he'd been making. "I don't know, but we'll find out. You mentioned you have photographs of Miss Smithe boarding a vessel owned by Romanowski?"

"Yes, they're at home. Ian had them developed yesterday."

"Let's drive over and have a look. Then I can wait for Miss Smithe to show up and see how she responds to a few questions."

It was dusk when Rafferty parked the squad car behind Gertie May's car in the driveway at Harris House. Laurel was glad to see Ian was home. She'd tried to reach him before she'd caught the cab to the police station, but the baby-sitter had told her he hadn't returned yet.

The baby-sitter looked at Rafferty with interest when they entered. Laurel didn't offer any explanations; she didn't want any rumors spread all over the cove. Everyone already knew the land search for Gertie May had been called off two days ago.

"I'm sorry I was out longer than expected, Tanya. I hope I didn't inconvenience you any," Laurel said, digging into her purse for some cash.

"No. Dorie was really good. But I think one of your guests checked out. She left some money on the desk in the office."

Laurel looked at Rafferty in alarm. Janet had flown the coop!

"Is Ian here?"

Tanya shook her head. "He came back just after you called, but then he left again in a taxi."

"Did he say where he was going, or leave a note?"

"Sorry."

"I know where Ian went, Mommy," Dorie piped in. "He told me he's on a airran."

Laurel gritted her teeth. Dorie meant an errand, of course. Here she'd uncovered the biggest lead they'd had so far and Ian was on a mysterious errand. An errand that required a taxi, no less. Why would he do that? Had he learned something else through the private investigator?

Laurel didn't have time to wonder what Ian was up to. She'd suddenly remembered that she'd left the pictures Ian had taken of Janet and Victor on the desk in the alcove last night. She'd forgotten about them in the bustle of getting Dorie ready for bed and setting up the video camera.

Laurel hurried into the alcove with Rafferty on her heels. On the desk blotter was the paperback novel Janet had had with her at breakfast, a stack of twenty-dollar bills, and a brief note from Janet explaining that she'd had a change of plans.

The packet of pictures was gone.

Chapter Ten

Laurel put dinner on the table at six. Ian's place at the table was empty. Outside, darkness blanketed the house, cutting them off from the rest of the world. Laurel forced herself to eat. She couldn't stop blaming herself for leaving the pictures lying around. Now they had no evidence to link Janet with Romanowski, and Rafferty had nothing to use as leverage to get Romanowski to talk.

"Is Ian coming back from his airran, Mommy?" Dorie asked when Laurel put her to bed.

Laurel smothered a pang of disquietude. "Of course he's coming back." She ruffled Dorie's bangs and kissed her forehead.

Dorie's arms tightened around her neck. "Just like Gertie May? 'Cause I don't like us being all alone, Mommy."

"I know, sweetie. Mommy's lonely without them, too. Go to sleep, now. Mommy loves you."

Laurel did a slow tour of the house, locking doors and windows. Then she spent the evening sorting and filing the papers in Gertie May's office. Everything seemed to be there, except for the petitions and the notes for the speech she and Gertie May had been working on to present to the district council. Laurel wasn't really surprised. She knew exactly what had happened to them; they'd been stolen. What she didn't know was when.

Had Romanowski staged the burglary to steal them? Or had Janet stolen them when she'd taken the pictures? The only way to find out was to ask Ian if he'd seen them when he'd picked up after the burglary.

At ten, Laurel double-checked the locks on the doors and engaged the camera. She also left a light burning in the hall and made up the couch for Ian. The blankets and the pillow smelled faintly of his lime shaving cream. Laurel smoothed the blanket. Dorie was right; it seemed very lonely in the house without Gertie May and Ian.

Laurel fell asleep worrying and listening for Ian's return.

In the morning, she flew out of bed minutes before the alarm went off to see if Ian had come back last night. But the couch hadn't been slept on. Pulling on her bathrobe, she ran upstairs to his room.

He wasn't there, either.

Laurel ran her fingers through her hair. *Where the hell was he?*

It took three cups of coffee to convince herself that Ian was fine. He simply wasn't the kind of man who made unnecessary phone calls. He never called Gertie May to announce his visits. Why should he phone her because he was staying out all night?

Laurel dumped the last dregs of her coffee in the sink and reached for the Yellow Pages. She had better things to do than worry about Ian—like hire a locksmith.

THE SHINY NEW KEY on her key ring made Laurel feel secure about leaving the house unattended while they walked to Chan's Market. It was a beautiful morning. The sun was shining brightly, melting away winter's ground cover. They blinked when they entered the store's dim interior. While Dorie chose a string of red licorice from the candy shelves for a treat, Laurel selected milk, bread, apples, and her favorite kind of brain food—a package of plain M&M's candy. Old Mr. Chan set aside his newspaper to ring up the sale as she plopped her purchases on the counter.

"I'm so sorry about Miss Harris and the break-in," he said, gesturing at the paper. "This last week has not been the same without Miss Harris coming in to buy her lotto tickets. Always the same numbers. Her birthday, your birthday and little Dorie's birthday.'' He shook his head sadly as he bagged her groceries. "Even Mr. Aames has not been buying tickets. I guess it's not fun if Miss Harris is not buying tickets, too.''

"Well, isn't there a draw tonight? I'll buy one for Gertie May.''

He handed her a ticket form and a pencil. "You have to darken the boxes that match your numbers, then give me the form and I'll slide it in the machine and give you a ticket.

"The jackpot is not too high this week. Someone won big last week—4.2 million dollars.'' He smiled broadly as he looked at the numbers and processed her ticket. "The lottery business is very good. I make lots of money—'' His smile suddenly faded into a frown as though he found his remark inappropriate for the situation.

Laurel paid for her purchases. When she got home she stuck the lottery ticket onto the refrigerator with a magnet as a symbol of hope that Gertie May would come back.

Ian didn't return for lunch—not that she expected him. There were no messages on the answering machine, either. Just after one o'clock Rafferty phoned to report that he'd questioned Romanowski, who'd denied any knowledge or involvement in Gertie May's disappearance. He'd even allowed a thorough police search of the *Venture* for Gertie May.

"Did he admit to knowing Janet Smithe?" Laurel asked, chewing on her lower lip.

"He said he's never heard of her.''

"He's lying—''

"Quite possibly. Though, without any evidence to corroborate your story, it's your word against his.''

"But Ian saw her get on the boat. That's something.''

"Yes, I would like to talk to him about that. Is he there?''

"No. He didn't return last night and I haven't heard from him.'' Laurel knew her explanation sounded lame. She could almost hear the gears turning in Rafferty's suspicious mind.

''Well, please relay to him that I wish to speak with him as soon as he returns.''

Laurel promised and hung up. Her body trembled with rage. Rafferty had made it plain that she had no credibility. Laurel marched into the office and scrounged through the drawers for a pen and a legal pad. While Dorie played office on the floor, Laurel rewrote the speech that she and Gertie May had been working on. A battle of words seemed to be the only way to beat Romanowski at his own game. Laurel only hoped that the district council would afford her more credibility than the police.

Her old dream of entering local politics and following in her parents' civic footsteps seemed even more unattainable as Laurel rearranged sentences and polished the opening statement of her speech. The scandal surrounding Steve's death had forced her to abandon those ambitions. Now she was continuing the business courses she'd started before Dorie was born, so she could give Dorie a future.

At four, Dorie ran out of staples and Laurel was ready for a break. They made a salad and baked muffins for dinner. Simon called from the Crow's Nest. One of the other waitresses had offered to cover her New Year's Eve shift, but he really needed her back on Friday, which gave her several days to find a baby-sitter.

''Where's Ian's plate?'' Dorie demanded, watching Laurel set the table.

''In the cupboard. We'll take it out if he comes.''

Dorie dragged a chair to the counter and started to climb up. Laurel quickly plucked her off.

''What are you doing? Counters aren't for climbing on. You could fall and get hurt.''

''I want a plate for Ian and Gertie May—''

Laurel hugged her daughter hard, sensing a tantrum starting. How was a preschooler supposed to understand why people disappeared and didn't come back? Laurel didn't understand it herself. ''How about if we eat dinner in the living room? We can watch a movie—it'll be fun.''

''Really?''

"Sure."

The phone rang while they were watching *Beauty and the Beast*. Laurel raced from the living room to catch it.

"Oh, Barb," she said, breathless, aware of a hollow ache of disappointment that it wasn't Ian. "How are you?"

"Hopeful. I'm beginning to feel everything's going to turn out for the best." Her voice faded out, then came back stronger. "More important, how are you holding up?"

Laurel's throat tightened convulsively as she tried to keep down the deep ache inside her. "Uh, the truth or the Dorie version?"

"Just between us girls."

"I'm so frightened. Each day that passes makes Gertie May's disappearance seem more permanent...and more disturbing. I don't want to think something horrible has happened to her, but it's getting harder to remain optimistic. It's been a week." Laurel glanced at Dorie, who'd followed her into the kitchen, to make certain she wasn't being overheard by little ears. "But I'm not giving up hope, because that would be giving up on Gertie May. I don't want to lose her, too."

"That's the right attitude. I'm not giving up, either."

"When are you coming to Vancouver? Have you got the test results back from the doctor?"

Laurel thought Barb paused a little too long before replying, "There have been a few delays in scheduling some of the tests because of the holidays. I'll let you know."

"All right, then. I wish you'd tell me what kind of tests. I'm worried about you."

"Don't. Gertie May needs your prayers more than I do. Laurel, there's someone here who'd like to talk to you."

Laurel frowned. "Wait—who, Barb?"

But Barb was gone.

"Hi, honey." A trace of dry humor reverberated in Ian's even tone.

"Ian?" Laurel nearly dropped the phone in pure astonishment. "I don't understand... What are you doing in Nelson? And with Barb? Don't you upset her. She hasn't been well lately. Why didn't you tell me where you were going? I was worried sick when you didn't come home last night," she sputtered.

Ian laughed.

Laurel didn't find anything amusing about their conversation. Maybe she was being completely unrealistic in thinking he could ever be honest with her. "What's so funny?"

"You. You sound so domestic. I always wondered what one of these phone calls would be like. You know, the 'Hi honey, I'm going to be late.' I have to say..." His voice lowered to a whisper—like silk sliding over her spine. "It was worth the wait."

"Ian!" She'd strangle him with the phone cord if he ever got within arm's length of her again. "What are you doing in Nelson?" she repeated through clenched teeth.

Dorie came running up to her and pulled on her skirt. "Mommy, I want to talk to Ian."

"Not now, Mommy's talking to him." Dorie started to cry. Laurel felt overwhelmed with frustration. "Oh, brother. Ian, would you mind talking to Dorie for a minute? She was very u-p-s-e-t about your absence last night. She could use a little reassuring."

"No problem. Like mother, like daughter, eh?"

Ian winced as Laurel's choked exclamation of rage was clearly transmitted over the telephone wire. Then he heard Dorie's hesitant greeting.

"Hi, kiddo," he said. "How are you?"

"Not fine. Are you disappeared, too?"

"Me? No-o. I decided to visit your nana Barb. She's a nice lady. I was telling her all about you."

"Goody! If you're at Nana's does that mean you're gonna be my new daddy? That's what I told Santa I wanted for Christmas—a daddy. Or a puppy."

Ian was stunned. She wanted *him* to be her daddy. Laurel was probably laughing her socks off at that revelation. He considered pointing out the advantages of a puppy, but he didn't want to hurt her feelings. "I think you'd better wait for Christmas to see what Santa brings you, okay? You don't want to ruin Santa's surprises.''

"Okay."

"I'll be back before your bedtime tomorrow, okay? Can I talk to your mommy again?'' Ian wiped his brow, feeling as though he'd safely reconnoitered a mine field. Not bad for a confirmed bachelor with no child-rearing experience.

He heard the low murmur of Laurel telling Dorie to go back to her movie.

"You deserved that, Ian. But thanks, it made her feel better.''

"I told Dorie I'll be home tomorrow night. Why don't you feed her a hot dog for dinner and I'll bring something for us? We can eat after she's asleep. Then, we can talk.''

"You're not going to tell me anything over the phone now, are you?''

"Not a chance. I thought you'd be grateful I phoned—''

Laurel promptly showed the depth of her gratitude by hanging up on him. Ian replaced the receiver with a rueful smile. Time to get down to business.

Barbara Wilson was more help than he could have imagined, a veritable pipeline into the community of Nelson. Having worked at the chamber of commerce for years, she knew most of the town's nine thousand inhabitants.

"Steve's murder sent shock waves through the community. Once his gambling debts became public knowledge, it was terribly humiliating for Laurel and me. Laurel sold everything she owned to make good Steve's debts—even the Limoges nativity set she'd inherited from her grandmother. I saw it on display in an antique store in town last week. The shadow of Steve's death is still hanging over her. I'm afraid it will continue to do so until Steve's murderer is found.''

Ian thought the shadow of Steve's death was still hanging over Barb, as well. Why else would she be living in this hovel of an apartment where the memories of her lifetime seemed to swirl in the dimness?

Barb helped herself to a glass of water and eased her pudgy body into a padded chair at the kitchenette table. Her hair was an indeterminate shade of blond, pulled into a straggly bun at her nape.

"You can only do so much for those you love. I miss them terribly, but I'm too set in my ways to leave Nelson. I like my own space, even if it's small. I had to sell my house—too much upkeep." She took a sip of water, looking as pale as the winter sun trying to break through the drawn curtains, and just as determined. "Explain this theory you have about a connection between Steve's murder and the Christmas cards you say Laurel has been receiving. What does it have to do with Gertie May?"

"I don't know yet. But I have a surefire way of finding out." He spread the money orders he'd got at the bank yesterday on the table. "There's a money order here for each of Steve's creditors. Payment made in full with interest. By the end of the day, Steve's slate will be wiped clean."

Barb gasped, squinting at the checks. "Oh, Ian, this is such a lot of money. Are you sure you want to do this?"

"It's the only way I can think of to flush out an unknown creditor who may be threatening Laurel—and, for all we know, may have killed Steve and abducted Gertie May. Nelson's a small town. If it's money the person's after, he or she will soon find out Laurel has enough of it to pay off her debts and the threatening cards will get more specific. It's a small sum to pay for Aunt Gem's life."

"I don't think Laurel will see it in quite the same vein. A male stranger whisking into town to pay off her debts. There'll be plenty of talk about it, if that's what you're after. And not the kind of talk Laurel would approve of." She eyed him critically. "But I think you're man enough to settle that with her. She has a lot of pride, you know. The Langs were fine, upstanding citizens. Penelope, her mother, was the last of the Laurels—one of Nelson's silver mining families. Penelope thought it quite fitting to give her daughter her maiden name. Bishop was another family name. The Langs were honest as the day is long, and civic-minded, too. Both Penelope and Hubert were awarded for their civic service. Their home is a museum now—they left it to the town...."

Barb unfolded a pair of reading glasses with shaking fingers and placed them on her nose. "I'm not certain I'm doing the right thing, but Gertie May is my dearest friend. Let's see what you have here..."

Ian leaned forward with interest. After the money orders were delivered, all he'd have to do is sit back and watch for developments. And explain to Laurel.

There'd be fireworks going off at Harris House tomorrow night long before the clock struck midnight, and they wouldn't be in celebration of ringing in the New Year.

Chapter Eleven

A promise was a promise.

Ian was determined to keep his promise to Dorie, but it was ten minutes past her bedtime when he walked into her bedroom the next evening. Laurel was reading her a story, and judging by the stack of books on her lap, she'd expected him to be late.

"I-an!" Dorie shrieked, lunging at him from her bed. She gave him a ferocious hug when he caught her against his chest and peppered his face with enthusiastic kisses. "You're back. I missed you."

"I missed you, too." He hugged her and kissed her forehead. "That's from your nana. I told her I'd give you one. Get into bed now." He deposited her on the bed with a bounce. She giggled and climbed under the covers. Then he risked a sideways glance at Laurel. His spirits sank at the ominous glassy set to her features—she wouldn't be welcoming him with open arms.

"You look great," he said warily, following her into the sitting room. His eyes skimmed appreciatively over her simple white shirt, red sweater and plaid skirt. She wore black nylons and black pumps and had a matching plaid bow on the end of her French braid. A pearl necklace was the finishing touch. He thought she was beautiful without makeup, but with makeup on tonight there was an allure to her primness that fascinated him.

"It's Sunday. I always dress for church," she replied in a matter-of-fact tone that curbed his prurient thoughts.

"Are you hungry? I brought Chinese. Will you join me upstairs after Dorie's asleep?"

She didn't answer him.

"Laurel?"

"Why don't you just dine alone? You manage to do everything else solo. You don't need anyone or anything, do you?" Her eyes glittered with cold accusation, creating a frosty veil of tension in the room.

He stared at her, wanting to say it wasn't true—but it was. The evening wasn't starting out the way he'd planned. "It's a lifelong habit. I've been on my own since I was younger than Dorie. Old habits are hard to break." He held out his hand and took a step toward her. "I'm trying now. *I have* been trying. I told you about the private investigator I'd hired."

"Only because I caught you in a lie. Don't you understand, Ian? I don't want to be suspicious of you, trying to second-guess every move you make. I don't want you to feel that way about me, either. The other day you said you cared about me—well, this is a strange way to show it." A pained expression crossed her face. "I needed you and I didn't know how to reach you."

She'd needed him? No one had ever said that to him before. He took another step closer.

"I left a message with Dorie to tell you where I was—"

"She's three and a half! Besides, telling me you're on an errand isn't exactly informative. Why didn't you tell the baby-sitter where you were going, or leave a note?"

"And have the baby-sitter read it—or broadcast what I told her all over the cove? Besides, I phoned you yesterday."

"I bet that was Barb's idea."

He shook his head. "No, mine. Cross my heart. Barb's couch wasn't nearly as comfortable as yours. I thought about you most of the night."

"Right, and how I've messed up your aunt's life."

"No, actually I was wondering what things would be like between us if Aunt Gem hadn't gone missing." He closed the gap remaining between them and wrapped his fingers around her hand. Her eyes widened with uncertainty, then ever so slowly melted all warm with honey. Cat's-eyes.

Her mouth trembled as his head lowered and he claimed the yielding softness of her lips, felt the soft sigh of her breath mingle with his. He loved how the blush of roses crept into her cheeks as she raised her eyes to meet his, questioningly.

"I came back tonight because I couldn't imagine spending New Year's Eve anywhere else but here with you and the lumpy couch."

She smiled grudgingly. But it warmed him through. This was more like it.

"Wait for me at the top of the stairs," he said gruffly. "I have a surprise for you. Then I promise I'll tell you about my secret mission to Nelson—down to the minutest detail."

"Great," she murmured, "because I have a little news of my own."

Her tone made him ill at ease. "What kind of news? Have you heard something from Rafferty about Aunt Gem?"

Laurel folded her arms. Did he actually think he could waltz in here after being gone for two days, give her a kiss and think everything was hunky-dory? "No, actually Rafferty heard something from me that might help us find out what happened to Gertie May. I hit pay dirt when I went down to the ship's registry. It seems Janet, our sweet-natured guest, was meeting Victor Romanowski—"

"You lost me. Who's Victor Romanowski?"

She told him about Gertie May's involvement in the Serenity Cove Heritage Society and its latest campaign to prevent the village from overdevelopment. "He wants to turn Panorama Park into a block of high-priced condos. Do you remember seeing some petitions in Gertie May's office when you tidied up after the burglary? I can't find them or the file containing the notes we've been making about the impact of the project.''

Ian frowned. ''I didn't throw any papers away. I piled everything on the desk. But come to think of it, I do remember seeing some petitions. Janet must have been looking at them the night I caught her in Aunt Gem's office. Are you suggesting the burglary was staged?''

''I think so. It was just a cover-up for stealing the petitions. It also explains why the guest rooms and the basement weren't searched.''

''Where's Janet now?'' Ian demanded, flexing his fingers.

Laurel shrugged her shoulders. ''She'd checked out by the time I got back from the ship's registry office.'' Her face reddened as she explained how she'd left the pictures on Gertie May's desk. ''Janet apparently found them and realized we were on to her or soon would be.''

''Damn! Why didn't you tell me any of this on the phone?''

Laurel's mouth fell open in disbelief. ''You still don't get it, do you? Communication is a two-way street. I asked what you were doing and you, Mr. Lone Wolf, refused to tell me. Why should I share with you? I called Rafferty instead. They're looking for Janet. Not surprisingly, Romanowski denies knowing her, but he allowed the police to search the boat and there was no sign of Gertie May. I've been pulling my hair out trying to decide what to do next. Rafferty's hoping you'll be able to identify Romanowski with Janet. He wants you to call him.''

Ian was silent for a moment, staring at her. Just when she thought they'd reached the same crossroad of distrust again, a broad grin creased his face.

''You did all that on your own?'' His eyes glowed with a sudden intense warmth that made her heart do crazy things as he took her hand and kissed her palm. His face felt rough against her fingertips. Laurel felt her anger and resistance toward him being supplanted by a stronger, deeper emotion. She realized how much she'd begun to count on him emotionally in the span of a week. "You're absolutely right, Mrs. Bishop. We'd make a damn fine team. I'll call Rafferty while I'm upstairs."

Laurel stared after him in amazement. Just what did he have in store for her upstairs?

He insisted she close her eyes when she met him at the basement door. He guided her by the hand to the dining room. Laurel could feel the pulse of attraction generating in their joined fingertips. "Open your eyes," he said softly.

The dining room was bathed in candlelight from the silver candelabrum. Two elegant place settings glistened on the mahogany table. A white rose lay across her plate and music played on the stereo. The Chinese feast he'd brought was set out in fine china bowls. But what made her gasp was the centerpiece—her Limoges nativity set. All ten pieces grouped around the baby Jesus. Tears welled in her eyes.

"Oh, Ian, I thought I'd never see this again. It broke my heart to sell it. How did you—"

"Happy New Year, Laurel."

Then suddenly it didn't matter how he'd found it or why. What mattered was that he was there with her and he'd obviously tried to please her. And he had. She caught his face between her hands and pulled his head down for a kiss that poured out all her jumbled emotions. A wonderful heat was flowing through her veins. Dimly she was aware that her red sweater had slipped off her shoulders and her blouse was undone. She slid her hands up under his sweatshirt, impatient to know the feel of his smooth, hard body. He had far too many clothes on. So did she.

She'd never done anything so passionately spontaneous as making love on a dining room rug. It was a frantic communion of bodies and souls. She had no regrets when it was over.

Ian stroked her hair with a shaking hand as he helped her dress. "You're the most beautiful, courageous woman I've ever met," he confessed. "Dorie's lucky to have you."

His admission brought a smile of pleasure to her lips. She felt bonded to him in a way she'd never felt toward Steve.

But she knew it was only temporary. "Thank you for the nativity set. I'll treasure it even more because it came back to me from a friend."

"Hmm." His arms tightened around her waist. "I don't think you were paying attention a few minutes ago—we exceeded the friend stage." The huskiness of his voice sent shivers up her spine.

Laurel blushed. "I certainly was paying attention."

They reheated their dinner and enjoyed what was left of the flickering candles.

Ian found it hard to sit across the table from her and not touch her, but he wanted her to eat. Their lovemaking had left him feeling shattered and reckless.

"You said you were on your own as a young child...I thought your parents died when you were in your teens," Laurel commented between bites of crispy egg roll.

"Oh, they were alive. I just rarely saw them. My parents were devoted to their work in archaeology." He explained their quest to prove Alaska was once a peninsula of Asia. "Even when I was with them, I was pretty much left to my own devices—playing in the dirt and looking for rocks— while they were becoming ecstatic over fluted points, burins and microblades." He smiled at her puzzled expression. "They were tools Palearctic Indians used to hunt herb-eating animals on the tundra."

Laurel laughed. "From a child's point of view, I can see why rocks would be more interesting."

"Actually, Aunt Gem was the one who turned me into a rock hound. She gave me a rock-and-mineral collecting kit when I was six. I started calling her Aunt Gem after I'd found a piece of rock crystal, which is just clear quartz—the commonest of minerals—but to me it was the equivalent of finding a rare diamond. By then I was in boarding school and only got to see Aunt Gem once a year—"

"I know. At Christmas," she teased him. "Gertie May's told me *that* story a few times. She loves you a lot, you know. I'm sorry, I interrupted you. Go on."

"Anyway, when I was fourteen, my parents died in a helicopter crash in Alaska." He popped a morsel of sweet-and-sour chicken into his mouth and glanced at her.

The candlelight gave her skin a delicate, white luster. Her teasing smile had faded, and now she looked as compassionate as the Madonna in the nativity set.

She touched his arm and he felt his heart slam against his ribs. How could she do that to him with such an innocuous touch? She was the first woman who'd ever made him feel this way.

"I'm sorry. I know how difficult it is to lose both your parents at once. My parents died within a month of each other, of unrelated causes. My mother died during gall bladder surgery. My father had a massive heart attack three weeks later. Of course, I'd been married over a year by then, so I wasn't as dependent on them. But still, it was rough."

"I didn't have it that bad. Aunt Gem became my guardian and the first thing she did was take me out of boarding school and put me in a private Catholic school, so I could live with her. When I was a kid, I always wished she was my mother. For a long time, I felt guilty for being glad that she'd become my legal guardian. I was sorry my parents were dead, but I was happy here."

"Gertie May definitely has a way of creating happiness around her."

Ian raised his glass of wine. "To Aunt Gem," he said reverently, the ghost of a little boy echoing in his voice.

Laurel raised her glass and joined in his toast. "To Gertie May."

A companionable silence settled over them as they finished off second helpings. Then Laurel handed him a fortune cookie. His fingers tightened around hers for a moment, making her breath quicken, then he let go.

"What does your fortune say?" she asked.

"'Your life is altering course.' The cookie must have seen me on that cabin cruiser."

Laurel groaned. "That was bad. A comedian you aren't. Mine says, 'Fortune awaits.'" She tossed the slip of paper onto the table. "I like the sound of that."

He grinned sheepishly. "That's one fortune I can guarantee will come true for you."

"What do you mean?" Her eyes narrowed with playful suspicion.

"Don't get mad, but the reason I went to Nelson was to pay off your creditors...."

"What?" Laurel's heartbeat skidded to a halt, then jump started into an erratic rhythm. She couldn't believe she'd heard correctly. "You're not serious," she whispered. "Please, tell me this is another of your bad jokes."

"No." He handed her the receipts. "All paid and accounted for."

She looked at the receipts, unable to believe her eyes or her ears. "Wh-why would you do such a thing?"

"Because I think Steve was in way over his head with the gambling. He probably got in so deep with a bookie that he couldn't pay up, and a matching pair of broken kneecaps wasn't enough to settle the score, so he had Steve killed. Then the bookie decided to lay low for a while until it was safe to try to get the money from you."

"Why would a bookie think I had more money than Steve?"

"Well, there's a museum in town with your family name all over it. It's an impressive-looking house."

"My parents weren't rich by any means. They gave most of their money away to worthy causes. They bequeathed the house and most of their estate to the town for a museum."

"Didn't that bother you?"

Laurel shook her head. "Not really. I was married and my parents thought Steve would be a good provider. He was an only child, too, and his parents were well-off. I planned to work as soon as I'd finished university, but Dorie came along and sidetracked my plans. Do you think this bookie traced me here to Serenity Cove and is trying to frighten me into paying him?"

"Possibly. What if he started his card campaign to intimidate you first, but Gertie May caught him leaving a card and he was forced to change his plans? Maybe he abducted her and he's waiting for the heat from the police to fade before he makes his next move? Or maybe this Romanowski character abducted her and the bookie is biding his time until he thinks it's clear to approach us again. I just wanted to spread money around Nelson, so people there know you have some ready cash. My guess is the bookie will hear about the loans being paid off and come calling. Then we'll know who we're dealing with."

"But, Ian, there's at least twenty thousand dollars' worth of receipts here—"

"I can afford it."

"Obviously." Laurel bit back the sarcasm in her tone. But the idea of being in debt to him annoyed her. So much for being in control of her own affairs. "I'll pay you back with interest," she said firmly, looking him straight in the eye—a difficult feat when they'd just made love two hours ago.

She didn't even want to speculate on his motivation for buying the nativity set. It was too disappointing to think it was another way of spreading money in Nelson. She felt very foolish for letting herself get swept away.

He nodded. "I know you will. As far as I'm concerned, you're a good risk. I'll give you a bank account number and you can make deposits whenever you're able. After tonight, we need never talk about it again." His tone and his manner seemed to imply that this was all quite reasonable. An impersonal business arrangement with no strings attached that saved her the bother of having to keep track of his whereabouts.

But it changed the nature of their relationship, especially now that she'd slept with him. It was all fine and good to say they'd never talk about it, but how could she forget that she owed him all this money? She couldn't. On the other hand, how could she fault him for committing a selfless act of love and generosity on Gertie May's behalf? She couldn't. Was he really convinced that the anonymous author of the Christmas cards was a bookie?

A chill stole over her. A bookie wouldn't stop at harming a child. Could Dorie be in danger, too?

Maybe she should be more grateful for what Ian had done. "Let's hope it pays off," she said, trying to sound positive.

"It will. It's almost midnight. Get your coat on and we'll go outside to see in the New Year."

"Okay. I want to check on Dorie first."

Outside, the night was sharp and breathtakingly beautiful. Icicles hung in frosty fingers from the eaves of the porch as they went down the steps and crunched across the snow to the edge of the front yard where they could look onto the cove. The sky and the water merged into a reflective mirror of Christmas lights, stars and the shining crescent of a first quarter moon.

"There are too many stars to make a wish," Laurel said, gazing up at the star-studded spectacle.

Ian slipped his arm around her shoulders and she looked at him. His eyes were as reflective as the stars in the shadows of his face. "Make a wish, anyway, and disguise it as a resolution."

"I resolve to find Gertie May." Her voice echoed, firm and clear.

A series of booms and crackling noises suddenly went off in the park. Red, blue and starry white cinders flared into the sky.

"Tradition demands a kiss," Ian said softly, nuzzling her ear. He cupped her chin, his fingers warm against her skin. Laurel felt torn with conflicting emotions. Despair and worry over Gertie May's safety. Gratitude over the money he'd laid out to pay her debts. Confusion over the gift of the nativity set. And desire to respond fully to the seductiveness of his kiss that told her she was alive and vibrant and still a woman.

When their lips met, she lost herself in the moment until they pulled apart breathless and panting, the acrid smoke of discharged fireworks drifting in the air.

"Happy New Year, Ian."

He touched the tip of her nose with his finger, his warm breath caressing her cheek. "This evening has been one tradition I could keep year after year."

Year after year. It was the nicest compliment he was capable of offering, but she wasn't going to count on it. Gertie May certainly couldn't. Four years of disappointment had followed in the wake of his last visit.

Laurel had already had enough disappointment in her life. But the memory of this night would hold a special place in her heart.

Chapter Twelve

Laurel awoke on New Year's Day thinking about everything that had happened between her and Ian last night. He'd ended up sleeping on the couch, insisting her bed was too narrow for the two of them. She needed a good night's sleep, which he'd promised she wouldn't get if she invited him into her bed. She needed to be strong and well rested if they were going to find Gertie May's abductor.

Laurel said a quiet prayer for her friend's safety, then headed to the bathroom to shower and dress.

Ian and Dorie surprised her by preparing breakfast. And, judging by Dorie's bright eyes and the whispering in the corner of the kitchen, they had a secret.

Laurel took a sip of coffee. "Okay, what are you two planning over there?"

Ian nudged Dorie's shoulder. "You ask."

"Can we please go sledding today, Mommy? Ian says he has a tra-dish-on on the mountain with Gertie May, and we can go too. Can we, Mommy? One of us *has* to go 'cause Ian's afraid to go on the sled all by himself. But I'm not afraid." Dorie shook her head.

Laurel tried to keep a straight face. "Hmm, I get the sledding part, but what's the tradition?"

"Ian says he and Gertie May always go up on the mountain to look at the world on the New Ears Day. Does everybody get new ears today, Mommy?"

Laurel couldn't help herself, she burst out laughing. "No. Only Ian—" she gasped, then another bubble of laughter escaped her before she could finish. "And apparently he gets a new mouthpiece today, too."

"Huh?" Dorie looked confused.

Ian felt his ears. "Yep, these feel much better than the old ones."

Laurel wiped her eyes. She'd been laughing so hard she was crying. Who'd have suspected Ian could be so silly with kids? Some of Gertie May's good example must have rubbed off on him over the years. "Never mind, sweetie. Yes, we can go sledding. How about if I pack a lunch to take with us?"

"Yeah!"

There wasn't much they could do today anyway. Everything would be closed. She and Ian could make a deliberate effort to keep the day lighthearted for Dorie's sake. After Dorie's bedtime, they could clarify the details of their visit to Romanowski's office tomorrow.

Before they left, Laurel turned on the camera. If the card sender was watching the house, he might take advantage of their absence to make another delivery.

A winding road bordered with majestic spires of Douglas fir, western red cedar, western hemlock and lacy cascades of tiny waterfalls led them to the top of Mount Seymour.

The warming presence of the sun took the chill off the air and softened the snowpack on the toboggan run, providing the courageous Dorie and the fearful Ian with a smooth coast down. There was only room for two on the red plastic toboggan, so Ian and Laurel took turns riding with Dorie. Laurel's heart swelled with motherly pleasure for her daughter as she watched Dorie and Ian pull the sled up the hill. Dorie was so happy and animated, pretending she was a horse. Ian egged her on with fake lashes of a whip and handfuls of snow oats.

This is what Dorie is missing out on by not having a dad, Laurel thought with a pang of regret. She tried to picture

Steve sledding with Dorie, but the image was fuzzy. Steve was always so competitive and sports-oriented, he would have skirted the run for younger kids and headed straight for the longer, scarier runs on the best toboggan money could buy. Someday, she hoped, Dorie would get the daddy for Christmas that she wished for. Maybe it wasn't too late to find her a puppy.

When the little horse had lost her gallop, they ate their lunch at the trestle tables in the ski lodge's cafeteria.

"That was fun, Mommy! This was almost my best day," Dorie declared, licking at the hot chocolate mustache clinging to her upper lip. "It's not my best day 'cause Gertie May's not here." She frowned at her sandwich, then took a big bite.

Laurel's appetite dwindled. "I know what you mean, sweetie. I'm always thinking about Gertie May, too, and wishing she were here with us." Feeling Ian's eyes on her, Laurel met his warm gaze and her breath caught in her throat as they exchanged an intimate smile. She suspected he was thinking about Gertie May, too.

After lunch they went for a walk in the "magic forest," as Dorie called it, steering clear of the downhill ski area and venturing into the domain of the snowshoers and cross-country skiers. It did look like a winter wonderland of stately trees and snowy carpets. Overhead, the heart-lifting sheet of blue sky that Vancouverites worship stretched from the mountains to the shimmering waters of the Georgia Strait far below.

Laurel filled her lungs with the evergreen-scented air and dodged a snowball that Ian chucked at her with blatant mischief in his eyes. She managed to hit him bull's-eye in the back before they stopped to build a snow bunny. Where did Dorie get these ideas? At least Ian didn't mind going along with it. She wondered if he felt as guilty as she did for having fun.

Finally, when Dorie's mittens were soaked through, they went home tired, wet, and emotionally fortified to deal with the reality that Gertie May was still missing.

"Look, there's Frederick!" Dorie said, leaning forward in her car seat.

"Oh, dear, he doesn't appear to be in a good mood," Laurel commented. Her elderly neighbor was confronting a well-groomed man wearing a tan overcoat, who'd parked on the street in front of Frederick's home. The man walked around to the rear of a white luxury sedan and opened the trunk, removing a House For Sale sign. "For heaven's sake, won't those Realtors leave him alone? They're trying to take advantage of Frederick because he's elderly." Laurel lost sight of them as they turned into the drive and the hedge blocked her view.

"Should we go see if he needs help?" Ian asked as he set the emergency brake.

"Do you mind?"

"No, you go ahead, and I'll get Dorie."

Laurel was already halfway out of the car. As she skirted the hedge, she could see the Realtor pounding the For Sale sign into the ground with a sledgehammer.

"Frederick, is everything all right?" she called.

He whirled to face her. Laurel thought he trembled, but perhaps he was cold. He wore his coat, but he'd left his gloves and hat indoors. He cleared his throat nervously. "Everything's fine. As you can see, I've decided to sell the house after all. I was just arguing with John about the necessity of putting up a sign. Selling your home is a private matter. I don't know why I have to broadcast the fact to my neighbors."

"Why don't we go inside and discuss it?" the Realtor suggested, offering Laurel a conciliatory smile.

Confused, Laurel laid her hand on Frederick's arm. "Are you sure you want to do this? You told me the other day you'd never sell."

"Ah, well, circumstances change," he said feebly.

The Realtor offered Laurel his hand. "John Waller. How do you do?"

Laurel shook his hand and glanced at Ian, who'd just joined her, carrying Dorie in his arms.

There was a sudden awkward pause in the conversation. "By the way, I dropped by this morning to inquire about Gertie May," Frederick told them, tucking his hands into his coat pockets. "I've been keeping an eye on the house for you. I noticed you went out this morning."

"Thanks, Frederick, we appreciate that," Ian said cordially.

Laurel looked at Frederick in concern. "You're shivering. Maybe you should get back inside or you'll be down with a cold like Anna." Maybe he was already coming down with a cold. He looked pale suddenly. "How's Anna doing?"

"Anna?" His eyes clouded over. "Oh, she's resting peacefully. No need to worry about her."

Laurel wasn't convinced, but there seemed to be no point in pursuing Frederick's decision to put his house on the market with Mr. Waller hovering over them like a hawk. "Well, we won't keep you."

But Laurel couldn't help glancing over her shoulder at Frederick and the Realtor as she and Ian went to unload their wet winter gear from the car. She couldn't rid herself of the eerie feeling that there was something odd about Frederick's sudden decision to sell his home. Had Victor Romanowski given Frederick an offer he couldn't refuse?

IAN STUDIED LAUREL with a critical eye as they prepared dinner, wondering what she'd look like pregnant. She needed a disguise for their venture into Victor Romanowski's domain tomorrow. A large belly, a beauty mark strategically placed an inch from her lips on her right cheek, and a mane of bleached, salon-styled hair should do the trick. All Romanowski would see is belly and hair.

Ian smiled as he chopped vegetables for the steamer. He wasn't much of a cook, but he could handle a knife. He sneaked a carrot stick to Dorie while Laurel popped a casserole that someone had made for them into the oven. Dorie gave him a conspiratorial smile and went back to kneading the biscuit dough. Her pink turtleneck gathered a collection of floury handprints as she tried to keep her fingers clean of the sticky dough. Laurel noticed the condition of her daughter's shirt, and frowned, but she didn't say anything. She put the biscuits on a pan, then let Dorie make "something" with the leftover dough.

He liked watching them together. He supposed Aunt Gem did, too. They probably kept her company, just like they were keeping him company now, in a way that made him feel less estranged from life. This was what a family was supposed to be like, he thought. It was comforting to know that what he'd dreamed about as a kid actually existed. He'd had a small taste of it when he'd lived with Aunt Gem. But that had been different. He'd been older, already a rebellious teenager.

Ian found he didn't even mind when Dorie slumped into a whine after swallowing three bites and ended up under the table, refusing to eat any more.

"She's exhausted," Laurel said with an apologetic note, climbing under the table after her. She held Dorie in her lap, one arm looped around her child, the other wielding a fork as she calmly finished her meal and coaxed Dorie into eating more.

Ian watched Dorie's eyelids droop. Poor kid was all tuckered out. A few seconds later she was asleep, snoring gently against her mother's breast. The scene was more poignant than a Norman Rockwell print. For the first time in his life, Ian wondered what it would be like to have a wife and a kid and a mortgage.

Who was he kidding? Ian shook his head. Making love to Laurel last night must have softened him up more than he thought.

While Laurel took Dorie downstairs, Ian did the dishes. Then he went into the office to play back the videotape from this afternoon. There was nothing interesting on it, only Frederick had approached the house. Good neighbor that he was, he'd even tried the doorknob to make certain the latch was secure. Laurel must have told him the door had been left open the day of the burglary. Ian rewound the tape and reset the video camera for the night. He was downright certain that something in the case would break soon.

When Laurel came back upstairs she was receptive to his idea of a disguise. They spent the evening assembling their getups and discussing their cover story.

"Are you sure Romanowski won't recognize me in a wig?" Laurel asked doubtfully. "Maybe I should wear one of your pairs of glasses—you've got six...."

Ian looked at her curiously as a warning bell went off in his head. How did she know he had six pairs of glasses? He didn't remember telling her that. Suddenly he knew...

She'd searched his room and he hadn't even noticed.

A clammy chill skated across his shoulders as all the suspicions he'd laid to rest about Laurel came back to haunt him.

She'd beaten him at his own game.

THEY DROPPED Dorie off at preschool the next morning at nine sharp. Laurel watched the sea gulls circling over the choppy waters of the Burrard Inlet as they joined the traffic creeping over the Second Narrows Bridge. She felt good this morning in her maternity dress with a pillow strapped around her waist. Empowered. Part of that had to do with Ian, with the feeling that they were working together.

Ian seemed serious this morning, his gray eyes hinting at an undercurrent of thought. What was he thinking? she wondered. Yesterday they hadn't kissed or made love again, or even talked about the intimacy they'd shared on New Year's Eve. He'd been warm all day, but as soon as they'd begun discussing their disguises she'd noticed a definite shift in his manner as he'd adopted a cool, remote air that held her at a distance.

It was difficult to tell, but she thought the man sitting beside her was the real Ian. A man of few words, who was most comfortable in his worn leather jacket and jeans. His features seemed harsher without the false, studious affectation of the glasses. But she liked that ruggedness about him.

It was a shock to see him an hour later clothed in a hand-somely patterned designer sweater complemented with a tweed jacket, brushed twill slacks, Italian leather shoes and an ostentatious gold watch. He'd even slicked his hair back. He oozed success and a healthy bank account.

"Nice watch," she commented, trying to get used to the change in him. She hadn't gotten used to the change in her-self yet.

"It's fake, and so are these," he told her, digging a flashy zirconia ring, a pair of gold earrings and a chunky gold necklace out of a shopping bag and handing them to her. She felt strange putting the ring on in front of him. He seemed so businesslike.

The office for Roma Developments Ltd. was on West Georgia Street. Laurel practiced a lumbering gait with her hands pressed nervously against her artificial belly. What if Romanowski recognized her?

Ian squeezed her hand as they rode up to the seventh floor in the elevator. "It's showtime," he mouthed to her as they entered a large reception area richly appointed in burgundy and oak. Several project models were on display through-out the room.

Laurel had to admit he was smooth when he talked to the receptionist.

"My wife and I are very interested in investing in the Se-renity Cove project," he explained.

"That project hasn't been approved yet, but I'll let Mr. Romanowski know you're here. He should be out shortly."

Then suddenly Victor Romanowski was in the room with them. Laurel smiled politely, holding her breath and rub-bing her tummy absentmindedly as they exchanged greet-ings. Romanowski sized her up in two seconds flat, then dismissed her as being a Barbie doll wife. He led them over to the architect's model. "Panorama Place is an exciting project. Serenity Cove has the quaint atmosphere of a wa-terfront village and that's what we're trying to emphasize in our models. Of course, they'll be luxury condos with qual-ity finishes throughout...."

"Which is precisely what piqued my interest," Ian said. "I'm considering the purchase of three condos as an investment. My wife and I have a residence in the British Properties."

Victor's eyes gleamed with dollar signs. "Well, let me point out some of the highlights of the project."

Laurel saw her chance to slip away. She glanced down pointedly at her belly and asked to use the ladies' room.

"Of course. Nancy, would you escort Mrs. Esterling to the ladies' room? Then bring me the floor plans for these models. From all indications, Mr. Esterling, approval of the project will go through next week."

Laurel lumbered slowly down the plushly carpeted hallway after the receptionist, taking note of the spacious office on the left. A brass nameplate on the desk indicated it belonged to Victor.

Laurel thanked the receptionist and stepped into the washroom, waiting a few seconds for the woman to leave before she darted out into the hall. The pillow strapped around her waist jounced up and down as she ran into Victor's office. She couldn't tell if anyone could hear her. Her heart pounded too loudly in her ears. She partially closed Victor's door, then flipped back through the pages of his desk calendar. The receptionist hadn't inserted the pages for the new year yet.

Laurel found December 23, the day Gertie May had disappeared. Janet Smithe had checked into Harris House earlier that day, and Laurel had spoken to Victor that night at the Crow's Nest. There were only two entries made on the page: 8:00 a.m. c.t.; 9:30 p.m. meeting—Hank. S.C. project.

Laurel had no idea what "c.t." stood for—circuit training? But the nine-thirty Saturday evening meeting had to be with the contractor for the Serenity Cove project. Though she could swear it was well after ten before Hank had shown up at the pub.

There were no notations on the pages from the twenty-fourth to the end of the month. Someone had drawn a line across them.

Laurel heard the warning jingle of keys out in the hall-way. She quickly sat down in a side chair and leaned forward with her head down. She could feel her wig slip.

"Mrs. Esterling?" she heard Victor say as he entered his office. Ian was with him, too. She recognized his shoes.

Ian crouched beside her and put his arm around her. "Darling, are you all right?"

"Yes," Laurel said weakly, putting her hand to her brow. "I suddenly felt dizzy and this was the closest chair I could find."

"You should have called out."

"I didn't want to disturb you, sweetheart. I know how important this investment is to you."

"I'll get you a glass of water," Victor offered. "Nancy!" he hollered down the hallway.

"She's in her eighth month," Ian explained. "We're hoping for a boy." He gently patted her stomach. Laurel seemed to be able to feel that touch through the thickness of feathers.

Nancy brought the glass of water. Laurel took a sip. "Thank you, I'll be all right now."

"Here, let me help you," Ian insisted as she tried to rise. Slowly they made it out into the reception area with Ian assuring Romanowski that he'd phone him later in the day. When they were alone in the elevator, Ian pulled Laurel into his arms and gave her a chaste kiss. "I had a feeling you were an accomplished actress," he said dryly. "That Romanowski character is pretty confident his project will be given the go-ahead. Did you find out anything?"

"I'm not sure." She told him about the appointments she'd seen written in Victor's calendar. While Ian wondered aloud what "c.t." meant, Laurel pondered over the significance of the kiss he'd just given her. Was it another performance? Another charade like the one they'd just executed in Romanowski's office? How could you tell with someone like Ian?

IAN GRIPPED the steering wheel tightly as they sped through the dingy streets of East Vancouver. They'd have to hurry if they were going to pick Dorie up at preschool on time. Beside him, Laurel had her dress hiked up around her hips and was struggling to remove the pillow from the elastic bandages that held it in place. She'd already discarded the blond wig and had wiped the beauty mark off with a facial tissue. He much preferred her natural beauty and hair color. He reined his thoughts in sharply—it was exactly that kind of thinking that had got him hopelessly tangled up in Laurel's problems in the first place.

Laurel tossed a pillow onto the back seat. "I think we've been looking at the time Gertie May disappeared all wrong."

"What do you mean?"

"All along we've been assuming that Gertie May disappeared between ten-thirty and eleven, because that's when Janet said she heard the doorbell. I think Gertie May actually disappeared earlier—sometime between nine-thirty and ten."

"What makes you say that?"

"Well, several reasons." Laurel ticked them off on her fingers. "One, Dorie saw someone peeking in her bedroom window twice, which means they were watching the house. Two, Romanowski's calendar says his meeting with Hank Morrison, the contractor for the project, was at nine-thirty. But I remember running into Romanowski at the Crow's Nest around ten. Hank didn't arrive until several minutes later. And three, Janet. She's obviously Romanowski's alibi. She said she came in around ten, and heard the doorbell between ten-thirty and eleven. Romanowski and Hank didn't leave the Crow's Nest until after eleven that night." Her eyes glowed with excitement. "I think Janet and Hank kidnapped Gertie May. Maybe they're only planning to hold her until after the district council meeting." The hope in her voice was contagious. Ian felt his own hopes burgeoning, and guilt that he'd started to doubt her again.

He squeezed her knee. "That's why we're holding Christmas, honey."

They both got out at the preschool. Dorie met them with a proud smile, a wet painting dangling from her hand.

"This is for you, Ian," she said shyly.

Ian felt the eyes of the other mothers on him. Laurel's, too. "Hey, a rainbow. Just what I need. Thanks, kiddo." He rolled the painting up carefully, not caring about the dribbles of paint that stained his pants. A man could never have too many gifts of love. Isn't that what Aunt Gem always used to say when she'd give him a hug?

Aunt Gem. He hurried Laurel and Dorie into the car, feeling a sudden urgency to share Laurel's theory with Rafferty as soon as possible.

Rafferty must have been on the same wavelength because he was waiting for them at the house. Ian felt a ripple of uneasiness as he invited the constable inside. Rafferty's expression struck Ian as being grave. Or was it just a shadow as a cloud blotted out the sun? "You're just the man we wanted to see. We have some new information—"

"Ma'am, maybe you'd like to get Dorie busy in another room, so we can talk privately," Rafferty suggested somberly.

Something was wrong.

An inexplicable heaviness descended on Ian's shoulders. He and Laurel exchanged a glance.

"O-of course," Laurel stammered.

Ian led Rafferty to the living room and made awkward conversation about the weather until Laurel joined them. "I-is it Gertie May?" she asked from the doorway, her hands clasped tightly in front of her.

"I think you'd both better sit down," Rafferty said gently. "I left a message on your answering machine, but you've obviously been out most of the morning. I wanted to tell you in person . . . We had a report late yesterday of remains being found by hikers on the Woodlands trail—the trail leads to several abandoned cottages higher up the mountain."

Ian felt the air being sucked from his lungs, the joy leaving his heart. "Remains?" He groped along the couch cushions for Laurel's hand. Her fingers felt like ice. He didn't want to hear this alone.

"Yes. We went in this morning and found partial human remains. This is very difficult... the body has been dismembered, by coyotes, we think, so a positive identification has yet to be made. An autopsy is being performed to determine the cause of death. We should have the results by tomorrow. But based on the fragments of clothing, we have reason to believe the deceased was female."

Ian felt Laurel's fingernails dig into his palm. He wished they would rip his heart out so he wouldn't be feeling anything. His mind was numb, incapable of thought.

He was vaguely aware that Rafferty was still talking. "The clothing fragments match the description of what Miss Harris was wearing when she went missing. But there was no ID. I've brought some samples with me and I'll have to ask you, Mrs. Wilson, to identify them. Are you up to that?"

Laurel made a small sound like a kitten mewing. Ian reached out for her as Rafferty left the room. His throat was tight with the ache of loss as he pulled her hard against him, finding comfort in the feel of her body. The pain in his chest dulled when her head rested upon it.

They clung to each other until Constable Rafferty returned, then pulled apart, still holding hands while Laurel examined the plastic bags of clothing Rafferty carried.

Ian felt the last gossamer threads of hope disappear when she mumbled, "These are—were—" she corrected herself "—Gertie May's pajamas. Her orange coat." Her voice cracked as she pointed at a torn, bloodied pair of rose-patterned underpants sealed in a plastic bag. "I don't know..."

Constable Rafferty nodded. "In any case, a DNA test will be done to positively identify the body, which means it won't be released for burial for about two weeks. You'll need to keep that in mind if you wish to commence funeral arrangements. I'll need to take her hairbrush . . . it'll contain hairs that we can compare against—"

Ian interrupted him. "Can't you use dental records?"

"Only partial remains were found—not the skull."

Ian felt sick to his stomach. Laurel sobbed quietly against his shoulder. He held her tightly and stared at Rafferty. *He wanted justice.* "If that bastard Romanowski killed Aunt Gem," he grated harshly, "just what the hell are you prepared to do about it?"

Chapter Thirteen

Silence weighed heavily upon the house. An omnipotent presence that forced Ian away from the solitude he'd thought he'd wanted this sorrowful evening downstairs into Laurel's arms.

He found her sitting up in bed in the dark, arms clasped around her knees. Rocking to and fro.

He felt the tears spring to his eyes. His heart ached with a tightness he didn't think he could bear alone, and there was only one person he could share it with. "Laurel?"

She lifted her head, opening her arms to him. "Oh, Ian. I was hoping you'd come," she whispered tearfully. "I didn't want to be alone tonight—especially tonight. Hold me, please."

"Oh, Laurel," he groaned, agony overwhelming him as his hands slid over the soft flannel covering her back, pulling her closer. He buried his face in the fragrant curls at her neck. "Oh, I need you, too."

They lay there together in the dark, grieving and holding each other. He told her things about Aunt Gem that he'd never told anyone before. He wasn't sure why he was telling her all this, but somehow it felt right. He just wanted to lie in Laurel's arms and drift away from reality. Forever...

Ian dreamed he was lost in a dark cavern and he couldn't find his way. Being alone had never felt so frightening. He reached out, trying to find his way in the darkness...and there was Laurel, reaching out for him, too.

His arms tightened around her as he breathed in her fragrant scent. He wanted to bury himself in the sweet warmth of her body, feel the release of emotions that had been building inside him and erase the fears that made him want to doubt her. His hands moved over her, slipping up under her nightgown to stroke her hips and breasts. Her skin felt like warm silk.

Suddenly her fingers were entangled in his hair. He kissed her deeply, terrified he might lose her in the darkness of the cavern. The dream took on a sudden urgency that Ian couldn't deny.

He tugged at his belt, groaning low in his throat when her fingers frantically pushed the jeans off his hips and wrapped around him, guiding him to enter her. Such exquisite feeling! Ian started to move. Passion lapped over him in waves, rising in crests as she locked her legs around his hips. Each thrust brought a comfort as forceful and soothing as a wave breaking on the shore... an eddy of sweet release, followed by a savage rush as the next wave broke. Then another. And another. And finally, a quiet joy that lasted until Ian realized it wasn't a dream at all. And in the heat of the moment, he'd forgotten his grief.

GERTIE MAY WAS DEAD. Laurel lay still with her head resting on Ian's chest, dreading the day ahead. Her eyes filled with tears. She wasn't going to speculate on how her dear friend had died—that was just too horrible. How on earth was she going to tell Dorie?

She wasn't, she decided staunchly. At least, not until the DNA test results were back in two weeks. Rafferty had advised them to hold off on a memorial service until then. By that time, she should have figured out how she and Dorie were going to live. And where. Laurel squeezed her eyes shut tight and prayed. It might all work if Rafferty didn't come up with the idiotic notion that she'd killed Gertie May.

Ian's sleep-warmed hands glided over her hips and belly, pulling her against him. She lifted her head as his eyes opened, seeing pain, grief and doubt reflected in his gaze. A mirror image of her own feelings.

She draped her thigh across his hips and snuggled closer, needing the comfort only he could offer. A hot clot of tears lodged in her throat. In two weeks, three weeks at the most, they'd be out of each other's lives.

IAN WASN'T SURE Laurel should be trying to keep Aunt Gem's death from Dorie, but he agreed that they should stay inside all day with the TV off so Dorie wouldn't see the news reports of the discovery of Gertie May's body.

The phone started ringing after lunch—neighbors and friends of Gertie May's, offering condolences.

"I can't take any more of this," Laurel told him after the fourth call, her eyes murky with grief. He tried to put his arms around her, but she brushed them away, glancing meaningfully in Dorie's direction.

The doorbell chimed and Ian went to answer it, prepared to do battle with journalists. The last thing they needed were reporters finding out about Laurel's past. Frederick stood on the porch, head bowed, looking like an old gray heron.

He held up a store-bought coffee cake. "I brought this by for you. I'm terribly sorry about your aunt. She was a fine woman. Is there anything I can do?"

"I think Laurel could use a friendly face. Do you have time to stay for coffee?"

"Today, I do. I've got a caregiver staying with Anna for a few hours so I can do errands and find a quiet place to sit and think."

Ian took Frederick's coat and led him into the kitchen. Dorie was making crayon etchings of the old keys to the house and Laurel was making a list—of what, Ian didn't know. Probably about the memorial service. Just something to keep her mind busy, he was sure. For a moment Frederick seemed rather lost, distracted almost, Ian thought, watching the elderly man glance around the kitchen, perhaps recalling the last time he'd seen Gertie May here. Then Frederick collected himself and sat down to admire Dorie's artwork and enjoy a slice of coffee cake.

"Mommy said I could have all these keys for myself," Dorie explained importantly.

"New locks, eh?" Frederick grunted dourly. "Doesn't surprise me." But he didn't comment further. Ian gave him credit for being savvy enough not to mention the burglary or Gertie May in front of Dorie.

"I'm going back to work at the Crow's Nest Friday night," Laurel told Frederick, switching topics. "But I have to find a baby-sitter. It's quite late to be coming home—too late to let the sitter go home by herself. I'd have to take her home, which means waking up Dorie."

Ian frowned. This was news to him.

"Well, you have all these guest rooms. Maybe your baby-sitter could stay the night and go home in the morning?" Frederick suggested.

"That's an excellent idea. I hadn't thought of that."

Frederick looked pleased. "Glad to help. I'm an old hand at arranging baby-sitting. My baby's just a little older." His face fell, then he brightened again and finished his mug of coffee. "I should be on my way."

The phone rang just then. Ian gestured to Frederick to stay when he recognized Rafferty's voice. Rafferty must have the autopsy results. Ian braced himself for the news.

"Your aunt's cause of death is hypothermia," Constable Rafferty informed him without preamble. "I'll spare you some of the details, but the coroner wanted me to reassure you that your aunt was dead before the coyotes found her body. One interesting note—your aunt couldn't have been dead for more than a few days. There's a bruise on her wrist that indicates she was restrained. We've brought Romanowski and his contractor, Hank Morrison, in for questioning, but without any evidence, we can't hold them. Morrison has an airtight alibi for Saturday evening. He and his wife were entertaining at their North Van home. I've got fifteen witnesses who say he didn't leave the party until ten o'clock, so that blows a hole through Mrs. Wilson's theory.

But it's still feasible that Romanowski and Morrison kidnapped Miss Harris *after* eleven. Once we find Janet Smithe, we'll have a few more answers." He cleared his throat. "I don't suppose you've taken a trip to Nelson recently?"

"As a matter of fact..."

"Spreading some money around, eh?"

"Yes," Ian said cautiously.

"Catch any fish?"

"No. But my line's still in the water."

"You get any nibbles, I want to hear about them. Understood? If someone is desperate enough to commit murder once, they don't usually hesitate to murder again."

Ian took Rafferty's warning to heart. As he hung up, his gaze swung from Dorie, who was stringing her keys onto a length of red ribbon, to Laurel, who was rubbing her arms as though a sudden chill had stolen over her. Neither of them was going to be next. He'd make damn sure of it.

"Well?" Laurel said.

Ian jerked his head, indicating they should leave the room. "She died of hypothermia," he explained when they'd reached the front hall.

Laurel sagged against the wall.

Frederick patted her shoulder. "Hypothermia? Does that mean they think it was an accident?"

"They're not sure yet," Ian replied. "But at least we know she didn't die cruelly."

"Yes." Frederick nodded sadly, putting on his coat. "One small thing to be grateful for in all of this. I'm sorry this happened...especially at Christmas."

Laurel gave a dry laugh. "I think I've forgotten what Christmas is all about. I haven't even given Dorie her gifts yet. We were waiting, you see—" She pressed her hand to her mouth.

Ian slipped his arms around her and waited until after Frederick had seen himself out to kiss her cheek and her eyelids. "We're gonna make it through this, honey. Aunt Gem didn't suffer. Let's hold on to that, okay?"

She nodded. He ducked his head, resting his forehead against hers, his fingers tangling in her hair. Quietly he told her the rest of what Rafferty had said. "Mr. Aames is a nice man with problems of his own. I didn't want to drag him into this. And I didn't think you'd want anyone else in Serenity Cove to know about Steve."

"I feel so guilty, Ian. Maybe if I'd taken the cards to the police earlier they could have done something. Then Gertie May would still be alive."

"There's no way of knowing that. Maybe she was killed because I showed the cards to the police."

"Oh, God. I can't believe she's dead."

"Neither can I."

She gripped his shirt. "We're not giving up. We're going to find out who's done this to her."

"Damn right. But we have to be careful. Dorie or you could be next on this person's agenda. Okay?"

She nodded.

"Now, what's this about you going back to work?"

"I have to. Or I'll lose my job. You know as well as I do that I haven't any savings."

She had a point. Offering her a loan seemed out of the question, too. She'd probably wring his neck for even suggesting it. "Okay. I'll baby-sit Dorie."

She tilted her head back to gaze up at him, her eyes filling with skepticism. "You?"

He grinned. "I put her to bed the other night when you were in the hospital. How tough can it be?"

"You're absolutely right. You're hired."

IAN SAT DOWN in the privacy of his room and opened his aunt's Bible to the page noting the births, deaths and marriages of five generations of Harrises. A white envelope marked the page. He'd been putting off the task of reading Aunt Gem's will all day, but he couldn't avoid it any longer. Funeral arrangements would have to be made. He needed to know about the house—what Aunt Gem wanted—so he could make some decisions about Laurel.

Ian swallowed hard as he opened the envelope. Sure enough, it contained the will and a handwritten letter. He unfolded the will first, his vision blurring when he came to the paragraph about the house. He couldn't believe it.

Feeling as though Aunt Gem had struck him with a club hammer, Ian reached for the letter.

Dear Ian,

I hope you'll forgive me, dear boy, for breaking my promise to leave you the house. You've been like a son to me and I know you love this old place, but as our visits have grown further apart and you've shown no signs of ever wishing to settle down, I've come to realize that the house would be nothing but a sentimental inconvenience for you. In my way of thinking, a house must be lived in to be a home.

By now, you've met Laurel and Dorie. Oh, how they've brightened up my life.

We're quite a jolly threesome. Just like you, this is the only home Dorie remembers. I want her to grow up here and fill the house with laughter. So I'm leaving the house to Laurel. She loves operating the bed-and-breakfast as much as I do. I can rest easy knowing that my two girls are taken care of.

Be happy.

Your loving
Aunt Gem

Short and sweet. He got the money. Laurel got the house. Why did he feel so dissatisfied? He fell back onto the bed, thinking. If he'd inherited the house as he'd originally thought, he'd been prepared to offer Laurel a job as caretaker. She could continue living downstairs and operate the bed-and-breakfast. They'd work out an equitable split of the profits and she could forget about her job as a cocktail waitress.

So why did it hurt so much knowing Laurel inherited the house? Did she know?

Ian closed his eyes with a groan. He didn't like the direction his thoughts were taking, the doubts that were resurfacing. The envelope was sealed. Of course, Laurel probably knew where the will was kept. Aunt Gem had probably told her in the event of her death. They were friends, for Pete's sake.

He stuffed the will and the letter back in the envelope. If Rafferty ever found out about this, he'd have the motive he needed to pin Aunt Gem's murder on Laurel. The house was worth five hundred thousand dollars. Laurel could sell it and be set for life. Why did that thought bother him even more?

Why did it make him think twice about the reason Laurel had slept with him again last night?

Chapter Fourteen

Ian leaned against the doorway of the alcove, watching Laurel punch at the computer keyboard. For some reason, today of all days, she seemed compelled to finish the speech for the district council. Ian didn't know whether her single-minded devotion to the speech was a device for coping with the shock of Aunt Gem's death or a clever act. Right now Ian felt as if Romanowski's involvement in Aunt Gem's death was a big *if*. Maybe Romanowski had planted a spy in the house and arranged the burglary to steal the petitions— that alone would have stacked his hand in winning approval for his development. He didn't have to resort to murder.

"Laurel?"

She looked up and gave him a halfhearted smile.

That smile pierced him and he hated the anger and the suspicion that curdled his thoughts. Laurel needed an accomplice to abduct Gertie May. Was her accomplice her lover? The P.I. hadn't come up with a boyfriend in her background check. "I'll be sleeping upstairs tonight," he said, keeping his face devoid of expression.

"Oh." Her eyes lowered for a second. When she looked up again, her smile was gone. "Are you okay?"

"I'm fine. I just need some space."

He saw the hurt flash like amber in her eyes and caught a glimpse of her confusion as her pale brow wrinkled. Was she disappointed? His pulse thudded in his temple.

She picked up a pencil on the desk. "I never asked you about Gertie May's will," she said softly. "Did you read it?"

"Yeah. It answered my questions about the funeral arrangements. I'll handle everything."

"Of course. You're her family."

It occurred to him that now would be a good opportunity to tell her about the house. To express his anger and disappointment. To get his suspicions out in the open. But he couldn't. The anger gripped his vocal cords too tightly. He needed time to think. But he hadn't been prepared for the chasm of unhappiness that keeping this secret from Laurel was causing him. He hesitated, unwilling to leave her for the loneliness of his bedroom just yet, but unable to reach out to her as he'd reached out to her last night.

The silence lengthened and for once she seemed to be able to conceal her feelings from him.

Finally she nodded. "Good night, then. Sleep well." Her head bent over the keyboard.

He slowly mounted the stairs, the hunt-and-peck rhythm of the computer keys sounding in his ears. Sleep tonight? He doubted it. How could he get so attached to a woman who wore a flannel nightgown to bed? He was at the top step when he heard a muffled sob.

He paused, listening.

Tap. Tap. The keys stopped. He heard another sob. She was crying. *Jeez.*

His stomach tightened. He clenched the balustrade and waited, waging a tug-of-war with his emotions.

Maybe he'd been wrong about the will. Maybe she didn't know Aunt Gem had left her the house. Maybe he was being a jerk and was using the house as an excuse. For what? To save him from the certain disaster of getting involved in a permanent relationship. The picket fence bit and a restricting nine-to-five job weren't for him. He'd suffocate.

He sat on the top stair and counted the steps down to the main floor. Fourteen. If he took them two at a time he could be at her side in ten strides, tops. *And what would you do when you got there?* he asked himself. *Pull her into your arms and make her a promise you couldn't keep just because you're afraid of spending the rest of your life alone?*

Ian put his head in his hands, trying to deny that brief feeling of joy, of emotional oneness with Laurel that he'd never experienced before. Why was he even thinking about this? Why couldn't he beat a hasty retreat to his room and leave her to mourn Aunt Gem in private?

The answer came to him swiftly. *Because he loved her.* In his thirty-five years he'd never met a woman equal to her gutsy strength, vulnerability and honey-eyed beauty. He probably never would again. He might not be capable of sharing her life with her, but he loved her all the same.

He waited, paying silent penance on the stairs, until the sporadic tap-tapping of the computer keys resumed.

LAUREL'S WORDS about baby-sitting came back to haunt Ian two nights later when she handed him a list of emergency phone numbers and outlined Dorie's bedtime routine.

"Is all this really necessary?" he asked, immediately regretting his question when her forehead wrinkled into a stern frown.

"Give her an inch and she'll take a mile."

"Don't worry about us. Dorie will take good care of me. And this Simon guy will walk you home, right?"

"Of course. I'd better get going. I don't want to be late." She kissed Dorie good-night. But she was awkward with him as he walked her to the door, where she pulled on her coat and boots.

Why shouldn't she be awkward? They'd hardly spoken to each other except to discuss the plans for Gertie May's funeral service. He still couldn't bring himself to tell her about the will. She certainly hadn't asked him how long she could stay in the house, which suggested that she already knew the house was hers. Ian watched her go down the front walk. Sooner or later she'd give herself away.

He glanced at the list in his hand. "Six p.m., bath." No sweat.

Dorie flipped and turned and splashed faster than any fish he could imagine. He gave up trying to soap her in favor of the whale splashing game, which was more fun. But then he had to mop up the spilled water on the floor and blow-dry Dorie's hair. By the time he had her dressed in a sprite-size flannel nightgown, he was only forty minutes off Laurel's schedule.

Snack next. He did the peanut butter and jelly crackers all wrong, Dorie quickly informed him. He was supposed to use the crackers shaped like four-leaf clovers, not the saltines. He made a funny face and ate them himself while he made new ones. Then he hustled her off to the bathroom to brush her teeth. She could sure talk a lot with a toothbrush in her mouth. Ian wiped toothpaste spray off the mirror and checked his watch. He was an hour behind, with just a story left to do.

"Two stories," Dorie corrected him, racing ahead of him into her room. "I get to pick them out." She dumped two books into his lap and scrambled up after them. "This one first."

"Oh, *The Three Little Pigs.*" Ian settled her more comfortably on his lap, where she wasn't liable to put pressure on the freshly knitted skin on his thigh. The doctor had removed the stitches just this morning.

He started to read—or tried to, anyway. Dorie coached him on the proper noises—"like Mommy makes." The book ended with a song about the big bad wolf. He was not a singer, he decided as he listened to his voice. He reached for the next book, *Goldilocks and the Three Bears,* and psyched himself up for more sound effects and bear voices. "You're really into threes, aren't you, kid? Three pigs, three bears."

Dorie giggled uproariously.

He got a kick out of listening to Dorie laugh at his deep Papa Bear voice. "That was much better than Mommy's," she said.

Ian closed the book and ruffled Dorie's silky hair. "Time for bed, kid."

"I gotta go potty." She hopped down and raced back into the bathroom.

Then he had to wait until she found her pink bunny to sleep with. Finally he tucked the covers up under her chin. She lifted her fragile, stick-thin arms and gave him a choke hold around his neck and a damp kiss. "Good night, Ian. I love you."

He hugged her back, reluctant to let go. "Good night, sprite." Suddenly he realized all those "musts" in Dorie's bedtime routine were very necessary. They made her feel cared for. Loved. And they had a rebound effect. "Love you, too," he whispered hoarsely.

He went upstairs to get a beer and the newspaper to keep him company until Dorie fell asleep, which shouldn't take long since he'd put her to bed an hour and a half later than usual. He heaved a tired sigh. Now he knew what he'd been missing the last ten years.

LAUREL ROLLED OVER and slid her hand out over the sheets, seeking the hard, reassuring warmth of Ian's body to chase the shadowy fears of her dreams away. But of course he wasn't there...and wouldn't ever be there again. Their sleeping together had been a definite mistake. Ever since it had happened the second time, she couldn't seem to talk to him. Maybe it was because they were both so distraught over Gertie May's death. But she'd have to talk to him soon. She couldn't go on living in his house rent-free, especially when she already owed him so much money.

Laurel sighed and burrowed deeper under the covers. She should get up, put on her bathrobe and slippers, but the effort seemed too great. She'd just sleep a few minutes longer.... She'd made it through two nights of work. One more shift tonight and she wouldn't have to worry about imposing on Ian's baby-sitting skills for another week.

Laurel drifted off again. When Dorie came and woke her, it was past eleven. Laurel scrambled out of bed and shoved her arms into the sleeves of her bathrobe. She hadn't known it was this late. Ian would think she was taking advantage of him.

"Look what I found on the beach, Mommy." Dorie opened her hand to show her a white, rough-edged stone. "Ian says it's milk quartz, but it doesn't come from cows. He says a long time ago people thought it was frozen ice, like a Popsicle, but it was really just a sparkly white rock. I'm going to put it in my treasure box."

"Good idea. Where's Ian?"

"Upstairs reading the newspaper."

Laurel took her daughter's hand. "Show me."

When they walked into the kitchen, Laurel's first impression of Ian as he lowered the Sunday newspaper was that he was furious. It was a big responsibility looking after a preschooler. She should have known better than to take him up on his offer. "I'm really sorry I overslept."

"You didn't oversleep. I turned your alarm off."

"Is something wrong, then?" Laurel suddenly felt afraid. What more could go wrong?

His tone gentled. "Maybe you'd better sit down. I don't know how to tell you this, but you've made the front-page news." He unfolded the paper and set it in her lap. "It's not a very flattering story."

Laurel stared at the large photo of herself in horror. Serenity Cove Woman Linked To Two Murders, the headline clamored. Blood pounded in her brain. She couldn't believe it. Her eyes sped over the words, hoping to find an impartial account of the facts. But there it was in black and white. Her alias. The facts of Steve's murder. The mystery of Gertie May's disappearance and the recovery of a body in the woods. All of it carefully woven together to make her appear guilty. Laurel started to tremble. For the second time in her life she'd been publicly convicted without a trial!

Chapter Fifteen

Laurel's mortification over the article slowly metamorphosed into full-fledged anger. Her parents had taught her to turn the other cheek, and because she'd endured the bad publicity in Nelson with her head held high, nearly everyone had thought she'd been involved in Steve's murder. Unless she did something, everyone in Serenity Cove would believe she'd harmed Gertie May.

This time she was fighting back. The reporter hadn't even bothered to interview her. So much for unbiased news reporting. Laurel checked the byline before she ripped the page out of the paper. Connie Tarlington. The name wasn't familiar.

She glanced at Ian. "I'm going to write a letter to the editor and tell my side of the story."

"Why don't you phone the editor and offer an exclusive interview instead? Or better yet, hold a press conference. There will probably be five other reporters camped out on the porch by nightfall."

"Because this way it'll be in my own words, not pieced-together quotes."

He rubbed the back of his neck. "Do what you have to do." He sounded exasperated this morning. She suspected the two-week wait for the DNA results was getting to him. He probably had a lot of work piling up.

"Well, writing a letter can't make things any worse than they already are. And it's the only way I can think of to salvage my reputation—or what's left of it. I wish I knew how this reporter found out this information about me."

"Me, too," Ian said darkly.

Laurel made toast and coffee, then sat down at the computer and polished up a statement for the newspaper, which Ian distributed to the reporters who trickled up to the door—just as he had predicted.

But Laurel's biggest worry was going to work that night. Sunday night was usually slow at the pub. Maybe there wouldn't be too many people. And maybe none of them had read their local paper this morning. Maybe.

WHEN SHE ENTERED the smoky interior of the Crow's Nest, she nearly ran into Victor Romanowski. "Excuse me," she muttered through clenched teeth.

"Well, well, look who's here. The mystery woman. My, what skeletons you keep in your closet."

"*My,* and how you liked uncovering them for all the world to see!" Even though she didn't have a shred of evidence to prove it, Laurel knew beyond a shadow of a doubt that Romanowski was somehow behind the article in the paper. Why else would he be here tonight?

His dark eyebrows rose. "I'm afraid I don't know what you're talking about. You must be delusional, or taking an extra sip or two of the drinks...."

"How dare you—"

"Is there a problem here?" Simon interrupted them before Laurel could wipe that smug expression off Victor's face with an insinuating remark about Janet Smithe.

"No, no problem." Victor laughed. His voice rose loud enough to be heard over the music. "I just want to clear out of here before she starts serving drinks. Being around her can be deadly."

The pub suddenly grew quiet. Laurel's face flamed with embarrassment. Everyone's eyes were concentrated on her. Condemning her. She lifted her chin. "How kind of you, Mr. Romanowski. I've lost my husband, and now, my best friend, under deplorable circumstances. If that's not bad enough, I also have to endure the callous comments of people like you who take it upon themselves to be both judge and jury."

Simon stepped between them, using his bulky frame as an intimidating buffer. "I know you're upset, Laurel," he said in a genial tone, "but if this goes any further I'll have to be paying you double for entertaining the customers." He turned his head and fixed Victor with a steady, hard-line stare that left no room for argument. "I believe you were on your way out, sir?"

"Gladly."

"And next time you're in, I'll thank you not to be stirring up trouble with my employees."

Laurel breathed a sigh of relief when Victor pushed through the door.

"Why don't you come into the back room?" Simon suggested gently.

"All right." She could use a quiet few moments to pull herself together.

Simon selected a white towel from a pile of clean linens and draped it over his shoulder, nervously fiddling with the ends of it. "Maybe it wasn't a good idea having you come back so soon, especially with the article in the paper today."

Laurel experienced a deep, sinking feeling. She licked her lips. "Simon, you don't believe any of that's true, do you? I mean, it's true my husband was murdered and that I lied to you about my name. But I was cleared of the charges in my husband's murder. And you walked me home the night Gertie May disappeared. She was already missing by then. How could I have done it?"

Simon avoided her gaze. "It doesn't matter what I think. The point is, customers may not come in if they think you'll be waiting on them."

"Are you firing me, then?" Her throat swelled with the humiliation of it all.

He patted her shoulder. "You're my best waitress. Why don't you take some time off? Who knows, maybe the police will solve it right quick?" He gave her a peppy smile. "Er, you've got some holiday pay due you. I can give you that to tide you over."

"I'd appreciate that." She felt numb. One uncouth remark from Victor Romanowski and she'd lost her job. She tried to find a bright side; she probably would have had to quit anyway.

Paycheck in hand, Laurel stumbled home.

"MOMMY, how come Ian wasn't sleeping on the couch this morning? He's s'pose to when you work at night," Dorie said, stirring milk into her oatmeal. "Did he go away again?"

Laurel stared glumly at her oatmeal, not hungry. She'd come back early last night so there was no reason for Ian to be sleeping on her couch with blankets that didn't cover nearly enough. "No, he didn't go away. He's sleeping upstairs."

"Where's he sleeping tonight?"

"Probably upstairs. Why?"

" 'Cause I want to ask him if I can wake him up tomorrow. He's more fun in the mornings."

Laurel made a face. "He is? Thank you very much, my darling daughter."

"He lets me watch cartoons that I *want* and I can eat cereal in the living room. Not yucky oatmeal."

"Ah. Well, I can see why you think he's more fun than me. You can ask him."

The doorbell rang and Laurel scraped back her chair, hoping it wasn't a reporter. It was Frederick.

He removed his hat. "Good morning, Laurel. I'm sorry to bother you. I was just on my way out and, well, it appears a graffiti artist has chosen the west wall of your house to leave a message."

Laurel blinked. "A message?"

"Not a very kind one, either, I'm afraid. Where are the police these days when you need them? You never read about donut shops being robbed."

Laurel glanced down at her slippers. "Would you mind keeping an eye on Dorie while I wake Ian? She's in the kitchen. I'll have to put some boots on...." Laurel ran upstairs and banged on Ian's door. "Come downstairs. Hurry. Frederick says—" Ian yanked open the door and she suddenly forgot what she was saying. He was buck naked.

She centered her gaze on his chest, trying to hide her embarrassment. They'd made love, after all, twice.

"What's going on?" he demanded, running his hand through his hair.

"Frederick says there's something written on the side of the house," she said, openmouthed. He reached for his jeans and she turned her head, waiting while he got dressed.

"I'm ready. Let's go."

In the front hall, they pulled on boots. Frederick came out from the kitchen. He'd unbuttoned his coat and had his hands thrust deep into his pockets. He nodded at Ian. "I'll watch Dorie while you two take a look."

"Thanks, Frederick." Laurel put her coat on over her bathrobe.

Outside, the cove was slumbering through a quiet gray morning. The sun was barely visible through a low bank of clouds. The boats on the water looked like models arranged on a glass shelf.

Her boot caught in the hem of her robe, causing her to stumble as she went down the steps. Ian caught her, his arms locking around her in a tight vise that she might have complained about were it not for the fact that it felt good to be in his arms again.

"Careful." His gray eyes reflected the coolness of the morning as he cautiously searched her face, leaving her feeling more uncertain than ever about what was going on between them. She sensed he wanted to say something—that something dark and unpleasant was going on in the deeper undercurrents of his thoughts. But he didn't.

He let go of her suddenly, leading the way with strong, sure strides that told her his leg was healing. She clutched the collar of her coat close around her neck, following him.

Her legs started to shake when she saw the writing.

MURDERESS

The thick, meter-long letters scrawled over the pale clap-boards shattered the tranquillity of the morning. From each letter, rivulets of black paint trickled down the wall like blood.

Laurel stared at the wall in absolute horror, feeling as though the word had been branded onto her back with a hot iron.

"It's the same person," she said dully through the numbness of her pain. "The same person who sent the cards. It has to be." *Why was someone tormenting her like this?*

Ian dabbed at a letter with his finger. "It's still tacky. We might be able to get it off—"

"No!" Didn't he understand that cleaning it away would mean it didn't exist? "Just phone the police, Ian." Then she turned and walked away.

DAMN! Ian stared at the black smear on his fingertip. He'd blown that. He hadn't offered her a word of encouragement or support. Or an apology, for that matter. She'd stood there wooden as a soldier in her blue coat with the red broad stripe of her robe underneath. Unmoving. Unblinking. Taking it all in.

He berated himself for leaving Laurel and Dorie alone last night—all on account of his foolish pride. If he'd been downstairs where he'd belonged, he might have heard this joker. He was a light sleeper. Instead he'd been upstairs thinking about Laurel until well after 3:00 a.m., then had slept deeply until the sound of Laurel pounding on his door had woken him.

He should be thanking his lucky stars that Laurel and Dorie weren't hurt by this creep. Laurel was right. He should call Rafferty and he shouldn't be walking all over the place. The can of paint had tipped over, making an inky puddle.

A paintbrush lay on the ground not far from where he stood. Ian viewed the mess as a good sign. The culprit was getting sloppy.

LAUREL AND DORIE observed the activity in the driveway from the bay window in the living room. Two police cars had arrived and a yellow police line stretched across the yard.

"The police are working very hard to find Gertie May, huh, Mommy?"

Laurel kneeled down and slipped her arms around Dorie's waist. "Yeah, sweetie." A dull ache throbbed in her breast. She'd have to tell Dorie the truth soon. She couldn't hide it from her much longer. She flicked her gaze warily out the window. At least the word faced the park rather than the street, not too many people would see it this time of year. But that yellow police ribbon was an attention getter.

Despite Ian's reassurances that the word could be painted over once the Ident team was finished, Laurel knew the harm was already done. Word of the incident would get around the cove. She'd already seen Ian chase off someone with a camera—probably a newspaper photographer.

Rafferty came in and spoke to her for a few minutes. The question of who was behind this hovered like a foreboding cloud from the ceiling. She found his focused determination to wrap up the investigation both alarming and reassuring. Unfortunately she couldn't tell him much about last night. She'd slept right through it.

"So, there was just you and your daughter downstairs last night," Rafferty repeated back to her, reading from his notes.

"That's right," Dorie piped in, listening from her window viewpoint. "Ian sometimes sleeps on our couch or in Mommy's bed, but not last night."

Laurel wished the floor would open up and swallow her whole. She flushed crimson with embarrassment. Rafferty looked up from his notebook and eyed her with keener interest. She could almost hear the gears turning in his mind, using this juicy piece of information to build a case against her. Or Ian. Or the two of them together, for that matter. Why hadn't she been more careful?

"I-Ian started sleeping on the couch downstairs after we got the prank phone call," she stammered, trying to extricate herself from Dorie's comment. "Sometimes I'd let him have the bed because it was more comfortable...but we haven't had any other calls, so he thought it was okay to go back upstairs." That sounded halfway plausible in her own mind. But policemen were born suspicious.

Ian entered the living room shortly after Rafferty had gone, bringing the smell of the wintry-fresh air with him. The sight of his bronzed, handsome face and windblown hair seemed just one more emotional onslaught after all of Rafferty's questions. Laurel sank into an armchair while Dorie latched on to Ian's legs with a squeal.

"Hey, hold on there, sprite." His eyes met Laurel's, but she noticed they still retained their distance. Cool. Unreadable. She remembered with a bittersweet pang the savage thrusts of his lovemaking. The hot, flowing sweetness of her release twining with the racking shudder of his own. Then the moment of complete and utter peace—of feeling like no one else but Ian could make her whole again. Had she imagined it all?

"I'm going to fix a sandwich and head out to the paint store. Are you okay?"

Laurel glanced down at her daughter, considering his question. *I'm a single mother. For Dorie's sake, I'll always be okay,* she thought willfully. She thrust her chin up. "I'm fine."

To her surprise, he picked Dorie up and settled her over his shoulder like a sack of potatoes. "Okay if I take this kid with me? I need a helper."

"Sure."

With both Dorie and Ian out of the house, Laurel felt insufferably lonely. She should have gone with them, but she didn't feel up to facing anyone yet. She wandered through the empty rooms gathering up Dorie's stray toys, then decided to phone her mother-in-law to cheer herself up. As always, Barb immediately honed in on her low mood and coaxed out an explanation.

"How horrible! Imagine someone writing that on the side of your house," Barb exclaimed in a shocked tone, wheezing on her indrawn breath. "I'm so glad Ian's there to protect you."

Laurel's spine went rigid. "I don't need a man to protect me, Barb."

"Not normally, no. But under these circumstances, I'm glad he's there. Why are you so defensive?"

"I'm not being defensive. I just—"

"He's grown into a very handsome man. I wonder if he's seeing anyone?"

"Barb, please." Laurel experienced a rush of panic at the same thought. Was that why Ian had pulled back from her?

"You're right, dear. I'm sorry. I've booked a flight for the sixteenth. I figured the memorial service would be after that. I wish I could come sooner...give you a hand with Dorie..." Her voice faded.

"I understand," Laurel reassured her. "It helps to know you're coming, and that I can still count on you."

"That will never change, dear."

Laurel replaced the receiver with a wistful sigh, wondering if she could still count on Ian.

ANOTHER INFERNAL LIST? How many lists could one woman write? Ian wondered sourly, taking a swig of beer from the bottle he'd been nursing for the past hour. He dragged his gaze back to the television screen visible over the tips of his socked feet. He had no idea what he was watching—some nature program.

He stole another glance at Laurel. She sat on the adjoining love seat—a suggestive name for a piece of furniture if he'd ever heard one—her slim legs curled up to one side. Her tawny hair draped in a glossy curtain over her cheeks as she bent her head in concentration over her notepad.

How was he going to explain his sudden willingness to sleep down here again tonight? There was one obvious answer, he thought, feeling the stirrings of desire throb painfully in his loins.

You're sleeping on the couch tonight! he told himself darkly, taking another long swallow. The liquid slid down his throat, doing little to ease the knot in the pit of his stomach. His unease of how to deal with the situation just served as further evidence at how inept he was at dealing with intimate relationships. She sighed softly and her faraway cat's-eye gaze landed on him. He shifted positions.

He made a small noise to catch her attention. "I owe you an apology," he said slowly, then paused, mesmerized by the graceful way she tucked her hair behind her ears and grew still, her eyes round and wary. Listening. "I never should have left you and Dorie alone down here...."

Her eyes suddenly glittered with a hard, amber sheen. Ian licked his lips.

"I don't need you to protect me, or Dorie. We got along fine before we met you and we'll continue to get along fine after you're gone. We haven't had a crank call in days and the police have a tap on incoming calls. But if your macho instincts insist, you're welcome to the couch."

His jaw clenched as their gazes locked in a silent standoff. If this was what being in love was like, he was better off without it. Sure, he'd give anything at this moment to tangle in the couch cushions with her—their passion would be fierce and frantic. A duel of flaring emotions. But how long could that last? Life would gradually intervene again.

"Oh, now you can hardly wait for me to leave.... Why doesn't that surprise me?"

She looked at him sharply. "What are you talking about?"

"The will, Laurel. Aunt Gem's will. You really had me going there for a while with your falsely accused widow story and the Christmas cards. Not to mention the phone call. It's odd how I never heard the phone ring when that call came in. It's odd, too, how those Christmas cards stopped arriving after we installed the surveillance camera. And one of the few nights I don't sleep downstairs, someone paints something on the house." He tilted his head back, finishing his beer in one gulp.

Laurel stood, her face pinched and white. Her fingers curled into fists. "Is that what you think of me? No wonder you..." Her voice trailed off. The strain pulsated between them, thick and heady.

Ian didn't blink. It felt good to finally get this powder keg off his chest. "Go on—" he encouraged her, his tone laden with contempt.

"What's in Gertie May's will?" she demanded.

"Aunt Gem left you her house."

"What? Is that what this is about? Gertie May left me her house." She tapped her forehead. "Oh, I see, the house is my motive for killing Gertie May, is it? Never mind Romanowski and Janet Smithe. Well, you can take my motive down to the RCMP detachment and see what Rafferty thinks of it. I had no idea Gertie May planned to do something like that. And even if she did, what of it? Maybe if you'd been a more caring and considerate nephew you'd have a legitimate complaint. You haven't spoken to Gertie May in four years! You've no one but yourself to blame for her decision. Now, if you'll excuse me, I'm going to bed."

Shaking her head, she stormed around the partition without even saying good-night. Hell, she probably knew he wouldn't have one. Ian tugged his T-shirt off over his head and tossed it toward the partition. He'd be back to his old self once he was a few thousand miles away. It was time he gave some serious consideration to his future.

Chapter Sixteen

Laurel's mood turned several shades darker when she scanned the Wednesday edition of the *North Shore News*. A color photo featuring the graffito attack on Harris House leapt out at her from the front page. *More bad publicity!*

She read the accompanying article. It didn't even mention a possible link between Gertie May's death and her involvement in the Heritage Society's fight to block Romanowski's condo development. Why wasn't it newsworthy that the developer had planted a spy in Harris House? Or that he'd been seen in Serenity Cove on the night Gertie May disappeared and the night *Murderess* appeared on the house?

She checked the editorial page; her letter hadn't been printed.

"When God was handing out miracles, I must have been standing in the line marked tragedies," she remarked dryly as Ian trod up the veranda steps.

"Then how do you explain Dorie? She's a miracle if I ever met one," he retorted, reading over her shoulder. He was just back from a meeting with the private investigator. What he'd gone to see him about, Laurel had no idea—he hadn't volunteered that information. Nor had he told her if he'd shown Gertie May's will to Rafferty. She was in no mood to ask. What difference would it make, anyway?

Laurel clenched her teeth, still seething from the hurt of the accusations he'd flung at her Monday night. Now she realized dully that what she had thought was an affinity forming between them had been nothing more than an act on his part. He'd seduced her to find out the truth. And she'd fallen for it.

His arm brushed her side as he pointed at the photo. Laurel felt the vibrations of his touch from her head to her toes. "Damn, I should have ripped the film out of that guy's camera," he said. "How'd he know so fast that it was there? He must have a police scanner or something."

Laurel folded the newspaper and leaned over the porch rail to check on Dorie, who was dragging her dolly around on a sled in the side yard. The last few days of sunshine had melted the snow away. Christmas was over. A New Year had begun. Gertie May's funeral service was scheduled for a week from Thursday. Laurel had to think about her future and Dorie's future. And how she was going to clear her name once and for all.

She gazed out at the water, seeking its calming influence. "I've been thinking about the house, Ian. If it means so much to you... it's yours. I'll talk to a lawyer and find out how to arrange it."

He gripped her coat sleeve. "No! Gertie May wanted Dorie to grow up here." His grip loosened and became almost a caress. "You were right. I wasn't much of a nephew to Aunt Gem, but I shouldn't have taken it out on you. I don't believe half of what I said to you the other night. You were probably more loving with Aunt Gem in the two years you were here than I've been all my life."

His apology knocked the anger out of her heart, but she knew he'd always have doubts about her. It just wasn't in his nature to trust someone. "Oh, Ian, don't punish yourself. Gertie May loved you for who you are. She respected your choices."

His eyes closed as he nodded. His jaw muscles were tight with restraint. She battled the urge to touch him, to share the painful feelings he was dealing with. She had no idea where their relationship stood now—what was real, what was pretend. She only knew that she cared for him, and she wanted to ease his grief. "We all have things we wish we could change in our lives. Sometimes I wish I'd never met Steve, but then, if I hadn't, I wouldn't have Dorie." Her voice shook. "The house will always be here, Ian. I know you're making plans to return to work, but you're welcome to stay as long as you need to—or to come back and reminisce."

Dorie, as though hearing her name mentioned, came running up the steps. "Mommy, Dolly and I want to play snow princess. But I need a crown."

Laurel looked at Dorie's pink cheeks and glowing eyes, and smiled past a veil of bleakness. Already in her short life, her daughter had lost two people she'd loved. Dorie had grown attached to Ian. She'd be hurt, too, when he said goodbye. "Let's go inside and make one."

"Hurrah! Mommy, can I put some jewels on it?"

"If you want jewels, you'll need me," Ian cut in. He winked at Laurel as he held the door open for them. "I need to stick around, anyway. The private investigator is digging into Romanowski's background. Checking out his finances. I told him to call me at home. I thought you could use the information for the council meeting Monday. He may come up with something."

"Even if he doesn't, Romanowski's still going to have a fight on his hands. The other members of the society are rounding up signatures again," Laurel replied, helping Dorie off with her snowsuit. But Ian's efforts cheered her immeasurably.

They went into the kitchen where Laurel promptly supplied some cardboard, gold foil wrapping paper, and sifted through Gertie May's button box for rubies, sapphires and emeralds, which Dorie attached to her crown with white glue.

"What, no diamonds?" Laurel teased Ian, thinking of the cubic zirconia ring he had bought for their sleuthing mission to Romanowski's office.

He lifted his hands, palms upward. "I don't deal in diamonds. I blame it on my foreverphobia."

Despite the faint twinge his frankness caused, Laurel threw back her head and laughed. Gertie May, if she were here, would have laughed, too. Sad, but true. She had to agree. Love didn't always last forever—even when you wanted it to with all your heart. But sometimes, Laurel thought stubbornly, it could be magic.

"Actually, the word diamond comes from the Greek word *adamas*. It means unconquerable. I wonder how many women would want diamonds for their engagement rings if they knew that?"

"Maybe it's a symbol meaning nothing is unconquerable if you have love," Laurel mused, glad that they'd reached an informal truce and were on speaking terms again. "If Steve had loved me enough to tell me about his gambling problem, we might have had a chance at beating it together."

Ian looked unconvinced at her logic. But then, by his own admission he knew nothing about love or relationships.

"So, if you don't like diamonds, what kind of stones do you think women should have in their engagement rings?"

"Simple. A gem that matches the fire in her soul."

"How come her soul—and not her eyes?"

"Because not all women are happy with their eye color or their hair color or their bodies... A woman can't change her soul. It's the essence of her being."

While Laurel pondered that for a moment, Dorie glued on the last of her buttons. "All done." She lifted the glittery, gluey mess and placed it on her head.

Laurel met Ian's gaze over Dorie's head. "Fabulous," they both said in unison.

IAN LOOKED at the princess in his rearview mirror and grinned despite the leaden feeling that reached deep into his soul. Dorie had insisted on wearing her crown to preschool this morning. She looked darned cute. The sight of her was just what he needed to lift his spirits. He and Laurel had an appointment at the funeral home in twenty minutes.

"I called Frederick to let him know we'd be out most of the morning," Laurel commented, sliding into the car. She was wearing a pale gray dress and her hair was tied back with a black ribbon. "It makes me feel better knowing he's keeping an eye on the house."

Ian nodded. "Good idea."

As they pulled onto the street, Laurel pointed out a red Sold sticker attached to the For Sale sign in Frederick's yard. "That was fast. He didn't mention it on the phone." She frowned. "Maybe he didn't say anything because he ended up selling to Romanowski."

"We can have the P.I. look into it," Ian suggested. "Unfortunately, he didn't find any shady business deals in Romanowski's past, or any money troubles, but he may come up with something by Monday. I asked him to check out Connie Tarlington, the reporter who wrote that article in the paper. Maybe we can find out her source of information." They dropped Dorie off at preschool, then turned onto a side street that connected with Serenity Cove's main street. Strangely enough, there was a lineup of cars at the stop sign. No one seemed to be moving.

After they'd been waiting a few minutes without budging an inch, Laurel climbed out of the car to find out what was causing the backup.

Had there been an accident? she wondered as she approached the intersection and saw a police officer halting traffic. Then she noticed the police vehicles swarmed around Chan's Market, and an ambulance. A crowd had gathered, watching the scene from across the street. A cold sense of dread pressed on Laurel's shoulders. Suddenly she had to know what was going on.

A friend of Gertie May's from the gardening club waved at her. Laurel joined her in the crowd, very much aware of the interested stares she received from several of the villagers. One woman with her two kids stepped farther away from her. Laurel suffered the humiliation with grace.

"Hi, Mildred. What's going on?"

Mildred shuddered in an ancient fur coat. Her sherry brown eyes bright with interest. "It's Mr. Chan. He was robbed last night. He didn't open the store this morning at seven-thirty like usual. The gals next door in the travel office got curious around eight-thirty, because they were desperate for cream for their coffee. They tried phoning, but there was no answer and no note on the door. So they called Mr. Chan's son, who came out to have a look. They found Mr. Chan upstairs. He'd been stabbed to death, poor man."

Laurel felt dizzy with nausea. First Gertie May, then Mr. Chan. What was going on in this town? Had the whole world gone crazy? She reeled away from Mildred and ran back to the car.

WHAT IS SO WRONG about wanting a wonderful Christmas? Laurel thought morosely, giving a silver globe suspended on the Christmas tree a tentative poke. A shower of dry needles rained to the floor as the ornament spun, reflecting the jeweled lights and ornaments surrounding it on its convex-mirrored surface. For a fraction of a second Laurel glimpsed the magic left in the tree. Her hand fell away. *There is nothing wrong with it. Just not this year. Dorie would have other Christmases. Happy ones.*

Ian entered the living room carrying several empty boxes in which to pack away the decorations. "The tree's a fire hazard," he reminded her, correctly interpreting her lack of motion as a change of mind.

Laurel sighed. She was still in a state of shock over Mr. Chan's death, because it suggested the possibility that Gertie May's death may have been a botched robbery attempt—a downtown gang singling out businesses in the smaller communities. Just what she needed—another theory to add to her perpetual state of confusion. She couldn't think straight. Was it her, or did everything in the house seem slightly out of order? Books not quite straight on the shelves, picture frames off kilter, and towels falling over in the linen cupboard. She couldn't remember moving anything.

Laurel shook her head, choking back tears. She just couldn't bring herself to take down the tree. It was too depressing. Her hopes were fading as rapidly as the tree's scent.

Ian put his arm around her. "Hard, huh?" He sounded choked up himself. "Why don't we start with the angel? You can give it to Dorie. Aunt Gem would like that."

She brushed the tears off the fringes of her eyelashes. "Okay." She held her breath as Ian stood on tiptoe and reached for the angel on top of the tree. Just as his fingers touched the angel's lacy skirt, the doorbell chimed. Laurel glanced at the grandfather clock. It was after nine.

Ian thrust the angel into her hands. "I'll get the door. You don't know who it could be at this hour."

The delicate porcelain face of the angel smiled sympathetically up at her. Laurel hugged it to her chest. Dorie would love owning it as a special memento of Gertie May.

"Laurel!" Ian's voice boomed from the hall, thick with panic. Laurel whirled around, nearly dropping the angel. "Call an ambulance! For God's sake, it's Aunt Gem!"

Chapter Seventeen

Ian stared in disbelief at his aunt's prone body swathed in blankets on the front porch. Her eyes were closed. Terror sliced through his exultation as he tried to find a pulse on her neck. "Aunt Gem? Can you hear me? It's Ian." *There!* He felt something.

"Laurel, she's alive!" *Just barely.* He lifted her carefully and carried her into the living room, laying her on the sofa. He tucked the blankets more securely around her. Her breathing seemed so shallow.

"Oh, God, Ian, I can't believe it. She's alive." Tears streamed down Laurel's cheeks as she took Aunt Gem's hand, rubbing it with her fingers. "Gertie May, please be all right. An ambulance will be here soon. You're back with us. It's going to be okay."

The wailing approach of an ambulance could already be heard. Ian gripped Laurel's shoulders, nearly brought to tears himself. "I'll meet you at the hospital. You get a baby-sitter for Dorie, then call Rafferty."

AN HOUR AND A HALF LATER, Ian prowled the perimeter of the hospital emergency waiting room. The adrenaline high from discovering his aunt on the doorstep like an abandoned baby had dissipated into worry over her condition. How long did it take to run tests? He checked his watch. Laurel should be here by now. Rafferty had already arrived with another officer from the Ident team. They were in with the doctors.

The automatic doors to the emergency entrance opened with an electronic whir and Ian caught a glimpse of honey hair. His heart lifted in his chest, his spirits rising again. "Laurel." Their eyes met, and he felt his breath being sucked from his lungs. *Damn, she was beautiful. An angel face with the inner strength of a lion.* She came straight into his arms.

He kissed her temple, breathing in the sweet scent of her hair.

"How is she? Can we see her?" Laurel asked, tilting her head up to see him. Hope shone in her face like sunshine. He held her tighter, afraid she would step away from him. He needed her here. Close. How could he have ever doubted her?

"I don't know yet. What took you so long? I got worried. I thought maybe..." He didn't want to think about her possibly being hurt.

"The sirens woke Dorie. It took a while to calm her down and take her to the Nichollses'. I thought she'd be safer at their house." A shadow flickered over her face and she chased it away with an optimistic smile.

They sat down, holding hands, to wait for the doctor. Ten minutes later Rafferty and a white-coated woman with a stethoscope draped around her neck approached them. Rafferty was smiling as he introduced Dr. Benson, a neurosurgeon.

"Your aunt is in a coma," Dr. Benson explained. "We've found a collection of blood between the skin and the skull, indicating an injury. A bump on the head in layman's terms. Her vital signs are good. Her pupils are responding to light. Fortunately, she's received good care."

"We found injection sites from an IV," Rafferty interjected. "Someone saw to it that your aunt received medical attention."

"Romanowski? He could afford that," Ian stated, a steely edge to his tone.

"That remains to be determined." Rafferty shifted his feet. "We've recovered the blankets and the clothing your aunt was wearing. The forensics lab will hopefully give us some clues as to where she was being held. You have to be patient. Don't go off half-cocked or you could find yourself in jail charged with assault."

"The nightgown Gertie May was wearing didn't belong to her," Laurel said thoughtfully. "The blankets didn't look familiar, either. But they didn't look new—"

"Did either of you hear a car pull up before the doorbell rang?"

Ian and Laurel exchanged glances. He'd been downstairs getting boxes from the basement. Laurel had been in the living room. They both shook their heads no.

"Whoever it was probably parked down the street and walked up."

Ian addressed the doctor. "Will my aunt recover?"

"Chances are very good. Unless she develops an infection or bleeding, she could come out of the coma at any time. At the moment though, we're not detecting any spontaneous activity, such as eye movement, that usually occurs before a person comes out of a coma."

"I've posted a guard on her room."

Laurel pushed her hair from her face. "That's reassuring. Can we see her?"

"Of course." Dr. Benson smiled. "Talk to her. Hold her hand. Pray. It all helps."

They took the elevator up to the intensive care unit on the fourth floor. A uniformed police officer stood outside the door.

"Hi, Aunt Gem." Ian leaned over the metal railings of the hospital bed and kissed her brow. Her pale, freckled skin looked two sizes too big for her body. "What mischief have you got yourself into?" He laughed gruffly and took her hand, being careful not to disturb the IV tube. "Christmases with you were always incredible, but this time you've outdone yourself. You'll have a great story to tell when you wake up."

He looked across the bed at Laurel. Her eyes were luminous. "Laurel's here with me, but we didn't bring the sprite. Maybe tomorrow."

"Gertie May, it's so good to see you," Laurel added softly, stroking Aunt Gem's shoulder. "The doctor says you're going to be fine. I can hardly wait until you wake up. Oh, the things I have to tell you about your nephew you're not going to believe."

"Wait a minute, you're not going to tell her you nearly knocked me out with a flashlight, are you?"

"Nearly? I'm going to tell her the truth. I knocked you out cold."

"Just what else were you planning on confiding to my aunt? You're going to ruin my image."

Laurel rolled her eyes. "I thought I'd tell her about the money and your visit to Barb. Oh, and the laundry—"

"The laundry?"

"Yes, the chemistry you have with sheets is worth repeating." She gave him a sultry smile.

He frowned, uncomfortably ill at ease. The sheets? Just what was Laurel referring to? She wouldn't tell Aunt Gem they'd slept together, would she? His Catholic aunt would have him scrubbing church pews for penance. But Ian didn't care about any of that now. He was too grateful for the second chance he'd been given with his aunt.

LAUREL GAZED up at the stars scattered across the inky sky and said a quiet prayer of thanks for the miracle of Gertie May's return. Everything would get better now. She was sure of it.

The night air was sharp and stimulating. She'd have a hard time falling asleep tonight. Maybe a glass of warm milk would calm her down, she thought as she stepped into the circle of golden light cast from the brass outdoor fixture and waited for Ian to unlock the front door. He pushed the door open. Harris House was dark and silent. The realization that she and Ian would be alone in the house for the rest of the night unnerved her.

"I should have left some lights on," she said inanely, searching for something to say.

Ian turned toward her and she slowly raised her eyes to meet his dark, probing gaze. A small noise in the shrubbery, like a cat moving among the dry stems of the hydrangeas, reached Laurel's ears, but it failed to distract either of them. She had the curious sensation as the gap in conversation lengthened, and the movement in the shrubbery subsided, that Ian was reaching some momentous decision.

He cupped the back of her neck, tilting her jaw up with his thumb as he lowered his mouth to her lips. His thumb stroked the pulse fluttering in her neck. His kiss was warm, deep, and oh, so-o persuasive. She felt a tiny explosion of pleasure in her chest, like a daffodil unfolding its petals before a bright spring sun.

He swept her up in his arms, bearing her weight easily. Laurel didn't resist. She held very still, her heart filling with hope.

"Ian?" Her breathlessness echoed her uncertainty.

"I want to make love to you tonight," he whispered huskily, kissing the soft skin of her neck. "Mmm-mmm. You smell so good, like dewy fresh flowers. Heavenly." Laurel shivered and caught his lean face between her hands. Her heart constricted with love for him. She might be very foolish for sleeping with him again, but tonight may be the last night they ever shared together. Gertie May would be getting well and coming home. Far too soon, Ian would be walking out of her life and returning to his work. Just this once, she wanted to show him how much she loved him.

Her tongue darted into his mouth with seductive intent. Ian needed no further invitation. He carried her into the hall and kicked the door closed with his foot. She tightened her hold around his neck as he slid the dead bolt into place. Then he strode upstairs and set her on her feet in his darkened bedroom. Faint starlight infiltrated the room from the window.

Ian unzipped his jacket and let it fall to the floor. Then he worked the buttons of Laurel's coat. "You won't be needing this. We'll generate enough heat of our own." Her body reacted instantly to the promise in his words. Her cheeks grew hot and her breasts ached with the heaviness of desire. She smiled and shook her head, pulling his shirttails out of his jeans and slowly undoing the buttons of his shirt, her eyes riveted on the broad expanse of his chest at her fingertips. They only had one night. She wanted to prolong the moment.

She spread his shirt and laved his nipples with her tongue until they beaded in response. Ian moaned and pulled her against his hips. She could feel the pulsing hardness of his arousal and a thrill shot through her.

She sent his shirt falling to the floor and lowered her tongue to his belly button. His groan of pleasure inspired her to release the top button of his jeans. Then, with a teasing smile, she fondled him through the thick fabric of his jeans, allowing her fingers to trail away as she bent to unlace his boots. Ian didn't let her remove them, he kicked them off, sending them crashing against the wall. Laurel devoted her attention to his socks, unrolling them with infinite slowness and slipping her fingers up his pant legs to caress his muscled calves.

"You're driving me crazy." Ian grinned. "But I like it."

She slid down the zipper of his jeans and inched them off his hips, allowing her hands to explore the sensitive places of his inner thighs. The hotness of his flesh warmed her cold fingers. She ran her fingers lightly over his legs, enjoying the sexy feel of the crisp hair coursing over the sinew and muscle and bone. He was so beautiful. His body glowed with the sheen of the starlight, cool and remote, but the heated glow of desire burning in his eyes told her of his deeper emotions.

Laurel rose to her feet and slipped her fingers into the waistband of his batik cotton shorts. "Now we're getting somewhere," he joked as his shorts joined his other clothing on the floor. She heard his sharp intake of breath when she palmed the shaft of his maleness and lovingly explored the velvety tip with her fingers and then her tongue. He clenched her shoulders, cursing his pleasure as she brought him perilously close to the edge of losing his self-control. Heady joy coursed through her.

"Stop, please...or I won't be responsible for what I do." He gently pulled her to her feet. "It's my turn." She stood as he turned his attention to the buttons on her tunic. They winked like golden stars in his fumbling grasp. She ran her hands over his arms, missing the feel of his body, and anticipating what was to come. Her tunic made a bright splash of color on the rug, followed by the cloud of her stirrup pants.

Ian kissed her breasts through the lacy camisole, pushing the spaghetti straps down off her shoulders. He swept the lacy fabric away, his mouth hot and devouring as his hands kneaded her buttocks. She instinctively moved her hips against him, feeling the ache of fulfillment build with sweetening intensity inside her.

With a deep sigh he carried her to the bed, whisking off her lacy panties before he joined her on the quilted comforter. "Oh, Laurel," he whispered, stroking her thighs. Her body responded to the rhythm of his caresses, arcing her hips upward. Laurel felt like the most beautiful, most desirable woman in the world as she lost herself in the magic of his skillful touch. She wanted it to go on forever....

"Oh!" Her eyes flew wide as his tongue touched her in the most intimate of places. Her thoughts grew crazed as wave after wave of delectable sensations went quivering through her. Never, ever, had she experienced lovemaking like this. She alternated between wanting him to go on forever and wanting him to stop the sweet torture he wreaked on her body.

He lifted his head and she ran her hands through his hair, frantically pulling him closer. He held back for a fraction of a second, his eyes locking with hers in the darkness. She could see the triumph gleam like silver in his gaze and she relished in the thought that he had the same control over her body that she did over his. Then his eyes closed as he entered her and Laurel forgot everything else but the joy of having him inside her. For this infinitesimal moment in time, he was completely hers....

Chapter Eighteen

Ian sat in the quiet hospital room listening to his aunt's steady, even breathing. "That's some roommate you found for yourself, Aunt Gem," he confided, believing she could hear him, even if she couldn't respond.

Laurel had gone to the cafeteria for coffee and sandwiches and Ian had been relieved to see her go. After the passionate abandon of their lovemaking last night, his feelings for her were so raw and powerful he didn't know how to handle them. He could barely look her in the eye. He needed to retreat for a while. Think. He gently squeezed his aunt's bony, freckled fingers.

"I'll tell you a secret, Aunt Gem. I've fallen in love, and I'm scared as hell. It would sure help if you'd wake up and tell me what happened. Who hurt you." He rubbed his hand over his tired eyes. "Don't worry, though. I'll take care of everything. And, I promise, you'll never be alone on Christmas again. I'll be there even if it means traveling halfway around the world. Four years between visits is too long."

LAUREL QUIETLY CLOSED the door to Gertie May's hospital room. The tail end of Ian's promises to Gertie May had knocked the wind out of her sails. She'd known Ian would eventually go back to his exciting job. So why did it hurt so much?

Tears stung her eyes as she stared down at the cardboard tray clasped in her hands. She took a moment to compose herself, then marched into the room, prattling about the poor choice of sandwiches the cafeteria had to offer.

They stayed two more hours. Then Ian suggested they take a break to see Dorie and return after dinner.

Laurel felt uncomfortable being alone with him in the car. Part of her wanted to lean her head on his shoulder, but she told herself it would be easier in the long run if she kept her distance. "I'll phone Barb when we get home, give her an update on Gertie May's condition," she said quietly. "We should change the Christmas tree this afternoon for Gertie May's homecoming. Where will we find a tree in the middle of January?"

"Don't worry. I'll cut one down from the backyard if I have to. I'll take the sprite with me—"

"Good. I'll dismantle the old tree, meantime. Why don't you pick up some hamburgers for dinner on your way home?" Laurel mentally calculated. "That way we can be back at the hospital at seven for visiting hours."

He pulled up at the Nichollses' house and stroked the inside of her thigh. "I hope your plans for this evening include a repeat of last night—"

She scowled. "We'll see," she said finally, unwilling to completely deny herself the pleasure of being with him again. Then she scrambled out of the car.

A few minutes later she waved to Ian and Dorie as they drove off in search of another Christmas tree. She was grateful for the time alone to sift through her thoughts. She called Barb first, then devoted her attention to the tree.

In less than half an hour she'd removed the decorations and had pulled the withered tree onto the veranda. She'd also reached the conclusion that she'd sleep with Ian again tonight—tomorrow night, too, and every opportunity available until he left, because she loved him. It was as simple as that. When the time came, she'd gracefully say goodbye.

She brushed fir needles off her corduroys and headed to the basement for the vacuum cleaner.

Laurel paused when she entered her suite, a silent alarm sounding in her head. *Someone had been down here.* She noted with dismay the empty bookshelves and the debris of books, papers and cushions strewn on the rug. All her framed photos had been taken off the wall and the backs removed. Had they been robbed again?

Numb with disbelief, Laurel walked around the partition to see what mess awaited her on the other side. Her bed had been taken apart, the drawers pulled from her bureau, and all her clothes removed from the closet.

Dorie's sleeping quarters was equally disturbed. Her clothes and toys littered the floor. Laurel quickly made up Dorie's bed, feeling supremely angry. For once she didn't care about Rafferty and his forensic evidence. The world had ceased to make sense to her. Gertie May was alive, but some poor woman wearing Gertie May's clothing had been found dead in the woods. Maybe the police would never figure out who that woman was or what happened to her, just like they'd never figured out what had happened to Steve. Regardless, her little girl wasn't coming home to a vandalized room. Laurel lined up Dorie's stuffed animals on her bed. That took care of half the mess.

She scooped an armful of clothing off the floor and dumped it on the dresser top, furious that some wacko had been pawing through her daughter's panties. Her arms jerked as she folded a tiny pair of underpants with pink rosebuds, remembering Dorie's proud, shining eyes as she'd told Anna that she was a big enough girl to wear real panties. No more diapers. And Anna had been so sweet. She'd said she had white underpants with pink rosebuds on them, too. *Pink rosebuds?*

Laurel blanched, remembering the bloodstained ladies' underpants Rafferty had shown her. *They'd had pink rosebuds on them!* She'd known immediately that they hadn't belonged to Gertie May. Did they belong to Anna? Laurel's hands stilled.

Was it possible the woman in the woods was Anna?

Both women had the same body build and gray hair. Laurel shook her head. No, it was too ridiculous to be true. Why she'd seen Anna... When? Laurel tried to think back. Boxing Day, December 26, the day of the robbery. They'd phoned the police from the Aameses' home. Anna had been in the living room. But surely she'd seen her since?

Laurel stuffed Dorie's clothes into the drawers, not bothering to fold them properly. Then she spent a few minutes straightening up the sitting room and trying to talk herself out of the notion that Anna was dead. It didn't work.

Armed with a plateful of Christmas cookies from the freezer, Laurel marched next door and rang the doorbell. She peeked through the sidelight. The house seemed quiet, but a few seconds later Frederick opened the door.

"Laurel. How nice to see you. Is everything all right? I saw the ambulance arrive last night... I hope Dorie or Ian isn't sick?"

"No, I've got wonderful news. Brace yourself. Gertie May's alive! She just appeared on our doorstep like a miracle from heaven." Laurel smiled broadly. "That's why I dropped by, I thought you'd want to know."

"Well, come in. I want to hear all about it. Is she all right?"

"She's in a coma. But the doctor says she should recover."

Frederick's bloodshot eyes glowed. He looked exhausted. Laurel felt ashamed for disturbing him. At least she would be less intrusive to the quiet order of Frederick's home than Rafferty. "This is cause for celebration. Have you got time for a cup of tea?"

"That would be lovely. Ian and Dorie are out running an errand. I brought chocolate-chip cookies. I know they're Anna's favorite."

Frederick took the plate of cookies so Laurel could remove her coat. "Anna's napping now. We had another tough night. Her coughing was keeping her awake, so I took her to the doctor this morning. He prescribed some new antibiotics and they've made her drowsy. I just woke up a few minutes ago—recharging my batteries so I can make it through the night ahead. Maybe she'll be up before you go."

Laurel nodded. "I hope so. I'd like to see her." He sounded so logical and yet... She followed him into the kitchen, looking for clues that Anna had been there recently. But there were no telltale signs of dirty plates or glasses stacked beside the sink. The tidy kitchen looked cheerful and normal as Frederick plugged in the electric kettle.

"I'll just use the washroom for a minute, if I may." It was the only excuse she could think of to get herself out of the kitchen long enough to check on Anna.

"Make yourself at home, dear."

The bathroom was at the end of the hall, the door standing open. Laurel looked furtively over her shoulder to make sure Frederick wasn't watching her. From the kitchen she could hear the scrape of a drawer. He was setting the table for tea. She flicked the bathroom light on and pulled the door firmly closed—loud enough for Frederick to hear. Then she quickly tiptoed toward the stairs.

Frederick had given her a tour of his home once, and Laurel knew their bedroom was on the second floor. The carpeted stairs muffled her footsteps. She'd die of embarrassment if Frederick caught her nosing around his house. How could she explain?

The bedroom door was closed. Laurel eased it open, wincing at the protesting squeak of hinges. She half expected to see Anna lifting her head off the pillow, awakened by the noise. But Anna was nowhere to be seen.

The two twin beds filling the cramped bedroom were neatly made, their bedspreads taut and unwrinkled.

Laurel surveyed the room in confusion, not wanting to believe the truth the empty beds implied. Goose bumps rose along her arms and up the ridge of her spine. Where was Anna? Had Frederick put her in another bedroom?

Something protruded from the end of the bed farthest from her. Laurel went to take a closer look. It was a leather suitcase with big brass latches and a sturdy leather handle. She tested the weight. Packed. Was Frederick going somewhere?

In the two years she'd known him, he'd never taken a trip. Only mentioned regrets that he couldn't travel because Anna was so sick. Laurel grew worried. It occurred to her that coming to Frederick's alone might not have been a good idea. She should get downstairs before he missed her...make an excuse to leave.

Behind her, the door squeaked. Laurel whirled around, hoping to see Anna. Her heart plummeted. Frederick stood in the doorway, wielding a very sharp and deadly-looking kitchen knife.

Chapter Nineteen

"I was afraid it would come to this," Frederick said sorrowfully, taking a threatening step toward her.

Laurel backed toward the wall. "I don't understand—"

"Don't move and I won't hurt you," he crooned. "I didn't hurt Gertie May, did I?"

"Gertie May? Frederick, please, what's this all about?"

"Not now, my dear. I need your cooperation." He came closer. The light streaming through the window glinted off the knife's steel blade. Was he going to kill her? Laurel fought the wave of panic that rushed through her. She had to escape.

She was younger, quicker than he. She could outmaneuver him. When he came within arm's length, she feinted left and went right, leaping over one of the beds. She almost thought she'd made it when his hand wrapped in her hair. She screamed, feeling the pain of thousands of hairs being ripped out at the roots as he yanked her backward to the floor. She landed flat on her back.

Her head throbbed. His grip was so tight the slightest movement caused more nerve-shrieking pain. The knife hovered above her chest and her heart pounded with terror as he pressed the tip of the blade near her collarbone until it bit into her flesh. She pressed her chin to her chest, whimpering at the bright red stain that appeared on her sweater.

"Listen to me. You're going to do exactly as I say and you won't get hurt. Understand?"

"Yes." Tears of pain welled in her eyes as she gazed up into his face. He looked wizened and desperate. His normally tidy, white hair stuck out in tufts on each side of his head like horns. She couldn't believe this was the same kindly old gentleman that she'd lived next door to for two years. Gardening had made him amazingly strong.

"We're going downstairs to the basement. If you try anything again, I'll slip this knife into your back and make your daughter an orphan."

"I won't, Frederick. I p-promise."

He stood, pulling her to her feet by her hair. Laurel bit her lip, trying not to scream. "Mr. Chan said the same thing and I ended up killing him." The unfeelingness of his statement terrified her further still. *Mr. Chan, the owner of the market? What did he have to do with her and Gertie May?*

Laurel stumbled down the stairs, her thoughts scattering in several directions when she felt the warm stickiness of her blood on her chest. She almost lost her balance once and pressed her hand to the wall to steady herself, leaving a bloody smear.

Frederick butted her toward the kitchen and they descended the basement stairs in the same fashion. Laurel managed to leave a bloody handprint on the doorjamb at the top of the stairs. Then Frederick steered her through a gloomy rec room to his music room.

Laurel had a hazy recall of this room: the upright piano and the special acoustical ceiling and carpeted walls that prevented his music from penetrating the rest of the house and disturbing Anna. Frederick had been the choir director at his church for years until Anna's illness had forced him to resign the position.

The music room was pitch-black when they entered, but the lights suddenly blazed on and Laurel blinked. The piano still held the place of honor on the north wall. But she didn't remember the cot and the table centered on the east wall.

"Where's Anna? What have you done to her?" she demanded as he nudged her toward the cot. On the table she saw a first-aid kit, an empty IV bag and a pair of handcuffs.

"Anna passed away. It was her last gift to me," Frederick said reverently, as though he were talking about a martyr or a saint. He reached for the handcuffs. "She put on Gertie May's clothes and went for a walk one night. It was snowing. Anna always loved a good tramp in the woods in the snow." He paused, and Laurel hoped to hear some grief for his dead wife or some regret over her death emerge into his tone, but there was none.

"I didn't notice she was gone until early the next morning. By the time I found her it was too late. She'd died of hypothermia. When I saw her lying in the snow, all dressed up like Gertie May, it seemed like an answer to a prayer. Anna was showing me in her own loving way how I could buy some time.... It was her way of telling me to take all the money and enjoy life for a change. I did the only thing I could—I carried her deeper into the woods where I was sure the coyotes would find her... then I kissed her goodbye."

Laurel shuddered at the horrible image he'd described. Poor Anna. "You said Anna put on Gertie May's clothes... Was Gertie May with you all this time?"

"Walk over to the piano," he commanded, ignoring her.

"I'll bet she was here in this soundproof room," Laurel babbled. "What are you going to do with the handcuffs?" He suddenly let go of her hair.

"You're going to fasten one bracelet on your wrist, then pass the chain around the piano leg and snap the second bracelet on your other wrist. That's a good girl. That should keep you out of trouble. It's worked on Anna more times than I can count."

Laurel noticed the deep scratches on the fluted piano leg and felt sickened. She sank onto the floor and pulled her legs up to her chest as he towered above her with the knife clenched in his right hand. Her legs were the only weapons she had if he came at her with the knife again.

She forced herself to sound calm. "Please, Frederick, tell me what's going on. Maybe I can help you. Why do you need to buy time? Is it because you abducted Gertie May?"

Frederick rubbed the back of his neck. "No, no, no," he snapped impatiently. "Because I can't find the ticket. She hid it before I came to the house."

Laurel moistened her lips, trying to make sense out of what he was saying. He'd gone completely bonkers. "What ticket?"

"The lottery ticket, dammit! She won the December 23 jackpot. Four point two million dollars."

She stared at him in disbelief. Gertie May had won the lottery? It sounded too fantastical to be true. Yet, if it were, Laurel felt only a deep pity that the quest for riches had conquered another man's soul. Had driven him to such violent extremes.

"Frederick," she said desperately. "We're all friends. I don't know where the ticket is, but I'll help you find it because I'm your friend. Isn't that why you released Gertie May, because you didn't want to hurt your friend?"

"Friend? Ha!" He laughed harshly. "I went to her because I needed help. I needed money or I was going to lose this house... the For Sale sign was going up January first. I couldn't keep up with the taxes and the bank won't loan me any more money." His face twisted. "I was born in this house. And Anna, dear Anna, this is the only home she remembers. But did Gertie May offer me any money? No! She told me it was time Anna was put in a nursing home, that the house and the garden were too much for me. Who was she to tell me what was too much?

"I grabbed her arm and demanded the ticket, but she wouldn't tell me where it was. She pushed me and I let her go. That's when she hit her head. If she'd just told me where the ticket was, she wouldn't have gotten hurt, and neither would Mr. Chan. He figured it out the other day after you bought a lottery ticket from him." The knife arced through the air. "He wanted a slice of the pie. The percentage he got for selling the winning ticket wasn't enough. I gave him a slice, all right. I only returned Gertie May to get you out of the house so I could search it."

Laurel fought against the terror that rose in a high-pitched scream in her throat. Her knees trembled against her chest. He was going to kill her. She could tell by the deadness in his bloodshot eyes. She had to give him a reason to keep her alive. "Gertie May usually puts her tickets on the refrigerator door—obviously it wasn't there. And you've searched her office and her bedroom. Did you look in her wallet and her coat pockets?"

"Yes. She had her coat on when I rang the bell. The wallet was in her pocket. I searched them both. I may be old, but I'm not stupid."

"You're very smart, Frederick, that's why I know I can help you find the ticket. I can see how well you've executed everything down to the last detail. The doctor said Gertie May received excellent medical care—not bad for a pharmacist. You probably used Gertie May's keys to get into the house." She took a stab in the dark. "Why, I bet you even took the petitions from Gertie May's office to make Victor Romanowski look guilty. That was brilliant."

"No, that was revenge. I've had a Realtor pestering me for weeks now about an interested buyer for my property. I finally had to give in because I couldn't find the ticket." He gave her a thin-lipped smile. "That bastard owns my house. I kept hoping I could back out of the deal, but I haven't been able to find the ticket. I searched the house the day you went to the funeral home. You probably never even noticed."

"You scoundrel." His chest puffed with pride, the reaction she'd been aiming for. "But how did you get in today?"

"I took one of the new keys the other morning while you and Ian were outside inspecting the grafitto."

"You wrote that?"

"Of course not. I would never do anything so uncivilized. I simply took advantage of an opportunity."

Did that mean he didn't know anything about the Christmas cards?

"We're wasting time—"

"I was just thinking that if I were Gertie May, I'd probably save the ticket for Christmas," she said quickly. "Maybe put it in the Christmas stockings or..." She paused as an idea suddenly came to her. "Did you look in Dorie's mouse hole?"

"Mouse hole?"

"The cubbyhole under the basement stairs. If you pull the toy kitchen away from the wall, you'll see a hole that gives you access to the space under the lower stairs. Gertie May and Dorie hid their gifts there." She glanced at her wristwatch. "Dorie and Ian are out shopping. If you hurry, you'll have time to look before they return."

"Hmm, Christmas presents..." Frederick's eyes gleamed. "That does sound like something Gertie May would do." He touched the tip of the knife with his finger. A chill skated across Laurel's shoulders as she realized that she'd been trapped inside his house long enough for her blood to dry on the steel blade. "What should I do with you?"

"I think we both know the answer to that," Laurel replied firmly. "I'll stay here. Someone has to see to it that Anna's given a proper church burial. I could last a few days without food. You'd need to phone Ian once you're safely out of the country to let him know where I am." She held her breath, hoping he'd agree. She wouldn't let herself be reduced to pleading for her life.

"No phone calls. They can be traced."

"A letter, then. If you drop it in the mailbox on your way out of the cove, it'll take at least two days to be delivered. You know how slow Canada Post can be." Laurel couldn't believe she was suggesting her life hinge on the delivery of a letter.

He stared at her, a blue vein pulsing on his forehead. "I'll think on it," he said. Then he left the room.

Assuming he had gone, Laurel pulled on the handcuffs. The metal rasped noisily against the fluted piano leg.

"I had a feeling you wouldn't cooperate." Frederick's dour voice tolled across the room. Laurel froze, then slowly swiveled her head toward him, knowing she was looking death in the face.

Frederick was holding a gallon-size plastic jug and what looked like a wet rag.

Oh, God, what is he going to do?

She watched helplessly as he removed the cap and liberally splashed a colorless liquid on the rag. The strong smell of ammonia ballooned into the room.

Frederick held the rag to his face. "I'm sorry, dear. I really have no other choice. I can't risk the police finding you here. So far, they can't connect me with anything. At my age, I've no wish to trade one prison for another. This ammonia works well in exterminating the raccoons that nest under my porch and pilfer my garden. If it's any comfort, I'll make sure you're dead before I leave you out for the coyotes."

Laurel screamed his name, her thoughts running rampant with the gruesome horror of his plans for her. Her lungs filled with ammonia fumes. He was absolutely crazy!

He dropped the empty container and backed out of the room. "Goodbye, Laurel."

Seconds later Laurel heard a key rattle in the doorknob. He'd locked her in, too!

She had to get out of here. The ammonia was overpowering, making her eyes water. It wouldn't be long until it knocked her out. And she didn't even want to contemplate what Frederick would do if Dorie or Ian got in the way of his finding the ticket. She tried to slip her hands out of the bracelets, lubricating the backs of her hands with saliva. The steel pressed into her skin, grinding against the bones in her hands. Her efforts were in vain. Her hands weren't slender enough.

She groaned in frustration and started coughing uncontrollably. She was never going to get out of these handcuffs!

She examined the piano leg through tear-filled eyes. A dull pressure was building steadily in her head as though it were being packed with cotton, making it difficult to think. The piano leg styling suggested it was ornamental rather than functional. The turned, fluted shaft was attached to a four-inch-thick wooden plinth at the base of the upright piano and to a similarly thick abacus at its top. The abacus was screwed into the underside of the keybed, but she'd need a fancy-head screwdriver to undo those screws. She didn't even have a dime in her pocket that she could make a feeble attempt with.

Her only option was to break the leg. The piano looked old. She ran her fingers along the joint at the top of the shaft, praying it was glued and wasn't too solid. Stretching her arms up as high as she could, Laurel pushed on the leg with both feet, using the weight of her body as leverage. Her chest was compressing painfully and she had to stop as another bout of coughing weakened her grip. The ammonia seemed to burn through her lungs and infiltrate every cell of her body. Laurel started kicking frantically....

"Is SANTA COMING tonight, Ian?" Dorie asked hopefully, bouncing in her car seat and twisting her head back so she could see the top of the tree poking out of the trunk as they neared home.

Ian chuckled. "Not tonight, sprite. But soon, when we can all be together. Tomorrow we can buy some carrots at the grocery store for the reindeer. Do reindeer eat oatmeal, too? I can't remember."

Dorie giggled. "Not oatmeal. But we need cookies for Santa. We can ask Mommy to bake some. Look! Mommy has the old tree outside," Dorie exclaimed as they turned into the drive. "Can I help decorate the new tree, Ian?"

Ian climbed out and reached into the back seat to unbuckle Dorie's car seat. "Sure. You can put the angel on top."

To his surprise, Dorie threw her arms around his neck and kissed him. "You're the best, Ian."

He lifted her out of the car and held her tight for a moment, his cheek pressed against her pink woolen tuque. Her words acted as a healing balm on an old insecurity. "So are you, kiddo. I hope Santa brings you what you want for Christmas. Let's bring the tree inside and surprise your mommy."

With Dorie's able assistance—someone had to tell him how many steps there were—Ian carried the potted pine tree into the living room and set it in the corner. The tree was on the small side, but it filled the room with a fresh, piney bouquet. Ian felt like singing. He tossed his jacket onto the sofa and called out to let Laurel know they were back.

When Laurel didn't answer immediately, he said to Dorie, "Mommy must be downstairs, let's go find her."

Dorie scampered ahead of him, singing a tune that sounded like, "We won, we won, we won." He recognized the melody, but not the words. Ian shook his head in amusement.

The lights were on in the basement. Dorie stopped singing suddenly. "You shouldn't be opening the presents. Those are for Christmas," she stated in a bossy tone.

Ian reached the foot of the stairs and made a sharp right. Dorie was three strides ahead of him, crouched down over a pile of shredded Christmas paper that lay at the base of her play kitchen, which had been pulled into the laundry area. On top of the play kitchen Ian saw a wooden-handled knife that could never be mistaken for a toy; the red-brown smear on the knife's blade looked anything but harmless. His nerves jangled a warning as Frederick rose out of the mouse hole and reached for Dorie's hand.

"Your mommy and I found the presents like this, Dorie," Frederick explained patiently. His mouth was smiling, but his eyes were far from friendly. "Why don't you help me wrap them?"

Ian's heart gelled. Frederick's other hand was dangerously close to the knife. He didn't know what the hell Frederick was doing in the house, but in a minute they'd be in a deadly tug-of-war over Dorie. "Dorie, honey, don't do that. Come to me."

Dorie looked back at him over her shoulder, confusion stamped on her face. Ian took a cautious step forward, his hands outstretched to her, arms shaking. "Trust me, honey. I love you. Frederick doesn't really want your help. I want *my* little girl right here." She straightened and took a tentative step toward him, but Frederick clasped the sleeve of her sweater.

"We don't need your help, Ian." Frederick's white-knuckled fingers curled around the knife handle. "Dorie, do you remember Gertie May hiding a ticket in the presents? It's a very special ticket and it's mine. Gertie May took it by mistake. I need you to find that ticket for me. There are some presents still in the back of the hole where I can't reach because I'm too big. You climb in and hand them out to me."

Dorie started to squirm. "I don't want to. I want Ian."

"Frederick, this isn't necessary," Ian cut in, afraid that if he moved again the old man would harm Dorie. The house was so damn silent. A cold wave of fear washed over him. He'd seen blood on the knife. Laurel's? Was she here somewhere? Her life seeping out of her? "Whatever this damn ticket is, take it and get out of here. Don't involve Dorie. She's just a child."

"Tell her to cooperate or she'll never celebrate another birthday."

Ian felt like the old man had hit him in the gut with a baseball bat. He squatted to Dorie's eye level and spoke to her reassuringly. "Dorie, baby, do what Frederick says.

Climb in the hole and get the presents way in the back. It's probably a small one."

"But they're your presents way in the back."

Ian smiled. God, he loved this little girl. "That's okay. I don't mind if Frederick sees them."

Dorie sighed heavily. "Okay, but we're not friends anymore, Frederick. It's not nice to take other people's presents."

Ian tensed, waiting until he was sure Dorie was safely in the hole before he sprang toward Frederick, butting him up against the wall. The old man was prepared for him. Ian blocked the incoming blow of the knife with his left arm, and buried his right fist into Frederick's stomach. Ian hoped that would be enough. He didn't want to hurt Frederick with Dorie watching. The old guy was surprisingly strong. He grunted, looking on the verge of collapsing to the floor. Instead his right arm snaked out and twisted toward Ian with a lateral movement.

Ian tried to grab Frederick's wrist to deflect the blow. But the knife glanced off his forearm. Ian felt the sting of pain shoot up his arm.

"Don't hurt him!" Dorie shouted, running out of the mouse hole with a small wrapped package in her hand. "Here it is! Gertie May said this is the most special present."

"Dorie, no!" Ian turned his head and a split second later he felt Frederick's knee drive into his groin. Ian gritted his teeth and tried to move between Frederick and Dorie, but Frederick had already grabbed the package and shoved Dorie sideways toward the washing machine. Dorie screamed and Ian dove toward her, catching her just before she hit the heavy appliance. He could hear Frederick escaping up the stairs.

Ian let him go. Dorie's needs came first. She was hysterical and calling for her mommy. Her arms wrapped tightly around his neck. He kissed her and stroked her hair, his own body trembling. He'd come perilously close to losing her.

"Are you hurt? That wasn't very nice of Frederick to push you like that. Don't worry, baby, he's gone now. We'll find Mommy."

Ian shifted Dorie's head into the crook of his neck. Blood dripped down his arm onto her clothes. As if she weren't traumatized enough already, he was going to have to take her with him to search the house.

He dialed 911 from the downstairs phone and demanded the police and an ambulance. Cold beads of sweat trickled between his shoulder blades as he combed the house, shouting himself hoarse as he called Laurel's name. Each unanswered cry made him more desperate to hear the sound of her voice, to hold her in his arms again. He checked closets and held Dorie carefully as he bent down to look under beds. Laurel had to be here somewhere. . . .

She wasn't.

"Don't worry, baby, we'll find her," Ian murmured huskily as he returned to the main floor. A waft of chilly air invaded the house. Ian shivered when it enveloped his clammy skin. Frederick had left the door open in his eagerness to get away. Dorie was growing heavy and more fretful in his arms. His injured arm felt numb.

But Ian didn't care. He had to find Laurel before it was too late. If she wasn't here, Frederick's house was the only logical alternative. But he couldn't take Dorie near Frederick again. It would terrify her. He'd have to wait for the police. Where were they, dammit? Ian shifted Dorie onto his other hip and bellowed Laurel's name one last time, praying for an answer.

He didn't know what he'd do if he lost her. Meeting her had made him see his life in a different light. From somewhere outside he heard a faint moan. He hurried onto the porch, his heart surging with hope. "Laurel?"

Night was covering the cove under her shadowy wing as Ian scanned the yard, listening. Then, from the long shadow at the foot of the steps, Ian heard another sound of distress. A weak, muttered cry. Shielding Dorie's eyes with his hand, he quietly moved to the edge of the porch.

Ian tensed. It was Frederick.

The old man lay in a fetal position on the concrete walk, muttering like a madman at a pair of socks that he'd removed from the small gift box Dorie had given him. "Damn, damn woman. There's no ticket..." The despair laced in Frederick's voice was pitiable. Ian looked for the knife. Its metal blade gleamed with a silver luster in the grass safely out of Frederick's reach.

Ian could hear the first faraway whine of the siren. He slung his legs over the porch rail. He'd have to move quickly. Once the police arrived he wouldn't be able to leave the scene. Seconds could count if Laurel were bleeding to death.

The inside of Frederick's house was eerie as a tomb. The door had been left unlocked. Ian turned on the lights and stumbled over a suitcase in the hall.

Dorie pointed at the hall tree. "There's Mommy's coat. Mom-my! We're here."

Ian added his own calls to Dorie's. He peered up the stairwell, trying to decide which part of the house to search first. Halfway up the pristine white plaster wall he saw a reddish brown smudge the size of a handprint. Ian charged up the stairs, his heart hammering painfully against his ribs.

It was a handprint!

Ian felt an explosive rage. If Frederick had harmed Laurel, he'd kill him....

"I don't see Anna," Dorie whispered as they toured the rooms and closets on the main floor. A strip of light glowed beneath the bathroom door, but the room was frustratingly empty. "Do you think Mommy rescued Anna because Frederick's being a bad man?"

"I don't know. Is there a basement in this house, Dorie?"

Dorie nodded. "There's a door in the kitchen, like our house."

Tea things were laid out on the table in the kitchen, but it didn't look like the party had started yet. Ian felt a prickly sensation at the back of his neck when they found the the basement door. They were on the right track. The doorjamb was marked with blood....

Chapter Twenty

Laurel pushed on the piano leg with all her might, feeling the joint start to give. She sucked in a deep breath of ammonia-tainted air, and pressed again, her arms and legs trembling as she fought against her ebbing strength and the overwhelming urge to cough.

Finally, Laurel heard splintering wood as the glue bond disintegrated and the leg snapped off. Laurel tumbled backward as the leg flew out of her arms, striking the opposite wall with a thunk.

Her head swam as she scrambled to her feet. She grabbed a bloodstained tea towel, which she recognized as Gertie May's, off the piano and wiped the tears and perspiration from her eyes, placing the dampened part over her nose. She needed some fresh air, fast. She took two steps to the window and pulled the heavy drapes open, dismayed to find that the narrow window had been painted shut and fitted with nonbreakable security glass.

The door was her only exit. Her only hope of saving herself and the two people she loved most. She staggered across the music room and tried the doorknob. It was locked. And the damn door was built of solid wood. Kicking it in would be impossible. But removing the hinge pins wouldn't.

She searched the room for something she could use as a screwdriver. There weren't any scissors in the first-aid kit. She pulled Frederick's metronome from a shelf. It had a thin steel needle. Would that work? She released the needle with a press of her thumb and wrenched it free of the box.

Then she retrieved the broken piano leg for protection.

Sinking to the carpet near the door, she bunched the tea towel on her knees, breathing through its layers of cotton as she worked the lower hinge pin. She was getting so tired.... She tried not to think about what could be happening at Harris House. At least Dorie was safe with Ian. He would protect her.

The first pin popped out of the hinge and bounced onto the navy carpeting. Laurel tried to stand, but her legs wouldn't cooperate. Her chest and shoulders ached. Her head felt fuzzy, like the picture fading to a tiny dot on a television set. She tried ineffectually to reach for the door-knob and pull herself up, but her hand fell away. She slumped against the wall, thinking of Ian and Dorie as her eyelids fluttered closed. One last regret materialized in the fuzzy reaches of her mind: she wished she'd told Ian she loved him....

She could almost hear his voice calling her back, telling her there was still time...

Beside her, the door caved inward with a thunderous sound. Laurel's eyes flew open in terror and her fingers reached for the piano leg. *The coyotes! Had Frederick come back?* She'd knock him to kingdom come....

"What the hell? What's that smell?"

"Mommy, we found you!"

Laurel stared straight up into Ian's eyes. He'd never looked so handsome or so wonderful as he did at that moment with Dorie's arms curled trustingly around his neck. Laurel dropped the piano leg and smiled weakly. "Ammonia."

Ian set Dorie down. "Sprite, I need to carry Mommy upstairs fast. You run up ahead of us." His strong arms lifted her gently. "You weren't going to knock me out with that stick, were you, lady?" he grumbled in her ear. He set her in a chair upstairs in the kitchen and opened the back door and the window over the sink. Laurel felt herself reviving as cold, fresh air filled her lungs. Ian pulled the collar of her sweater down to look at her cut. "Are you okay?" he asked, his eyes dark with concern.

She nodded. "It's stopped bleeding. Just give me a minute."

He smiled and planted a firm, possessive kiss on her cheek that assuaged the trauma of the past two hours until she noticed the blood on Dorie's clothing and panicked.

"She's fine," Ian quickly assured her. "Frederick got me, too. It's just a scratch."

"Frederick?" Fear lodged in her throat. Ian's cavalier attitude didn't fool her one bit. She examined his wound. "A scratch? You're probably going to need stitches."

"Mommy, Frederick's a bad man." Dorie launched into an exhaustive account of her fright. Laurel listened, amazed that Dorie didn't burst into tears or seem overly distraught by what she'd just been through. She had Ian to thank for that. She loved him all the more for making her daughter feel safe and secure. Laurel's eyes misted with tears. Why couldn't Ian see what a nice family they made together? He had everything he needed to be a good father: love, patience and enthusiasm.

He could be a good husband, too, if he wanted. They'd already been through enough tough times to tell her that he could be emotionally supportive.... Suddenly, it all seemed just too much to handle. Her chin sank to her chest and she lost consciousness.

LAUREL CAME TO in a hospital bed to find Ian's warm, strong fingers curled around hers. His eyes were liquid gray, like mercury. "The doctor says you're going to be okay. No permanent damage—we got you out in time. Thank God."

Her head throbbed and the rest of her body ached. She felt worse than she had after thirty-six hours of labor with Dorie. And her throat hadn't felt sore after childbirth. "Oh, Ian," she said hoarsely. "Thank you for protecting Dorie and saving me. I thought I was going to die before I could tell you…" She paused, suddenly afraid to say what was in her heart. How could she tell him she loved him without driving him off to the next continent?

"Tell me what?"

"How much you mean to me. You're a true friend and—"

A frown started to knit along his brow and Laurel worried that she'd already gotten too personal.

"Laurel, I—"

A sharp rap sounded on the door, then the door swung open and Rafferty entered her hospital room. Laurel was relieved at the interruption. She wasn't sure she wanted to hear what Ian had to say. He looked decidedly unhappy and she hadn't even gotten to the "I love you" part. Maybe it was best left unsaid?

Rafferty's expression was as unflappable as ever. "Mind if I ask a few questions?"

Laurel expected herself to tense up, but for the first time in two years she felt unafraid that every word she said would land her deeper into trouble. The whole story slowly tumbled out. Then Ian added his two cents' worth.

"That poor man," Laurel murmured. "I think the strain of caring for Anna affected his thinking. Is he badly injured?"

"Physically he's okay." Rafferty referred back to his notes. "There are several loose ends that need clearing up—the lottery ticket. Frederick Aames never found it, obviously. Should either of you find it, I'd advise you to put it in a secure place. Once the press gets wind of this story you could have a lot of crazies turning up on your doorstep asking for a handout."

Laurel hoped the ticket was lost forever. It had caused too much heartache.

Ian shrugged. "As far as I'm concerned, the ticket remains wherever it is until Aunt Gem personally retrieves it."

His easy dismissal of the money pleased her immensely. The corner of her mouth twitched up.

Rafferty promptly burst her bubble of happiness with his pragmatism. "We also don't know who sent the Christmas cards. Frederick only admitted to breaking into the house and stealing the petitions. And Romanowski's possible involvement remains to be proven. We may still be dealing with the person who murdered your husband. This person may have let up for a while, fearing that he might inadvertently be charged with Miss Harris's abduction. So, please, watch your back."

Laurel felt an icy draft sweep through the room as though someone had opened a window. Would Steve's murder haunt her forever?

Ian squeezed her fingers. "Don't worry, I'm not going anywhere until we find out who's behind these cards."

Laurel closed her eyes, feeling disheartened. Losing Ian was a high price to pay for a life of peace.

IAN CHECKED the east-end address he'd jotted down on the notepad. The narrow, stucco house cramped between two narrow brick structures looked seedy. Was this where Connie Tarlington was hiding out? Ian tossed the notepad onto the dashboard and climbed out of the car. The streetlights flashed on as he hurried up the broken concrete walk. There was no time to waste. The district council meeting was in two hours. He hoped Laurel would see the note he'd left her on the hall table. Tracking down Connie Tarlington was the least he could do for a true friend like Laurel. True friend, hell! He was still smarting from the "let's be friends" line she'd tried to lay on him at the hospital. Well, he wasn't buying it—at least, not yet anyway.

The doorbell didn't work. Ian rapped loudly on the screen door. Inside, he could hear footsteps approaching.

Then the door opened.

Ian sucked in his breath. This was the last person he'd expected to find.

THE BUZZ of hundreds of voices filling the district council chamber halted abruptly into silence as the mayor called the meeting to order. There was a good turnout tonight of Serenity Cove residents. A point in their favor, Laurel thought, trying to dispel the nervous butterflies in her stomach. Across the room, Victor Romanowski glowed with the confidence inspired by the men in expensive suits flanking him on both sides. His experts: architects, lawyers and the pink-faced contractor. Laurel craned her neck toward the door as the agenda was read. Where was Ian?

She felt mildly disappointed. He'd been so secretive since she'd been released from the hospital two days ago. She knew his promise to stay was interfering with his job. She'd overheard him turn down an assignment on the phone yesterday. She knew instinctively by the way his eyes lingered on her when he thought she wasn't looking that this was one promise he might not be able to keep. Now she was glad she'd never told him she loved him. It would make their parting that much easier. He certainly hadn't told her he loved her.

He'd been gone when she and Dorie came back late this afternoon from a visit to the hospital. He didn't even know Gertie May had moved her hand today. A good sign she was coming around.

She'd do best to forget about him and concentrate on her own life, her own concerns. The council meeting.

The development was the second item on the agenda, and Laurel leaned forward with interest as Victor Romanowski and his team made their presentation. They made it sound so wonderful. Improving the community as a whole. Increasing the tax base and property values for local residents.

Then it was Laurel's turn to present the Serenity Cove Heritage Society's arguments. A murmur taut with speculation rippled through the room as she took her place at the speaker's podium. Her knees were quaking and her heartbeat sounded hollow in her chest, but the thought of Gertie May counting on her gave her strength.

"A condo development would change the nature of our community from a quaint, peaceful village to an exclusive enclave of rich commuters—to the detriment of local residents," she argued. "The waterfront park is the heart of Serenity Cove. Residents enjoy its rocky beaches, wooded trails and gently sloping lawns year-round. To think that an architectural masterpiece of cream stucco and green-tinted panes would improve the community is ludicrous."

"Your Worship," Victor Jacek Romanowski responded, rising to his feet and addressing the mayor and the six councillors. "Ms. Bishop's views are representative of a small interest group only. Her remarks are clearly as questionable as her reputation. Why, anyone who's read the paper lately knows that Ms. Bishop is presenting herself this evening under an alias."

Laurel saw red, but she refused to be baited. Her actions would speak for themselves. She held up the stack of petitions that Rafferty had recovered from Frederick's house. "I'm expressing the views of over six hundred residents who've signed this petition to save our park and prevent the overdeveloping of our community."

A commotion at the entrance to the chamber interrupted the proceedings as several people tried to enter the packed room. Two police officers emerged through the wall of spectators, followed by Constable Rafferty, Ian and—Janet Smithe? What was she doing here?

Laurel stared at Ian, trying to comprehend what was going on. He winked at her and she suddenly knew that everything would be all right.

"Your Worship, I apologize for interrupting these proceedings," Rafferty said as he approached Romanowski and placed a hand on his shoulder. "Victor Romanowski, I have a warrant for your arrest on charges of uttering threats, willful damage to property, criminal libel and conspiracy."

The mayor tried to call for order as Victor Romanowski was led away in handcuffs, threatening to sue for false arrest.

Laurel made her way to Ian's side. He squeezed her hand. Laurel didn't want his strong, supportive fingers to ever let go. "Sorry I'm late. But that was worth waiting for, wasn't it?"

"I don't understand," she whispered, shaking her head.

"Janet here can explain, or rather, the 'c.t.' on Romanowski's calendar. Her real name is Connie Tarlington."

Connie lowered her pale blue eyes, ashamed. "I'm not very proud of it, but Victor paid me to stay at Harris House to keep tabs on the Heritage Society's efforts to stop the development. He knew you'd put up a good fight, so he had you and Miss Harris investigated to see if there were any skeletons he could use to his advantage. That's how he found out about your husband's death. He had me deliver those Christmas cards to shake you up, keep you from focusing on the project.

"I got scared, though, when Miss Harris disappeared. I thought Victor had something to do with it and I'd be an accessory. When I saw those pictures on the desk, I knew you could eventually link me to him, so I decided it would be a good time for me and the pictures to disappear."

"How did you find her, Ian?" Laurel asked.

"I guess you didn't read my note. The private investigator found her. You know, the guy you thought it was a waste of time for me to hire. I thought there might be a connection between 'c.t.' and Connie Tarlington. It came as a surprise when I went to see her—"

"He paid me a visit at my sister's house," Connie explained. "I wrote the article in the paper about you, but I didn't write 'Murderess' on the side of your house. One of Victor's cronies did that. I've been hiding out at my sister's because things were getting too crazy. I saw Victor for the kind of man he really is—a bulldozer who'd run over anything and anyone to get what he wants. Ian convinced me to come forward." She flashed him a grateful smile. "I just needed some protection."

Laurel felt a prick of territorial jealously. She wanted to be the only woman in the world who had the right to look at Ian like that. "Well, I'm glad you came forward. Shh, now, the council's ready to vote." Laurel held her breath. Ian compressed her fingers in a firm grip.

One by one the councillors voted to officially designate Panorama Park as parkland. The crowd cheered. Ian pulled Laurel into his arms and kissed her temple. "You did it." He grinned as they were surrounded by neighbors and friends offering congratulations.

"No, we all did it," she said, flushing with pleasure. She tugged on the lapel of his leather jacket. "Let's stop by the hospital and tell Gertie May."

His arms tightened around her again as he whispered for her ears only, "Agreed. Then we go home to celebrate."

She buried her face in his neck, loving the fresh lime and male scent of his skin. She wanted nothing more than an evening's celebration with him. "Agreed."

Chapter Twenty-One

Gertie May thought it was time she stopped dallying with her thoughts in this nice, dark cocoon and had a peek at the world. She'd been hearing voices for the last little while. Familiar voices. The words confused her.

Someone was holding her hand. *Laurel?*

"I love him and I don't know what to do...."

Yes, it was dear, sweet Laurel. "In love," she'd said.

"Please, wake up. I need someone to talk to."

Gertie May slowly opened her eyes, but her eyelids fluttered closed again at the brightness of the room. *This wouldn't do. This was one conversation she wanted to be a party to.*

"Gertie May?"

She tried again. *There. Much better.* Her vision slowly focused. Suddenly, Laurel's beautiful face was in front of her. Tears running down her cheeks. *Why was she crying?* Gertie May tried to speak. "A-about time..." Her voice sounded unnaturally weak to her ears.

"You're awake! I'll be right back."

Gertie May watched in amusement as Laurel flew toward the door. *Oh, dear, where was she going in such a hurry?* They hadn't finished their conversation.

Then the door swung open again and Gertie May saw him. Her Ian. Strong and handsome as ever. *Oh, dear boy, he hadn't left her alone. What is this? He's holding Dorie's hand? Darling Dorie.*

Gertie May smiled delightedly, lifting her hands to draw her loved ones closer. Ian kissed her cheek and she knew he was real. This wasn't a dream. Then he hoisted Dorie up in his arms so she could say hello, too. The three of them were smiling and talking at once. Gertie May couldn't comprehend a word of it. She just absorbed the beauty of the picture they made until her sharp eyes caught something interesting.... Laurel was rubbing Ian's arm in an absentminded way, a loving smile curving her lips as she and Ian exchanged a dewy-eyed, intimate glance. *Ah, so that's what was in the air.*

Gertie May beamed. She'd come back just in time.

LAUREL SURVEYED the fresh floral arrangement on the dining room table with a critical eye. She wanted everything to be perfect. Eight days had passed since Gertie May had rallied from the coma and she was coming home this morning. They were finally going to celebrate Christmas.

Laurel grinned. It should be quite a Christmas. Gertie May's memory had returned gradually and selectively. After a few days she'd finally recalled the events of the night she'd disappeared. She'd gathered her pruners and put her coat on over her pajamas, intending to pop outside to cut a few sprigs of fresh holly, and had encountered Frederick at the door. Frederick had obviously put Laurel's rain boots on her by mistake. Then Gertie May clammed up, swearing that was all she remembered, but Laurel presumed by the mischievous twinkle in her eyes that her friend remembered where the lottery ticket was hidden. She just wasn't saying—yet.

"The table looks lovely," Barb remarked, shuffling slowly into the dining room. Laurel could tell from the dull sheen in Barb's hazel eyes and the gray tinge to her skin that she was in a lot of pain. Barb hadn't been telling her the truth about her diagnosis. Instead of arriving on the sixteenth, Barb had changed her reservations to a week later. Despite Laurel's gentle badgering, Barb hadn't talked about her health in the two days she'd been staying with them.

"Thanks." Laurel hugged her mother-in-law. "I'm glad you could make it for our Christmas. But you should be resting, saving your strength for Gertie May's homecoming. Dorie is tireless."

"I wanted to talk to you privately, before the others returned."

"All right." They slowly moved to the living room to see what Santa had brought in the night. The pocket doors had been kept closed to keep Dorie from peeking until Gertie May was home to join them in unwrapping the gifts. Excitement shimmered in the room. The tree glowed merrily, a mountain of brightly wrapped packages tucked beneath its fragrant branches. Christmas stockings bulging with enticing surprises were hung by the cheery fire. Candles burned on the mantel. The air smelled deliciously of evergreens, pecan pie and a turkey roasting in the kitchen. Laurel smiled in spite of her misgivings about Ian's as-yet-unannounced departure. *It really felt like Christmas.*

"I have a confession to make to you, darling." Barb took in the gaily decorated room and sighed heavily. "This place is fitting. I didn't want another Christmas to go by without making things right. So this year I'm giving you the gift of truth. You've had to pay for my mistake and it's not fair."

Laurel patted Barb's hands. "We've been over this before. I haven't had to pay for your mistakes, they were Steve's mistakes."

"No, no. I killed him, you see. I killed Steve."

Emotions welled in Laurel's heart. "No, Barb," she whispered in stubborn disbelief. "You're not responsible—"

"Laurel, dear, listen to me. I came to the house that night to see if I could help you with any Christmas preparations. I knew Dorie had been sick and you were tired. I just wanted to help." She sniffed as a tear coursed down her plump cheek. "I let myself in and started tidying up the kitchen. Steve was supposed to be at work, but I heard him on the phone in the living room so I went to say hello. That's when I found out..."

"Found out what, Barb?" Laurel felt cold as a numbness stole over her body.

"About the money. I heard him on the phone. He was telling someone he'd already spent all the money his father left me. The money he was responsible for as trustee of Charlie's estate. Gambled it away. He was asking for more time, saying he'd get the money somehow. I confronted him when he got off the phone. You should have heard him lying to me, making up a story that he'd invested the money in a business deal that would make me rich. Then he had the gall to ask if I had any other savings that he didn't know about—he needed some cash to tide him over until after the holidays. I refused. I was so angry." She swallowed hard, her bosom rising and falling rapidly with each breath. "Then... I'm sorry, Laurel, but I lost control.

"I realized that from day one he'd never appreciated a single thing I'd done for him. I wasn't thinking straight—just reacting. He turned his back on me to walk away. I picked up the tennis trophy he was so proud of and I hit him. I didn't know I had so much strength." Barb pulled a handkerchief from her sweater sleeve and blew her nose. "I killed my stepson."

Through a haze of shock Laurel knew Barb was telling the truth. She should have suspected something sooner. "But why—"

"Let me finish," Barb interrupted her. "It feels good to get it off my chest. I know there's no excuse for what I did. But afterward, well, it occurred to me that we were better off without him. You, me, Dorie. Steve was never a very good husband or father or son. He was too into himself."

Laurel felt her eyes brim with tears and she couldn't hold back the tide of angry words. "How can you say that?"

"I can say that because I loved him and I knew his faults." Barb choked back a sob. "I was so afraid the police would arrest you, or they'd find out what I did, but they didn't. I didn't know I was such an accomplished liar until the police questioned me about him. You were innocent and the police knew it. I just didn't reckon with the way the town would react. That's why I sent you here to Gertie May. That way you'd never know the real reasons I sold the house and my car and moved into an apartment." She clutched Laurel's hand. "You've been happy here, haven't you?"

"Yes. We love living with Gertie May."

"I know. I thought it would all work out.... Then Gertie May went missing and Steve's death exploded in your face again. It made me realize that I can't expect you to bear the burden of my actions any longer. It's not fair to you or Dorie. I went to the police last Thursday and confessed. I gave them the trophy—"

Laurel's mouth dropped opened. "You did what?"

"I confessed."

"Wh-why didn't they arrest you?"

"They did. My arraignment hearing was on Monday. My lawyer put up his house as a surety so I could be released on bail. The preliminary hearing is set for April, but they won't have to waste the court's time. You see, dear, I'm dying and I know it. Lung cancer. The doctor says it's hard to predict when, but I know in my heart it'll be soon. Please, don't cry. I'm ready to go. I can't live with myself anymore."

Laurel sobbed quietly, feeling Barb's arm tighten around her shoulders. Barb's confession felt like the ultimate betrayal. She loved her and trusted her, and Barb had been lying to her all this time. Damn Steve and his gambling! His addiction had destroyed their life and their family.

"I know it's asking a lot of you, dear, but I hope someday you'll find it in your heart to forgive me for the misery I've put you through."

Laurel lifted her head and looked her mother-in-law straight in the eye. Being angry with Barb would serve no purpose and they had so little time left. Dorie was going to lose yet another loved one. Laurel struggled to regain her composure. "You're already forgiven. I'll stand by you the same way I stood by Steve. You're at least trying to right your wrong."

"Thank you, dear. I can rest easy now, knowing you and Dorie will be fine. Ian's a good man. He'll make you happier than Steve ever did."

"He already has." That much, at least, was true. Laurel didn't have the heart to tell Barb she was mistaken in thinking she and Ian would have a life together.

"It's Christmas. Enough tears," Barb said, noticeably winded. "We'll be happy and enjoy this day. I'll leave it to you to decide when, and if, you want to tell the others what I've done. Help me to my room now. I'd like to lie down."

Arm in arm, they went upstairs to a guest room as Laurel pondered over Barb's confession. She couldn't condone the violent means by which Barb had dealt with Steve. But her confession finally freed Laurel from the past. Had given her peace of mind. For that she would always be grateful. She helped Barb off with her bathrobe and tucked her into bed like she was Dorie's age, kissing her tired brow. "Thanks for the gift. For now, we'll keep it between just us girls."

"MOMMY! NANA! We're back! Gertie May's here. That means it's Christmas. Did Santa come?" Dorie shrieked, racing into the house just after eleven. Ian and Gertie May followed along behind at a more sedate pace, laughing at Dorie's boisterous excitement.

"Oh, it's lovely to be home again." Gertie May enfolded Laurel in a heartwarming hug. "I trust the secret mission was a success?" she asked in a stage whisper.

"All taken care of, down to the letter of your instructions." Laurel grinned. Then she sobered, remembering Gertie May had just been released from the hospital. "Are you sure you're up to this? You could rest first—"

"Oh, pooh, pooh. I'm fit as a fiddle. Dorie's had to wait long enough for old Saint Nick. Barb, my old friend, give me a hug. That's better. Marvelous, we're all here. Ian," Gertie May commanded regally, "open the doors."

Laurel watched with a full, glowing heart as Dorie skipped into the room and stopped, her eyes round with awe at the first sight of her Christmas. Laurel snapped a photo, certain the picture would be out of focus because of her own watery eyes. This Christmas was all she'd ever dreamed about for Dorie. Her gaze shifted to Ian, who was helping Barb and Gertie May to comfortable seats on the sofa. Well, almost. She'd like to amend her dream to include one more person. But it was too late to talk to Santa Claus about that.

Dorie held up a half-eaten carrot from a plate left on the hearth the night before, and chattered on about reindeer tooth marks. The fun had officially begun.

Ian and Dorie distributed the Christmas stockings at Gertie May's insistence. Oohs and ahhs, exclamations of delight, and gentle jokes, created an atmosphere of cheer as small packages were torn open and examined. Finally, underneath the orange tucked in the toes of their stockings, each of them found a small, white envelope.

"Open yours first," Gertie May urged, almost beside herself with glee.

"Imagine that," Ian drawled, reading the card he withdrew from the envelope. "An I.O.U. from Santa Claus for two hundred and fifty thousand dollars."

Laurel looked at her card. "Mine says the same thing. Only Santa insists I use the money to finish my business classes and finance the career of my dreams."

"What would that be?" Ian's shoulder brushed hers as he leaned over the back of her chair to read her card, sending a current of sensual awareness swooshing through her body. She breathed in the fresh male scent of him, feeling dizzy by his nearness. This was the closest they'd been to each other in days—since the night before Barb had arrived. Then they'd moved to separate beds and their separate lives by an unspoken agreement. Laurel tried to remain aloof.

"Local politics. I thought I'd start with councillor or a school board position and work on up to mayor." She could, too, now that her reputation was unblemished.

Barb chuckled. "You'll go far, dear. I just know it. Santa wants me to go on a cruise with an old friend. Santa's providing the pocket change."

"What does mine say, Mommy? Santa forgot I can't read." Dorie held up her card to Laurel.

"Santa's given you a trust fund for your education, sweetie." Laurel looked at the monetary figure on the card. Gertie May was being overwhelmingly generous. "Santa's very, very good to us."

Dorie looked unimpressed. "Can I open my real presents now?"

"Gertie May hasn't opened her card yet," Laurel replied gently, tapping the impish tip of Dorie's nose.

With a flourish, Gertie May opened her card. "Santa has decided that my I.O.U. would be well spent on a cultural center for Serenity Cove. We've been trying to raise funds for one for years without much success."

"Wonderful!" Laurel enthused. "I should have known you would do something to benefit the community."

Ian rose and kissed his aunt's cheek. "I'm proud of you, Aunt Gem. You're one in *four* million. But, aren't you forgetting something?"

Gertie May laughed. "Oh, yes! The ticket. I've had an angel of mercy keeping an eye on it for me. Ian, if you and Dorie would be so kind as to take the angel off the top of the tree—"

"Come here, sprite."

Gertie May inverted the angel in her lap and poked at the cone-shaped cardboard insert with a fingernail. A second later the insert loosened and a lottery ticket floated onto her lap. Gertie May kissed the ticket. "The luckiest numbers in the world. Now, let's see about those *real* presents. Is that big box for me?"

Everyone laughed, and some serious ripping and tearing of wrapping paper ensued. The big box for Gertie May contained a new orange wool coat from Ian. A separate box, from Laurel, contained leather boots dyed to match.

Dorie and Laurel gave Ian a wallet-size photo of themselves. "So you won't forget us," Laurel explained softly. Ian thanked them both so solemnly that Laurel wondered if she'd done the wrong thing. Maybe he didn't want to remember them? But then he pulled out his wallet and slipped the photo in the first plastic sleeve where it would be visible every time he opened it. His thumb grazed the photo as he inspected the pose. Then he grinned. Laurel immediately felt better.

There were still a few gifts remaining under the tree when the doorbell suddenly pealed. Laurel looked up from inspecting a new fitness outfit to see Ian checking his watch. "I wonder who that could be?" he said, winking at her as he went to answer it.

Something was afoot. Laurel's heartbeat accelerated. Did Ian have a special present for her?

"Ho, ho, ho. Merry Christmas!" a jolly voice cried out. Laurel reached for the camera as Santa Claus bounded into the living room with a puppy in his arms. The puppy had an enormous red bow tied to her collar.

Dorie gazed at Santa and the golden cocker spaniel in awe. "Is the puppy for me?"

Santa nodded. "Just like you asked for. My elves have been looking after her for you. Do you promise Santa you'll take good care of her?"

"Yes!" Dorie squealed. Santa placed the puppy in Dorie's welcoming arms. Laurel snapped another picture of the puppy licking Dorie's face. Her own reaction to Dorie's puppy was bittersweet and she was glad to have the camera to hide behind so no one could see her face and sense her disappointment. Dorie had told Ian she'd asked Santa for a daddy or a puppy...Ian had obviously chosen the latter gift.

Santa departed with another hearty round of ho, ho, ho's and Laurel took several pictures, purposefully avoiding looking at Ian. Her insides ached....

The last few presents under the tree were unwrapped. More toys and books for Dorie. Laurel rose from her chair to gather the wrapping paper. The puppy was chewing on it.

"Wait," Ian said, taking her hand. "There's something else."

Laurel raised her eyes to meet his warm gray gaze, trying to read into his soul. Impossible. He seemed just as secretive as ever. He put a small, red velvet jewelry box in the palm of her hand and her body quivered. Was it...

His strong, tanned fingers shook as he opened the box. Laurel gazed down at a necklace glittering on a bed of red velvet. It was a large oval stone, an unusual brown-and-amber color, set in gold. It was exquisitely beautiful. She couldn't keep the tears from rushing to her eyes.

"It's a cat's-eye," Ian explained in the gentlest of voices, and pleaded with her to hold still so they could get this public show of exchanging a gift over with as soon as possible. Light struck the pendant and the stone flashed a fiery amber and gold. "I bought it because it reminded me of your eyes. Your soul."

He slipped the chain around her neck and fastened it. Gertie May and Barb made appreciative cooing sounds. Laurel wanted to run and hide. To bury her hot face in the cool linen of her pillow. But his hands had slipped to her shoulders, preventing her from making an excuse to leave the room as he looked from the pendant to her eyes with a critical gaze. She averted her gaze, trying to form a thank-you past the burning sensation in her throat.

"Do you remember the conversation we had about engagement rings?" he said huskily. Suddenly it seemed very quiet in the room. Laurel could hear the snap of the fire over the sound of her heartbeat thrumming in her ears. Her eyes crept back to his face, wary. He was smiling. Her heart squeezed painfully. "I said, I thought a woman's engagement ring should match the fire in her soul. As I recall, you were more in favor of diamonds." His hand slipped into his pocket and he removed a second red velvet box, identical to the first.

Laurel didn't even dare let herself hope again. Tears flowed freely onto her cheeks as he went down on one knee.

"I love you, Laurel Bishop Wilson. You knocked me off my feet the moment I met you and I'm a happier man for it. You changed my life. I feel like I've been lost all these years and I've finally found what it is I've been looking for. You. Dorie. A family. Heck, everyone else has been getting their Christmas wish answered. Why can't I?" He laughed dryly. "Open the box."

With trembling fingers, Laurel eased the lid of the velvet box open. A white card was folded in a tent shape over what she hoped was a ring. She pulled the card away. An unconquerable diamond solitaire ring winked at her. Laurel tried to read the card through her tears. "A Realtor's card?" she whispered, uncomprehending.

"Hey, I took a big chance picking out a ring you might not like and getting a new job. I wouldn't dare pick out a house without consulting my partner. My wife."

Laurel could hardly believe her ears. It was all too wonderful to be true. "A job? You got a new job?"

He nodded. "I'm negotiating a contract to write a training manual for gem dealers. Then, in the fall, I'll start teaching full-time gemology courses at Vancouver Community College." He took the ring out of the box.

Laurel put her hand on his wrist to stop him from slipping the ring on her finger. "Ian, I can't ask you to give up your job and your life-style for me."

"I'm doing it for me. I want you. I want your problems and your political fights. I want to be the reason for your smiling face. I want a house with a lawn that always needs mowing. I want to be Dorie's father and teach her all the stuff dads are supposed to teach their kids." He looked at the others, his eyes and husky voice brimming with love and hope. "I want Dorie to be a big sister and Aunt Gem to have lots more kids in her life to love. All you have to do is say you'll do me the honor of becoming my wife, my friend, and most definitely . . . my lover. Will you marry me?"

"Oh, Ian. Yes, yes, yes, yes. *Yes!*" Then she let him slip the diamond ring on her finger, knowing it was indeed the perfect symbol of his love.

As Ian stood and pulled her into his arms for a kiss, Laurel heard Dorie squealing in the background.

"Mommy! Look! There's a 'gagement ring tied onto my puppy's bow. I get to marry Ian, too!"

Laurel sighed contentedly. Santa had really outdone himself this year.

UNLOCK THE DOOR TO GREAT ROMANCE AT BRIDE'S BAY RESORT

Join Harlequin's new across-the-lines series, set in an exclusive hotel on an island off the coast of South Carolina.

Seven of your favorite authors will bring you exciting stories about fascinating heroes and heroines discovering love at Bride's Bay Resort.

Look for these fabulous stories coming to a store near you beginning in January 1996.

Harlequin American Romance #613 in January
Matchmaking Baby by Cathy Gillen Thacker

Harlequin Presents #1794 in February
Indiscretions by Robyn Donald

Harlequin Intrigue #362 in March
Love and Lies by Dawn Stewardson

Harlequin Romance #3404 in April
Make Believe Engagement by Day Leclaire

Harlequin Temptation #588 in May
Stranger in the Night by Roseanne Williams

Harlequin Superromance #695 in June
Married to a Stranger by Connie Bennett

Harlequin Historicals #324 in July
Dulcie's Gift by Ruth Langan

Visit Bride's Bay Resort each month wherever
Harlequin books are sold.

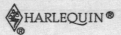

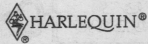

HARLEQUIN®

Don't miss these Harlequin favorites by some of our most distinguished authors!
And now you can receive a discount by ordering two or more titles!

HT#25593	WHAT MIGHT HAVE BEEN by Glenda Sanders	$2.99 U.S. ☐ /$3.50 CAN. ☐
HP#11713	AN UNSUITABLE WIFE by Lindsay Armstrong	$2.99 U.S. ☐ /$3.50 CAN. ☐
HR#03356	BACHELOR'S FAMILY by Jessica Steele	$2.99 U.S. ☐ /$3.50 CAN. ☐
HS#70494	THE BIG SECRET by Janice Kaiser	$3.39 ☐
HI#22196	CHILD'S PLAY by Bethany Campbell	$2.89 ☐
HAR#16553	THE MARRYING TYPE by Judith Arnold	$3.50 U.S. ☐ /$3.99 CAN. ☐
HH#28844	THE TEMPTING OF JULIA by Maura Seger	$3.99 U.S ☐ /$4.50 CAN. ☐

(limited quantities available on certain titles)

AMOUNT	$
DEDUCT: 10% DISCOUNT FOR 2+ BOOKS	$
POSTAGE & HANDLING ($1.00 for one book, 50¢ for each additional)	$
APPLICABLE TAXES*	$_____
TOTAL PAYABLE	$_____

(check or money order—please do not send cash)

To order, complete this form and send it, along with a check or money order for the total above, payable to Harlequin Books, to: **In the U.S.:** 3010 Walden Avenue, P.O. Box 9047, Buffalo, NY 14269-9047; **In Canada:** P.O. Box 613, Fort Erie, Ontario, L2A 5X3.

Name: _____

Address:_____City: _____

State/Prov.: _____ Zip/Postal Code: _____

*New York residents remit applicable sales taxes.
Canadian residents remit applicable GST and provincial taxes.

HBACK-OD2

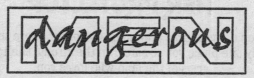

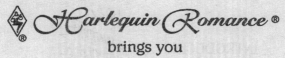

Harlequin Romance ®

brings you

HOLDING OUT FOR A HERO

Some men are worth waiting for!

Beginning in January, Harlequin Romance will be
bringing you some of the world's most eligible men.
They're handsome, they're charming, but, best of all,
they're single! Twelve lucky women are about to
discover that finding Mr. Right is not a problem—it's
holding on to him!

In the coming months, watch for our Holding Out for
a Hero flash on books by some of your favorite
authors, including LEIGH MICHAELS, JEANNE ALLAN,
BETTY NEELS, LUCY GORDON and REBECCA WINTERS!

HOFH-G

INTRODUCING...

A collection of award-winning books by award-winning authors! From Harlequin and Silhouette.

Falling Angel
by Anne Stuart

WINNER OF THE RITA AWARD
FOR BEST ROMANCE!

Falling Angel by Anne Stuart is a RITA Award winner, voted Best Romance. A truly wonderful story, *Falling Angel* will transport you into a world of hidden identities, second chances and the magic of falling in love.

"Ms. Stuart's talent shines like the brightest of stars, making it very obvious that her ultimate destiny is to be the next romance author at the top of the best-seller charts."
—*Affaire de Coeur*

A heartwarming story for the holidays. You won't want to miss award-winning *Falling Angel*, available this January wherever Harlequin and Silhouette books are sold.

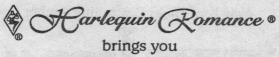

ℋarlequin Romance ®

brings you

How the West Was Wooed!

Harlequin Romance would like to welcome you **Back to the Ranch** again in 1996 with our new miniseries, Hitched! We've rounded up twelve of our most popular authors, and the result is a whole year of romance, Western-style. Every month we'll be bringing you a spirited, independent woman whose heart is about to be lassoed by a rugged, handsome, one-hundred-percent cowboy!

Watch for books branded Hitched! in the coming months. We'll be featuring all your favorite writers including, **Patricia Knoll, Ruth Jean Dale, Rebecca Winters** and **Patricia Wilson**, to mention a few!

HITCH-G

New York Times Bestselling Author

PENNY JORDAN

Explore the lives of four women as they overcome a

CRUEL LEGACY

For Philippa, Sally, Elizabeth and Deborah life will never be the same after the final act of one man. Now they must stand on their own and reclaim their lives.

As Philippa learns to live without wealth and social standing, Sally finds herself tempted by a man who is not her husband. And Elizabeth struggles between supporting her husband and proclaiming her independence, while Deborah must choose between a jealous lover and a ruthless boss.

Don't miss CRUEL LEGACY, available this December at your favorite retail outlet.

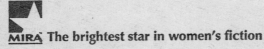

MIRA The brightest star in women's fiction

MPJCL